THE HAUNTING

ALSO BY NATASHA PRESTON

The Cellar

Awake

The Cabin

You Will Be Mine

The Lost

The Twin

The Lake

The Fear

The Island

THE HAUNTING

NATASHA PRESTON

DELACORTE PRESS

This is a work of fiction. Names, characters, places, and incidents either are the product of the author's imagination or are used fictitiously. Any resemblance to actual persons, living or dead, events, or locales is entirely coincidental.

GetUnderlined.com

Educators and librarians, for a variety of teaching tools, visit us at RHTeachersLibrarians.com

Library of Congress Cataloging-in-Publication Data is available upon request.
ISBN 978-0-593-48151-6 (trade pbk.) — ISBN 978-0-593-48152-3 (ebook)

The text of this book is set in 11-point Janson MT Pro.
Interior design by Michelle Crowe

Printed in the United States of America
10 9 8 7 6 5 4 3 2 1
First Edition

For Joseph

1

SATURDAY, OCTOBER 23

What's the best way to ask your boyfriend how he feels about the one-year anniversary of his father's Halloween murder spree?

Your *ex*-boyfriend, because, oh yeah, you're forbidden to ever see or speak with him again.

Nash never returned to school after five of our classmates were slaughtered by his dad, a man who made me hot chocolate with a mountain of marshmallows whenever I came over.

Jackson Whitmore was two people: the welcoming dad and the cold-blooded killer. It took a long time to merge them.

The memory of what he did is all over town, haunting the residents with constant reminders wherever you look. The memorial statue for his victims sits proudly in the square, in the center of town, visible from every angle—the same location where some of them were found.

I stare at it now. A bronze phoenix with its large wings splayed toward heaven. Five names are engraved underneath the bird. I trace each one with my finger.

Mac Johnson

Caitlin Howard

Kelsie Allen

Brodie Edwards

Jia Yang

There's no getting away from what he did. A reminder is carved into stone.

Jackson's killing spree lasted a week, but it feels like it never ended. The mayor had flowers planted in every inch of soil in the spring. It still smelled like death to me.

Figuring out what to say to Nash has been plaguing me for the past few weeks. Everything I think of sounds totally stupid. Forgetting him has been impossible, and with Halloween coming up, he's on my mind even more than usual.

Still, it's been about five months since we last spoke—on a rainy spring day when we ran into each other outside school. Me leaving late for the day, him going to collect a jacket that had been in the lost and found.

It was a short conversation once we'd asked what the other was doing. Short and *super* awkward. I can still remember the way he tried to avoid eye contact, as if looking at me hurt, and how I felt so guilty for writing him off like the rest of the town.

Dark gray clouds, the same color as my eyes, cover the sky, as likely to rain as I am to cry. I've been finding it increasingly difficult to trap my emotions inside. I'm not supposed to think about Nash. My feelings for him were supposed to disappear along with our contact.

I walk away from the statue and toward Gina's restaurant to

meet Adi for breakfast, still clinging to my phone in case I come up with something good to say. I pass a couple of dressed-up scarecrows, one draped in white like a ghost with smudged black circles for eyes. The other dressed in a tattered black cloak with a distorted face and pointed hood. It's the more sinister one that I have a hard time looking at. You can tell the ghost was made by the elementary school kids. The creepy *thing,* high school.

When I step inside the restaurant, everyone turns their head to watch me. A few people whisper, still not over getting a glimpse of the killer's son's ex.

I feel like a one-woman show.

The one-woman coward show where I ignore my instincts and pretend that I'm fine not talking to Nash anymore.

I duck my head and take a seat at an empty table. Gina's is a country-style restaurant, with red-and-white checkered tablecloths. I scroll on my phone to distract myself from the fact that Nash's name is suddenly on everyone's lips.

My parents were thrilled when I stopped seeing Nash—after forcing me to—and I need them to believe I've given up wanting to. It's much easier if they don't know anything. If I send him a message and my parents find out, they will freak. It will be a freak-out of epic proportions. Their straight-A daughter, headed for a great college, fraternizing—a word my dad *actually* used—with a Whitmore.

It's not something I should even be thinking about.

Everyone in our tight-knit community, including my best friends, thinks it's better if the remaining Whitmores keep to their large property on the outskirts of town.

But what Jackson Whitmore did last year wasn't Nash's—or his sister, Grace's—fault. Not that it matters because apparently everyone here believes they're guilty by association.

It's all bullshit.

I think I might be the only one left who cares about Nash and Grace.

But I'm not allowed to do anything about it and it's slowly eating away at me.

I need to reach out to him, to let him know that he's not alone, but, yeah, I don't know what to say.

Okay, come on. Think of something. . . As hard as it is for all of us to deal with the anniversary, it must be ten times harder for them. I can only imagine how it must feel to be blamed for something you didn't do.

They lost everything because of what their dad did.

Penny:

i know it's been a while but i still care about you.

Delete.

No, that's absolute crap.

Penny:

How are you and grace doing? I know everyone else blames you but i don't.

Delete.

Penny:

Please don't hate me.

Delete.

I couldn't make these suck more if I tried.

Penny:

Can we meet?

Delete. Delete. Delete.

This shouldn't be so hard! We used to talk about *everything.* We'd send messages, from long essays to full conversations using only GIFs—sometimes no words were needed. I don't think that would be appropriate in this situation. *I'm sorry your dad is a killer but here's a GIF of Tom Hanks waving on a boat.*

Yeah, I don't think so.

So, I end up sending nothing at all. Every time. Which is way worse.

"Penny," my best friend, Adeline, says, sliding into the booth. "Gina has pumpkin-shaped sprinkles on the ice cream sundaes."

I place my cell facedown on the table, ignoring the simmering frustration in my gut. I half feel like I'm waiting on Nash to reply . . . to the nothing I sent.

"You ordered us one, right?" I ask, though I'm not hungry. That seems to be a theme recently.

Can't eat properly because of the big ball of anxiety.

Can't sleep properly because of the big ball of anxiety.

Can't focus well at school or piano practice because . . . well, you get it.

I haven't tried ice cream for breakfast, though.

"Duh," she says, tying her tight red curls on top of her head. "Sundae eating is getting serious."

"You know it is. I ordered us the doubles." She pauses, taking me in. "What's going on? You look shady and you're playing 'Für Elise' on your cell."

I look down and realize I've been anxiously tapping on the back of my phone. I curl my fingers into my palm. "Everything's fine. I'm just always practicing."

Usually I can convince almost anyone of anything—you've just got to say whatever the lie is with conviction—but my most useful talent does not work on Adi this time. Plus, I haven't played piano in a while.

She raises her brows, her pale green eyes full of suspicion, and leans back against the dark wooden booth. A move that I recognize means she's ready to kick ass.

Adi doesn't have any time for pretending when she knows it's a lie.

"I was thinking about him," I tell her, sighing.

She doesn't need a name to know who I mean. *Him* is pretty much his name now.

Him is Nash.

Her is Grace.

That Man is Jackson.

As if saying their names will release Jackson from federal prison and send him on another spree.

"Don't go there, Pen," she warns.

My heart sinks to my toes. It's not the reaction I was hoping for but it's pretty much the one I expected. Nash is the one thing we will never agree on, the one thing she doesn't have my back on.

"It wasn't his fault."

"I'm with you on that but you probably weren't going to marry your high school boyfriend anyway. You're off to Juilliard and he would rather die than live anywhere near a city. It was never going to work."

That doesn't mean I should write him off. Besides, I don't know if I'll get into Juilliard, not anymore, or if I even want to pursue music professionally. I've let it go in the last year, but I'll save that little confession for another time. My parents won't be too excited.

"What's your costume going to be?" I ask.

"Nice subject change but it wasn't very smooth. I don't know yet. I'll see what Party Town has. You still dressing as a corpse bride?"

"I think so," I reply. I'll never tell her that Nash was supposed to be a corpse groom this year.

We'd been together for a year before last Halloween and had our costumes picked out . . . but we never got to wear them because trick-or-treating was canceled, and his dad was arrested. We were going to be prisoners.

Ironic.

Now the only prisoner is Jackson Whitmore. Nash and Grace, too, if you count being ostracized by the town and isolated in your home. Which I do.

"Penny, try not to think about him." Adi's voice is soft and understanding, but it's easy for her to say that. Nash was her friend, but it didn't take her long to stop checking in with him. Same as our other friends Zayn and Omar.

"I want to text him."

"That's the opposite of not thinking about him."

"I can't just turn my thoughts off. Like you said, it's the anniversary. How must he be feeling?"

She shrugs. "Not your business anymore."

This is getting me nowhere. I wish Adi was on my side with this one. She usually is, but Adi only likes drama that she's not involved in.

We eat our ice cream, her devouring hers and me picking at mine, and then head to Party Town just in time for it to open. The street is heaving with people. Our small town comes alive during any holiday and Halloween is the biggest of the year.

Pumpkins, spiders, ghosts, and bats adorn every shop window and door. Small children are already running around in costume despite it not being Halloween until next weekend. To be fair, they've been at it for the last two weeks.

I remember dressing up the second October began when I was younger.

I loved the lead-up, the costume shopping, and the decorating. Mom and I always got spooky designs painted on our nails. Mine were black with white ghosts. Hers white with pumpkins.

It used to be my favorite holiday.

Adi and I walk past a group of people apple bobbing on the

square, some sort of fundraiser. The mayor is dressed in a Cruella de Vil costume and filling buckets with bright green apples.

It's hard to believe that our town was tainted with horror only a year ago when you see people celebrating. Jackson had always been a bit of a loner, nothing like Nash and Grace, who were popular in school. He owned a scrapyard on his property rather than farming on it, and kept to himself.

He never came into town much, only to get groceries or run errands. My parents never loved me going to Nash's house because they hadn't really met his dad. But he was kind to me, and you can hardly hold it against someone for being a private person.

That is, until they start murdering kids.

Nash said that his dad was happy and had friends who weren't nearby.

I never saw them, and how could he have been happy when he was all alone? But I was always met with a smile and a hot chocolate. He made small talk and encouraged me to go for Juilliard.

We pass the phoenix again and I keep my eyes down this time, not wanting Adi to say anything else about Nash.

Just past the statue is the pretty yellow-brick grocery store with its stack of newspapers outside.

The headline on the front page today reads ANNIVERSARY OF FIRST BRUTAL HALLOWEEN MURDER.

Adi links our arms. "Look, are you okay with the Nash Situation? You know, not seeing him?" she asks, spotting me looking back at the memorial.

My friends all refer to the murders as the Nash Situation. I want to scream that it should be the Jackson Situation, but each time I've brought that up, it didn't end well.

People our age died and that's all that will ever matter.

Nash and Grace are collateral damage.

It *sucks.*

"Why do you care? You told me to forget him thirty minutes ago."

I sound like a whiny five-year-old.

"That's what you *should* do. I'm trying to be a good friend here. I'm sorry I was so abrupt earlier. You can talk to me about him if you need to."

"Why the one-eighty?"

"Because you look sad."

Great, now everyone can tell how I feel with one look. I can't count the number of times I heard whispers of "that one's Nash's girlfriend" since Jackson was arrested.

"Penny?" Adi prods.

"I'm fine."

"Cool, so you can start dating again," she says with a small smile, calling my bluff.

No, thanks.

"Looks pretty quiet in Party Town," I say. "It shouldn't take long to find something."

"Another dodge."

I ignore her and reach for the faded, chipped blue door. Some gargoyle-looking thing hangs on the glass like a wreath.

"It's locked."

Adi peers through the window. "We're right on time. Mrs. Vanderford must be running late."

I lean back against the brick, between the ghosts and skeletons, and wait. "She's probably dealing with Karter's latest stunt."

The shop owner's son, who I unfortunately share three classes with, is a huge bully. He walks around angry, picking fights and telling others what to do. Adi dated him for five minutes when we first started high school, but she soon realized he's a douchebag.

"Girls, I'm coming!" Mrs. Vanderford calls from across the road.

A few more people join us to wait for the store to open. Another girl from school, Mae, her group of friends, and some younger kids.

"So sorry, everyone," she says, panting as she unlocks the door. "Car trouble this morning. Come on in."

We filter into the store and hear her mutter something to herself about the alarm not being on and how her son, Karter, must've forgotten again.

I look over my shoulder to see her shaking her head and ranting about him being irresponsible. Her bad for trusting him, really. I wouldn't trust him to babysit an egg.

Costumes hang from every wall and on racks in between. There's a long section for decorations. Creepy organ music drifts through the store as Mrs. Vanderford slips behind the counter.

Cobwebs hang from the ceiling above me, adorned with black plastic spiders.

Adi leads us deeper into the store and we split up, each of us going to opposite sides of the same rack.

We start in the middle where all the big costumes are. There will be puffy corpse bride dresses along here, I'm sure.

Mae walks past, stopping beside me. "Hi, Penny."

"Hey. What're you here for?"

"We're all going as blood-soaked cheerleaders this year." She rolls her eyes. "Not my idea but it'll be fun."

"Nice. Hey, did you need my environmental science notes?"

"Please! Can I grab them at school Monday?"

"Sure."

She gives me another wave as she heads to her group; one girl is holding up a blue cheerleader costume and the other red.

There's about to be an argument.

I scrunch my nose and call over to Adi on the other side of the rack. "You smell something weird?"

"Probably that," she replies, pointing to Mrs. Vanderford, who's scowling and dumping a takeout box into the trash.

Karter's dinner probably.

"Babe, here's a good one. Mix of black and white," she says, holding it up, but I still can't see a lot of it. We're right in the middle of the aisle that stretches almost the length of the store.

I part the costumes in front of me because it'll be quicker than going around.

As I step forward, my foot kicks something solid.

"Ah. Hold on," I mutter to Adi, and look down.

The first thing that I see is an arm and my brain tries hard to convince me it's a mannequin.

But it's not. I can tell from the red patch of blood seeping through his white shirt.

Screaming, I leap back and slap my hand over my mouth.

"Penny, what the hell!" Adi's voice sounds like she's suddenly miles away.

I back up, almost tripping over myself until I hit the wall and slide to the floor. My eyes fix on the body in front of me. I can't even blink.

Mrs. Vanderford and another employee run toward me, and other shoppers crane their necks to see what the dramatic girl is screaming about.

I gag against my fist as I spot the body's dead eyes staring up at nothing. I recognize him—Noah. Another classmate of ours.

Adi screams and grabs hold of me, pulling my arm up as she tries to get me to stand. "Oh my god! What the . . . Is he *dead*?"

I vaguely hear her words over the ringing in my ears.

Yeah, he's *really* dead. There's blood all over his chest and now I can see that there are a couple darker patches. And the smell. That's what it was, not Karter's takeout.

I think he was stabbed.

"Stop looking, Penny!" Adi scolds, yanking me to my feet. I stand, wobbly, my legs almost unable to support my weight.

"Everyone outside," Mrs. Vanderford says, her voice robotic after the shock. "Come on, outside now. Karen, call . . . call the police."

Adi and I stumble through the store. I walk in a daze as we make it outside and into the crisp fall morning air. I gasp a mouthful of oxygen and my hands tremble in my pockets as I stare at the phoenix in the square, trying to make sense of what I just saw.

"It's happening again," Adi whispers, huddling close to me.

I blink a few times and listen to my pulse thumping in my ears. I'm only semi-aware of my surroundings, the small crowd that's forming outside the store and the whispers of disbelief.

Mae and her friends exit with tear-stained cheeks, no doubt having seen *the body* on their way out.

"Penny!" Adi calls, shaking my arm. "Snap out of it!"

Shaking my head, I turn to her and mutter, "Wh-what?"

"It's happening again. The murders."

"No," I breathe. Straightening my back, I say, "No. Jackson's serving a life sentence in a *federal* prison in Pennsylvania. He's locked up and two states away."

"Yeah . . . but his kids aren't."

I yank my arm out of hers, wishing I could walk away from here, away from her and everyone else. I stare at Adi in disbelief. "Nash isn't behind this."

My lungs resist as I try to suck in enough oxygen. The feeling of being totally helpless is all-consuming.

Adi doesn't respond but she does move away from me and closer to Mae's group, who are now outside with us.

I can't believe that Nash would ever hurt anyone.

This can't be him.

He's *nothing* like his dad.

He wouldn't do that.

I turn around to put as much distance between me and Adi's confusing accusation as possible. That's when I see him. Between the little bookstore and the pharmacy, facing Party Town and staring straight at me.

Nash.

2

My heart sinks as we make eye contact. From across the street, I see his familiar pained expression. Before he asked me out, we were friends. I've known him since kindergarten. There's so much distance between us now, and I'm not talking about physically.

What is he doing here? He *can't* be here.

With a shake of his head, which tousles his mop of dark brown hair, he slowly turns around and retreats into the shadows. I curl my hands into fists and wish I could run after him.

If it had been anyone else who'd seen him, he would already be in the back of a cop car.

Two of which screech to a stop outside the store, making me jump. Blue lights bounce off the store window, making the ghosts on the glass glow.

This time I don't hesitate to press send, because I have something to say that's nothing to do with how much I miss him or how sorry I am for staying away. Sliding my cell out of my pocket, I send Nash a text before I can talk myself out of it.

Penny:

are you okay?

He must be worrying. Last month a window was smashed at the grocery store and Nash was blamed. Despite the total lack of evidence and the fact that Karter had been seen in the area.

That has to be playing on Nash's mind.

He'll be scared, and he only has his sister on his side. The two of them against the whole town. Those aren't great odds.

"Penny, the cops want to speak with us," Adi says, cutting through my thoughts and bringing me straight back to the dead body in Party Town.

"Yeah," I reply, taking one last look at the empty spot where Nash stood.

Adi and I both speak separately with cops outside the store. I don't have much to tell them other than I accidentally kicked Noah's dead body when I discovered him, and it was the worst moment of my life.

The cop makes it sound like the fact that I found him is suspicious. But if I hadn't, someone else would've.

When I point this out, he softens, but only a little. He still looks at me like he's going to underline my name three times on his pad and stick my photo on a board of suspects. Or maybe I'm being paranoid and reading too much into it.

Both my parents called, but they're hours away in the city for meetings, so it'll be a while until they can get back. I've never been so grateful that they're not home.

I don't need to be smothered right now. It takes a lot to convince them that I'm fine. I'm not allowed to be on my own, so I promise to go home with Adi until they're back.

Obviously that's not what I'm going to do.

As soon as I manage to ditch Adi, I'm heading straight out to Nash's farm.

"Babe, this is so surreal," Adi says. Her mom is holding on to her as if Noah's dead body is about to jump up and eat her brain.

"I know. Are you okay?" I ask, trying to keep still. I'm on edge, antsy, and desperate to get the hell out of here.

"I think so. I wasn't the one who found . . ."

I wave my hand, moving my weight from foot to foot. "I'm feeling fine. Shocked, but I'm okay. As soon as we're allowed to leave, I think I'll go home and take a shower."

To be fair, I *do* want to do that.

"I just spoke to Officer Gray, and he says we're free to leave. They might have further questions, but they know where we live," Adi's mom says. "Do you want to come to our house, Penny?"

"Yeah, I think I do." I have to in case my parents ask. "But I'll go home to shower and change first. I'll be about an hour."

It'll take me, like, twenty minutes really. Which means I'll have plenty of time to go find Nash.

"Okay, darling. Adi, let's get you home. I want you off the streets."

Adi rolls her eyes at the way her mom says "streets."

Though the serial killer last year and dead body this year has her, understandably, freaked out.

We're all freaking out.

I get in the old jeep my grandpa passed down to me and drive toward my house. Nash's place is on the opposite side of town but if I take a left and Adi sees, she'll wonder where I'm going. Actually . . . she'll know *exactly* where I'm going.

I'll go out of my way and take the long route up to Nash's.

I drive out of the town square to where stores give way to houses, then farther out to the surrounding farms and cornfields. I follow a tractor for a mile until I turn off onto the long gravelly drive.

The uneven road to his farm is so familiar. I could be going there to watch a movie or ride ATVs in one of the fields. The scrapyard is on the left, still taped off. I don't know what Nash and Grace plan to do with the farm, but I don't think they'd get much support if they tried reopening the yard.

A cloud of dust follows me, so they'll know someone is approaching. Grace can't stand me anymore. The last time I spoke to Nash on the phone, she was in the background telling him to hang up because I was trash and had no loyalty.

No loyalty.

And I proved her right.

I park outside the large red farmhouse and get out. The plants that used to grow in the front have all died. Jackson was an avid gardener.

How do you go from watering sunflowers to stabbing high school seniors?

I lock the car and walk to the front door. Mud clings to the wood; they've not bothered to wash it off. Wringing my hands, I pray that it'll be Nash who answers and not Grace.

She should be at college now, but the rumor is that she couldn't get in after what her dad did.

That seems unlikely, though. The other rumor is that she wouldn't leave Nash on his own. That one I believe.

They're only a year apart and have always been close. When their mom died five years ago, Grace stepped up. At one point she was like a sister to me too. She cares about everyone and trusts easily until you give her a reason not to.

The doorbell no longer works when I press it, so I knock and wait.

Inside I can hear someone moving—a door bangs, something scrapes on the floor. Maybe Nash has seen it's me and is running to hide, the chair he was sitting on now lying on the floor.

I wouldn't blame him.

A second later, the front door opens and Nash is scowling at me.

He stands with his arms crossed, his form way more muscular than it used to be, like he spends all of his spare time in his dad's home gym.

It takes an embarrassingly long time to be able to form words. His eyes are a striking deep blue with lighter flecks that resemble constellations, but right now they look angry.

Like, *really* angry.

He runs his hand through his messy hair and exhales. "What do you want, Penny?"

Why do I feel as stupid and giddy as when I first had a crush on him? If I could stop myself liking him, I would have done it by now. It sucks to miss someone you have to stay away from.

"I . . . I saw you in town?"

"Well done. I was in town. Now, *what do you want?*"

"Noah is dead," I whisper.

"Who the hell's Noah?" His expression is cold, eyes hard, jaw tight, waiting for the accusation to come. He knows who Noah is.

"We go to school with him."

You still should be at school with us now, but you switched to online classes.

None of the teachers at school will tell me how he's doing. They're respecting his privacy apparently, so I get nothing, and I hate it. I'm left with my imagination, which seems to always veer to the negative side.

He shrugs, still holding the door with a grip so tight his knuckles are two shades lighter than the rest of his tanned skin.

"He was on the football team," I remind him. *With you.*

"Right. That's what was happening in town. Why are you telling me this?"

In this moment, I'm unsure. I'm a fool for coming but how could I not?

"I don't know. It just seemed . . . right to. I'm sorry, this was a mistake. I shouldn't be here."

I start to turn, but he steps outside and blocks my way. "Then why did you come? Why now? Do you think I had something to do with it? My dad is a cold-blooded killer so that must mean I am too. Right?"

"No."

He arches a brow, challenging me, pushing me. It's like he wants me to agree and tell him that I'm just as small-minded as the rest of the town. "No?"

"Nash, if I thought you were the killer, I wouldn't be here right now, would I?"

"If I was on a murder spree, I wouldn't kill you. That'd be the quickest way to get myself caught."

Ouch. "That's the only reason you wouldn't kill me?"

Why the hell are you asking him that?

"Forget it," I say, holding my hand up before he can respond. "I'll go."

"Straight to the cops to tell them that I've been discussing who I'd kill?"

"Is that really what you think of me?"

He doesn't blink as he stares at me like I've said something incredibly stupid. He's the one being dumb here. I want to be gentle with him, but I also want to whack him with something hard.

Sure, he's mad but at least he's speaking to me.

"It's complicated, Nash," I say, answering his unspoken question. "I didn't want to stay away, but what else could I do?"

"Yeah, it's all about you, Penny."

"No, I'm not saying—"

"You're right, you should go. If Grace comes down and sees you, she'll freak."

I almost ask him how she is, but something tells me I don't want the answer.

"I like the new truck," I say, pointing to the red Chevy in the drive.

"Not mine."

I figured it belongs to Grace since her old car isn't here, and Nash's black truck is in the open barn.

He follows me to my car and watches as I open my door.

"I'm sorry I came," I say over my shoulder. "But I do miss you, and I hate this. I hate this so much."

As soon as the words are out, I leap into my seat.

That's why I came. Because he was always the one I went to, even before we were dating. Because I know he's hurting, and I want to make it better. Because I'm scared that there could be a copycat killer, and I don't know what it means for him if there is.

I watch him in my rearview mirror, staring after me with a hollow, unreadable expression.

3

By the time I shower and get to Adi's, my parents were calling me again. At least I was able to legitimately tell them I was at her house, so they didn't suspect anything.

Adi and I sit in her deep purple room. She's turned on the fairy lights that drape across the ceiling and lit the cherry-scented candle.

She picks up a fluffy pink pen and doodles on her notepad.

I look at the heading: SUSPECTS.

"Adi—"

She interrupts me. "How long did it take the cops to find Jackson last year?"

"The cops were on it for nearly a week, but the feds arrested him on their second day here. Put the notepad away, Nancy Drew."

Adi knows this already. Everyone does.

Will the feds return now? It was wild when they turned up. A total circus. I'd never seen so many people walking around town before; everyone wanted to watch them work. Some were happy to see them, while others thought our own cops would get him eventually.

Maybe, but it's not like they could take that risk with more teens' lives.

"Yes, but if his hair wasn't left behind, would he have been caught? Are we really relying on this killer making a similar mistake?"

I raise my hand. "I have questions."

"Come on, Pen, it's happening again. That much is obvious."

"Is it?"

"Duh."

"Great argument, Adi. You should join the debate team."

"What else are we going to do this weekend? It's a week until Halloween, same as last year. The timeline fits Jackson's. You can't deny that."

No, that I can't deny.

I wish I could think of something to come back at her with. But I can't because she's totally right. The timeline is identical. All we can do is hope that the cops find whoever it is before he copies the next kill. Last year, there were two more murders in the week leading to Halloween: a double murder on Devil's Night and, finally, an arrest in the early hours of Halloween.

Nash had called me at six o'clock that morning, panicked, telling me the feds had busted the door open and arrested his dad. I told him not to worry, said it had to be a mistake and his dad would be back home soon.

Adi turns on her vintage-style radio and we listen to live coverage of the murder on the local station. People keep calling in to have their say. It's all completely unhelpful and only spreading hate and fear. I'm grateful for Adi's aversion to TV news stations because I don't want to watch people I recognize being interviewed on the street.

The first thing I hear is Nash and Grace being mentioned straightaway, not quite by name but by people's not-so-subtle "you do know he has children," and it makes my stomach burn with anger.

Adi can sense my mood and, so far, has refrained from blaming them again. It's written all over her face, though. And she's now angled the notepad away from me to scribble in.

I can tell she agrees with the callers because her eyebrows rise every time someone says the cops need to knock on their door.

Has she forgotten she was Nash's friend too? She was the one who encouraged him to ask me on a date and helped him pick out my birthday present.

I want to shake her.

We're both on our phones as we listen, her flitting between that and her notes. I don't know who she's messaging but it's not a group I'm in. Our chat has been crickets since Omar and Zayn told us that they'd be straight over once they arrived back in town later.

Omar and Zayn, the two who complete our group—now that Nash is . . . gone—were both away for the weekend. Omar was with his family while they organized his sister's wedding. Zayn was with his mom visiting his grandparents. Neither of them were due home until tomorrow, but I think both of their parents want to know what's happening here.

As horrific as the murders were last year, they did give everyone something to talk about and memorials to organize. I'd never seen the town so alive as when it was drenched in death.

It's kind of sick.

My phone dings. Adi looks up but doesn't say anything. She would usually ask who it is, so that makes me think she's talking about Nash to someone. If she asks me, I get to ask her.

I almost gasp when Nash's name appears on my screen.

He's replied. I *never* expected him to, especially not after seeing him this morning. He looked like he wanted to chase me off his property with a pitchfork.

Nash:

i didn't kill him.

I sag in relief. Of course, I already knew that, but I *needed* to hear the words. I had to hear it from him. And, for reasons that I shouldn't overthink, he felt the need to tell me he's innocent.

Penny:

i already know that. are you okay?

Nash:

you shouldn't be talking to me.

Penny:

no, i never should have stopped talking to you. i'm sorry.

Nash:

i get it.

The fact that he gets it makes me feel even worse. I should get an award for the crappiest girlfriend ever . . . *ex*-girlfriend. There just wasn't a way to stay with him while every person in my life ordered me away.

Penny:

what can i do, nash?

Nash:

meet me tonight.

Penny:

when and where?

Nash:

the old movie theater. midnight.

Midnight. It'll be October 24 then, exactly one year since Jackson took his second victim's—a girl named Cait—life. If the new killer, if that's what's even happening here, is copying Jackson, someone might die at midnight.

Nash:

??

Penny:

I'll be there.

My parents are in bed by ten every night because they're always up at five for work, so sneaking out won't be an issue. Nash knows that. We spent a lot of time in the summer before the murders sneaking out and hanging around the local park.

He doesn't reply after I agree to meet, so I put my phone down and focus on Adi, my mood suddenly lighter than before.

"Apparently the cops are headed to the Whitmore farm," Adi says.

That didn't take them long but it's to be expected. Someone was murdered on the anniversary of their dad's first kill. It was only a matter of time.

Jackson's chosen method was stabbing, and Noah was stabbed. At least I think he was. There were definite marks on his chest that looked like stab wounds to me.

"That was always coming," I reply, picking my phone up again.

Nash won't be shocked that he's getting a visit, but I want to warn him that it's happening right now. I send a quick message that he reads almost immediately. There's no response but at least he knows.

"Do you think they have a decent alibi?" Adi asks, looking at my phone, knowing what I've done. It's the first time she's genuinely seemed concerned for them.

"I don't know. I hope so because if they were just at home, I don't think the cops will accept that."

"They'll be able to track their phones."

"All that proves is that you didn't take your phone out," I tell her.

"They won't be able to convict them on that alone. Don't panic, Pen."

"I hope not. Judging by the radio callers, everyone would love to see the next generation of Whitmores in jail, just like their dad."

She tilts her head. "Babe, that's not true. They're scared. Can you blame them after last year?"

"If you think *we're* all scared, can you imagine how Nash and Grace must feel?"

"I get it." We sit in silence for a moment before Adi perks up. "Hey, someone's posted on the town Facebook group that two cop cars just turned into the farm. That was quick."

We all revived our neglected Facebook accounts last year because the adults were using a town group to discuss the murders.

Everyone will be glued to their windows, waiting for something to happen, phone in hand so they can update the town the second it does. I hate it.

"I think I'm going to head out," I say. "My parents will be home soon, and I said I'd meet them there."

"You sure? You can stay here as long as you want."

I stand and grab my phone and bag. "Thanks, but I just need to chill before they get back. They're going to have a lot of questions."

And as president of the Nash Is Bad News Club, Dad is going to have a lot to say about him. Which will result in him making me promise that I will *never* go near him again.

A promise that I'll break within hours of making it.

I'm not just a terrible girlfriend . . .

"You should take some time to relax. I mean, you were the one who found Noah. Last week we were sitting in class with him and now he's . . . you know."

Yeah, dead. I very much get it.

"I promise I will."

Adi and her parents wave me off . . . along with an inflatable ghost that's swaying in their front yard. I drive the long way again, passing my road and heading back toward Nash's place. I won't go down the drive because the cops might see but I need to know what's going on.

As I approach their street, I pass a cop car.

No!

Nash is in the back.

I brake a little too hard and pull over on the side of the road, my heart in my throat, but the car is gone. What the hell? Grace wasn't with him, so where is she? Why would they only question Nash?

My mind instantly goes back a year, to when Nash told me the feds had taken his dad. *He's in the back of their SUV right now, Penny. I don't know what to do.*

Why would they take him in? He can be questioned at home. Grace must have been, because I didn't pass anyone else and there are no more cop cars outside their house.

Why only him? The question loops in my mind.

He wouldn't hurt anyone. I know it.

I take a breath and think about what I should do next, about how I can help him, if that's even possible. Whatever I do, it needs to not make things worse for either of us.

Going to the station would be pointless, so I stick my car in drive and continue to his house. Grace is likely to tell me to get lost, but I have to try to talk to her. There might be something I can do.

She's outside when I pull up.

When she spots my car, she folds her arms and her dark blue eyes narrow into tiny slits of destruction. She looks like she wants to strangle me and throw me in the river.

I'm so not welcome here.

I hop out of my car and without giving her the chance to yell at me, I ask, "Why did they take him?"

She scoffs, curling her lip. "Don't pretend you care."

"I do care. Why did they take him?"

Has he been taken for questioning, or has he been arrested? Two very different things.

She pushes her wavy brown hair behind her ears and huffs. "Someone said they saw him in town, watching the costume store, apparently. As if it's a crime even if he was there! They've taken him in. Go on, you go back and spread the gossip. It's already all over social media. Everyone thinks Nash is guilty."

"That's not what I'm here for. I saw him in town too. I didn't realize anyone else had."

Her back stiffens, making her taller. "Where was he?"

Grace didn't know that he was out then. Not that she would—they were always close but didn't check in much. But they're not often in town anymore. It doesn't look great for Nash that on one of the rare days he's there, someone gets murdered.

"Opposite Party Town, between the bookstore and pharmacy."

Her eyes widen and her anger over seeing me transforms into worry for her brother.

"God, Penny. If that's where someone else saw him, it doesn't look good. He's all I have left. They're going to pin this on him," she says, and takes a long, ragged breath that sounds as if she's about to hyperventilate. I'm no good in medical emergencies. "The whole town would *love* it if Nash was guilty."

"Breathe, Grace. I won't let anyone blame him. He didn't do this."

She snorts again. "You won't let them? I dare you to say Nash is innocent to anyone but me or him."

Turning abruptly, she goes back inside and slams the door. I hear her shout, "I can't lose him too!"

4

It's late afternoon when I pull up to the police and fire station, but I park in the lot of the stationery store across the street. I want a good view of the station, but I don't want to be seen.

The stationery store is heavily decorated with Halloween characters and orange lights. The other side of the road is a stark difference. There's not even a cobweb on either station.

Without a plan beyond where I'm going to wait, I sit and watch, chewing on my lip as the ball of anxiety in my stomach grows again. Things would be so much easier if I could forget about Nash like everyone wants me to. But I wouldn't give up on Adi, Omar, or Zayn either.

There are a few windows that face the street but only one you can see through. That's the one I'm currently fixed on, but I can only see a small slice of the front desk.

No Nash yet. He might already be in the interview room.

God, he must be so scared. Grace didn't mention getting a lawyer, but he must have someone with him. He's still a minor.

My heart beats erratically at the thought of Nash going down for this. I'm getting way ahead of myself here; I don't even know what happened today. There's so much speculation, and I can feel myself getting sucked into it.

It'll be fine. The cops will question him, check CCTV, and realize it wasn't him.

A car pulls into the police station lot and a man with short white-blond hair and a poorly fitting suit gets out. That must be the man representing Nash; he said last year that his dad's lawyer's hair was super light.

He goes inside but I don't see him through the window. He was probably escorted straight to Nash.

I tighten my grip on the steering wheel, sitting as far forward as I can . . . waiting.

As I'm watching the window like a stalker, I see a flash of red speed past. Jolting, I do a double take, noticing it's Grace's new truck. It's slightly past me before I can properly see the driver, but it doesn't look like Grace. Too tall and the shoulders are too broad.

No way.

The hairs on my neck stand up. It can't be.

The driver is wearing a dark blue cap with familiar tufts of ash-brown hair sticking out from under it.

No. Freaking. Way.

Jackson?

Nuh-uh. That can't be right. He's serving life without the chance of parole. He was only sentenced two months ago, so there's no way he could've been released.

I grip the steering wheel harder, debating whether I should follow the car, but that feels like the dumbest thing I could possibly do. Follow a potential serial killer.

No. It can't be him.

Nash and Grace don't have any other family. Their mom is dead, their dad is in prison, and both sets of grandparents died when they were really young.

Maybe Grace has a boyfriend.

Or . . . maybe it *was* Jackson.

Oh my god. Don't be stupid. We would've heard if he'd been released. It took all of three seconds for people to find out that the cops were on their way to Nash's farm. No way could Jackson be walking the streets again without there being an uproar.

Everyone in town would be marching along that dusty road with pitchforks.

But it's not him, so who the hell was it?

It has to be Grace's boyfriend. I didn't think she had one but it's not like she'd suddenly call me after months just to announce her relationship status. There was a guy she was interested in at her work. I vaguely remember some coy smiles when she was messaging someone last year.

I slow my breathing and try to reason with myself. I've seen a dead body, we have a potential copycat killer on the loose, and I've just spent all morning listening to conspiracy theories.

I'm obviously not thinking straight.

The relentless dinging sounding from my phone pulls me back to reality—one where a killer in federal prison hasn't escaped without anyone finding out.

This is a much better place to be. *More focus on staying grounded, Penny.*

My group chat is going off. Omar and Zayn are now at Adi's, and I'm not there. I can't bring myself to face them. Zayn will keep asking how I'm doing, and Omar will make one too many jokes.

I don't pay much attention to my phone, but the conversation is being held via our chat and not between them in person. I've only seen snippets as they're typing constantly but Adi's telling them that I need space after my trauma.

My trauma.

That's what we're calling it. I mean, it's fairly accurate, but I can't think about what I've seen yet. Besides, Adi and Mae saw the body too. I don't need any special treatment.

Having something else to focus on is probably the reason why I'm not having a meltdown. As cold as that sounds.

I'm worrying about Nash and now his dad or Grace's Jackson-look-alike boyfriend.

Would Grace go out with someone who, from the side at least, shares a striking resemblance to her imprisoned, murderous father?

She wouldn't.

I'm going crazy.

Since there's no one I can call and Nash is still inside the station, I use Google to indulge my downward spiral and search Jackson Whitmore's release date.

Because obviously logic isn't something I can trust today.

There is no date that comes up because, yeah, he's serving a life sentence and will die in prison.

There's no record of him being mysteriously released or breaking out. The feds are keeping him locked up. That would have to be public information anyway, surely?

If he'd escaped, the news would be everywhere. And if he escaped, why would he come back here to kill again? Quickest way to find yourself back in jail.

While I search and scroll Google, half losing my mind, the door of the station opens across the street and Nash walks out, followed by the white-haired man. They quickly go their separate ways, the man straight into his car, peeling away like he could catch something from sticking around.

Nash holds his phone up, probably ready to call Grace, but then he spots me and freezes. His expression is hard for a moment, and I wonder if he thinks I'm the one who turned him in.

I'm not sure what his next move will be. It will either be asking Grace to pick him up or coming toward me. My heart flutters wildly as I wait, hoping that he will walk over here and we can talk.

Please, Nash. I just want a chance.

After a quick deliberation, he crosses the road and walks toward my car.

I sit up straight and unlock the doors, ready to let him in. He runs his hand through his hair, the light bouncing off his surfer-styled brown locks. He always styles his slightly wavy hair a little disheveled, but this is the first time I've seen it as messy as it is now.

Nash slides into the passenger seat and blows out a long breath. His legs stretch to the end of the footwell. He fills my car more now. He's so much bigger; he must be working out daily.

"Are you okay?" I ask. "What happened?"

"You came," he says, and laughs at himself. Probably for stating the obvious, but I'm not sure it was something he meant to say aloud. Shaking his head, he turns to me, and I can see a thousand questions in his eyes and a bit of anger too. Actually, a lot of anger. I deserve every ounce of it.

For a second I can't help but stare. He's real and he's here. His dark blue eyes are stunning against his tanned skin, but they're filled with sadness.

"I was on my way to your place after Adi told me the cops were coming to you. I never thought you'd be taken away. You weren't in there very long. Was that your lawyer?"

He smirks the way he always does when I ramble. "Yeah, that was Beckett, the lawyer. They questioned me about why I was in town today . . . as if that's a crime." He scoffs and shakes his head. "They took my fingerprints."

"What, you were arrested?"

"No, I did the prints voluntarily. They just wanted to know why I was in town, where I was in the early hours, and what my relationship with Noah was like. That kind of stuff."

"They couldn't have asked that at your place?"

"Oh, they absolutely could have. I think they wanted to scare me. The cops in this town aren't my biggest fans. Every time a car is broken into or a store window is smashed, they knock on my door. Beckett wasn't happy about that and told them to back off unless they had evidence."

"Do they know it wasn't you?"

"What if I told you one of the store windows was me?" he asks.

"I don't care about that! I'm talking about the *murder*."

"I don't know what they think. They're investigating. Which I guess means they're trying to find a way to make this my fault."

"That won't happen. There's CCTV all over town, Nash. Soon they will see it's not you."

The mayor went on a huge crime-prevention spree last fall, installing more cameras on almost every building and some around the square. It was really distressing because suddenly adults were obsessed with watching over us, and my dad even bought a gun.

My parents have calmed down checking in on me . . . until now.

I bet they start obsessively checking the doorbell camera again.

I lay back against my seat. Whoever is copying Jackson will probably be masked, though. If they're from town, they'll know about the extra security measures. "Who could it be? Do you know if your dad gets any weird mail from superfans?"

"You still listening to crime podcasts?"

"Nash!"

"I don't speak to him, Penny. Okay. I have *no* contact with him. He murdered five people and despite what everyone is saying, I'm not goddamn proud of him!"

"All right," I say, raising my hands in surrender. "I'm sorry. It's just if they don't figure out who's doing this . . ."

"It's worse for me. I get it," he replies, shoving his hands through his hair again. "I had nothing to do with this."

"I know. Can you think of *anyone*?"

"No. Grace has spoken to him a couple of times, so I'll ask her."

"She has?"

He turns his nose up. "She wants to *understand* and can't accept that he's just a sick bastard. She has all these questions, the same as mine I guess, but she can't relax until they're answered."

"What kind of questions?"

"How? Why? What made him snap? Did he always want to do it? How did he . . . you know, decide who to kill? As far as I'm aware, he didn't know any of them. Had he always wanted to hurt people? Why people the same age as his kids? You were over so many times. . . ."

He turns away and looks out the window.

The temperature in the car plummets, and I rub the goose bumps on my arms. "You've wondered if he wanted to kill me?"

"I don't ever want the answer to that question," he replies. His voice is dark and cold, and sends a shiver down my spine.

I know Nash, so I know he wouldn't forgive his dad, but I didn't realize he hated him. Jackson's still his dad after all and you don't get to choose how you *feel* about someone.

"I like the highlights," he says, changing things up. Neither of us wanting to consider what his dad may have wanted to do to me.

My blond hair is a few shades lighter now, brighter. I wanted, needed, a change and my hair was the one thing that I had any power over.

"Thanks. Nash, I don't have long. My parents are on their way home."

He doesn't respond for the longest time, so I almost repeat myself, unsure if he's heard me. He's somewhere deep inside his head and I've not been allowed in. All my own fault.

Suddenly, he turns back and startles me. "I should go."

"Yeah, we do need to leave, but I'll drive you."

"Grace won't be happy."

"I've seen her today. She wasn't happy then, so it doesn't matter. I don't care."

"You went back to my house?"

"Briefly. Before I came here. Let me drive you. It's the least I can do."

"Okay," he replies, but makes it sound like he doesn't quite understand why. I've not offered him a lift for a long time. "Are we still meeting at midnight?"

I turn the engine on and glance around to see if anyone has spotted us. We're good. The only people around are too far away or too engrossed in their own lives to notice.

"Yes," I reply. "Hey, does Grace have a boyfriend?"

He does a double take. "What? Why would you ask that?"

"The car outside your house."

"It's hers, remember?" he replies, glancing out the window.

"Right."

He's lying to me. Someone who isn't Grace was driving that car. Why would he hide that?

I try to push away an uneasy feeling in my stomach. Nash doesn't lie. Not to me. We had a pact. One I'm sure ended when I cut off contact. It's a bit hypocritical of me to feel hurt that he's not opening up, I know that.

A lot has changed in a year. Everything he says to me now might be a lie.

"Why does Grace need two cars?" I ask.

"She's going to sell her old one," he replies, still avoiding looking at me.

Did he forget that I can tell when he's being dishonest? Why is he protecting whoever was in the car? The weird tension between us weighs heavy.

"I don't know if she has a boyfriend. We don't talk as much anymore, but she meets some people from work."

Okay, the guy she was crushing on was from her work, so that makes sense.

Nash ducks down as we drive, passing car after car in a display of my bravery . . . or stupidity.

"Why do you still want to meet me at midnight now that we're both here?" I ask. "I mean, I'll do it. I'm just curious."

My shoulders lose some of the tension when I turn down their driveway to the farm. We're alone here. No one saw us. I can't believe I have to behave like a criminal just to see him.

"You asked to see me—that's why we're meeting."

"Why are you acting weird?"

"Is that a serious question, Penny?"

I jam the brakes, and we slide to a stop with a cloud of dust engulfing us.

Nash slams his hand on the dash and stares at me with wide eyes. "What the hell was that?"

"Enough bullshit."

He opens the door and gets out.

"Nash!" I shout.

"Midnight or don't bother. Lose the attitude too. You're not the one on trial here."

He slams the door so hard that the car rocks.

Well, at least he's getting all that anger and resentment out. I smile, pleased with how that went despite the mini argument at the end. Once he's past the anger stage, we can have a real discussion about everything that's happened.

I can ask more questions. He can be more honest.

He can tell me what the hell is going on.

5

Mom and Dad fussed over me the entire evening, talking through safety measures . . . and by that, I mean they told me everything I can and cannot do and offered to start me with a therapist. It took a few rather dramatic yawns before they finally let me go to bed. I heard them follow soon after.

Then I waited, watching Netflix on my phone until almost midnight.

At ten minutes to, I slip on my shoes and open the back door and disappear into the backyard. My parents' window faces the front of the house. Dad was always happy about that, said he was able to see if anyone was approaching. He has no idea I use that to my advantage when sneaking out.

I walk close to the wall around the side of the house and slap my hand over my mouth, jolting backward at the large figure in my yard. A scream almost rips from my throat, one that would land me in a hell of a lot of trouble.

The whites of the freaking werewolf's eyes glow against the light of the moon.

It used to be my favorite Halloween decoration. I knew it was there because I helped put it up, but it still scared the crap out of me.

I hate that thing now.

On my way back home, I need to remember it's there. Along with the stupid skeletons and headstones.

I've already had enough of this holiday.

Fluffy pretend cobwebs stretch from branch to branch on Dad's perfectly maintained trees. Throwing my arms out, I rip some of it down, my heart still thudding from the scare, and tiptoe to the front of the house.

Why did I ever like this holiday?

Dad even trimmed a small hedge into the shape of a pumpkin. I refrain from kicking it. He might notice if I do any damage. Or a neighbor might. There's actually a neighborhood group that will put passive-aggressive notes in your mailbox if your yard is overgrown.

We're a cute, close-knit town . . . haunted by murder.

The walk to the old movie theater will only take me five minutes, but I gave myself extra time to get out of the house. And, to be honest, I wanted to arrive first and watch out for Nash.

That sounds a bit creepy, but I don't like being watched. Not after Jackson. There were occasions when I was alone with him, when I'd arrived at Nash's before he got back from football practice. Jackson never made me feel uncomfortable but once he was arrested, I couldn't help but stress at how easy it would've been for him to kill me.

I'd sit at their kitchen table while he made hot chocolate and a sandwich. We'd make small talk about college or piano. All that time, he could've been daydreaming about sticking a knife into my gut.

It's only when I'm half a block away from home that I realize how incredibly stupid it is of me to walk around in the dead of night alone. Thoughts of Jackson are not helping me feel better about being alone.

Someone was murdered today and every house I pass has some sort of gruesome character in the front yard. It's like a never-ending haunted hayride. I keep my head down and walk through the chilly, silent night.

One of those yards would be a great place for a killer to blend in. Hiding in plain sight.

My heart thuds harder as I pick up my pace, my mind conjuring scenarios of a serial killer stepping out from someone's yard and following me.

I turn the corner and look in each direction, my breathing now the same as the time I tried running a 10K. The decorated streetlights ensure that the town isn't in complete darkness. The moon is bright, bouncing off storefronts ahead and reflecting off puddles from the downpour an hour ago.

I'm almost past the houses now. Just a few more and I won't see as many creepy statues. I can't take a more direct route because of people's stupid doorbell cameras.

Don't move, don't move, don't move, I chant to the Halloween decorations in my head.

Tension curls my shoulders as I huddle to make myself as small and inconspicuous as possible.

The last house on the left before I cross the road and into the town center has five dark figures in the yard. Vampires maybe. It's kind of dark . . . and I'm trying to ignore them. In my periphery, I see a cloak sway.

It's just part of the costume.

You're fine.

Keep walking.

I clench my hands into fists and power on.

It's getting colder by the second. I'm bundled in my woolly hat and gloves with my coat zipped to my chin, but I still feel the icy wind stinging my cheeks.

When I'm level with the vampires, I wrap my arms around my stomach and push against the queasiness. Why couldn't we have met in my backyard?

I'm acutely aware of every sight and sound around me, despite trying to ignore the creepy holiday decorations. In daylight they're not at all scary.

Crossing the road, I breathe a little easier. The display of Halloween characters has given way to the more subtle window displays and hanging lights. Which are unfortunately off now that it's almost midnight.

The town is filled with the scent of pumpkin. They're everywhere, outside every shop and house, some carved with sinister faces and designs, the others cute or untouched.

As I step onto the sidewalk, I hear footsteps behind me.

My heart misses a beat, and I whip around on the spot.

What the hell?

It could be Nash—it's likely Nash—but in the dead of night, my mind goes elsewhere.

This could be the killer.

I step back into the doorway of the library, listening to the thudding of my pulse, and press my hand to my mouth. I'm hiding until I know exactly who it is.

It's okay. No one was behind me when I turned around. I'm pretty sure of that. Which means no one knows I'm here. If it's Nash, I'll step out. If it's not . . .

I don't even want to consider that I'm out here alone with a killer.

Where's Nash and why did I think getting here early would be a good idea?

The footsteps grow louder as the person closes in.

I sink into the wall, half hiding behind a mountain of pumpkins and promising myself that I'll never do anything stupid like this again.

There is just enough room here for me. I wish I'd risked waking my parents by taking my car now. Better to be grounded than stabbed.

I'm *such* an idiot.

Heavy boots thump on the ground. I crouch lower. They sound like they're on top of me, and then suddenly they stop.

Crap.

I keep my eyes open, holding my breath so I don't make any noise, and wait. The doorway is wide so I would have a chance to escape if whoever it is spots me. I could run forward or in the opposite direction to them and maybe make it away. But for how long and where would I go?

A few people live above some of the businesses, but most of the apartments have been turned into more store space.

I'm confident that if my life depended on it, I could scream the whole town awake. I've only had a quarter of an ice cream sundae and a few bites of dinner today, so I'd probably faint before outrunning him.

Thud, thud, thud.

Nash wears sneakers most of the time. These sound like thick boots.

The steps retreat, and I listen until I can barely hear them. I think they went back the way they came from.

Why?

If it was the killer and they knew I was here, I wouldn't be alive now.

I stand, leaning my palm on the wall so that I don't do anything stupid like trip and knock the pumpkin pile over.

Slowly, I peer around the corner and my heart stops.

Ahead, just disappearing around the side of the launderette, is a hooded figure with a white mask.

I leap back, my head banging on the glass pane of the library door.

Wincing, I freeze and pray to god that whoever that was didn't hear me.

This is not so unusual for Halloween, I try to convince myself. If we'd never experienced murders here, I wouldn't even think twice about someone walking around in costume in the middle of the night.

But there had been five murders. And now there was a new one.

Jackson wore a plain white mask with two holes for eyes and no mouth.

I didn't get to see much of the mask this person was wearing; it looked similar, but it might be a different one.

Wait . . . could that person have been in one of the yards?

Hell no, do *not* go there.

I hate where my mind takes me.

I look across the square to the little alleyway that leads down to the old part of town. Empty buildings waiting to be renovated.

Benji's movie theater is crumbling but will soon be turned into an indoor skate park and arcade—to stop so many people from jumping off benches with their boards. Nash was pretty good on a board and taught me. I've not seen him skate since his dad's murders.

There is almost enough money from fundraising. Adults keen to give us somewhere to go. Stop us turning out like Jackson, I guess.

Looking both ways, I contemplate making a run for it to try and get away.

The masked dude is gone. Or gone as far as I can see. I can't stay cowering here forever.

Nash should be at the theater now. I only need to make it to him and then we're two on one, and those are odds I like.

My stomach twists tight, my body in total disagreement with

this plan, but what am I supposed to do now? I'm safer with Nash than walking home alone. I have to get home somehow, and I would really rather it be with another person.

I look down, assessing my path to the other side. A road, the town square, which is filled with Halloween decorations, then another road.

That's it.

As soon as I'm past that point, there will be no decorations. I won't constantly think I'm seeing a real person and not just a statue.

Not going to lie, I'm looking forward to that. It'll be much easier to convince myself that sneaking out wasn't a terrible idea.

I take a breath and shove myself off the wall, sprinting as fast as I can.

Wind whistles past my ears as I run, spurred on by adrenaline. I hear nothing else and the thought that someone could be behind me without me knowing is suffocating.

I leap clean over a bench and land heavy on my feet but I don't stop. I pass a graveyard of headstones, skeletons, a fake corpse in a suit, and make it across the grassy square and to the next road.

The alleyway feels smaller, more cramped, as I run between the walls and out onto the old block. Twisting, I make a sharp left and run up the steps of the movie theater.

My lungs heave for oxygen. Bending over, I hide behind a half-wall and suck in cold air. I grip the railing so I don't slip as black spots dance in front of my face. I've never wanted to be tucked up safe in my bed more than I do right now.

Tears spring to my eyes but I push them back and swallow. I'm here now, stupid as that is, and I need to figure out what to do. There is no Nash.

My watch illuminates as I twist my wrist. A few minutes past midnight.

• • •

SUNDAY, OCTOBER 24

I wait for Nash, hiding behind the wall and watching obsessively in every direction. If he doesn't come, I need to figure out how to get home without being seen.

There are two options that I flat out refuse to consider, even though they keep popping into my head.

Nash has been killed.

Nash is the killer.

There's a third, I suppose.

This was someone messing around in a costume around *Halloween,* and I'm losing my mind. I think I've slowly been losing my mind since last year, so I'd bet on that.

My watch shows 12:09 a.m.

"Where are you?" I whisper, and the words disappear into vapor.

He wouldn't stand me up. Unless he's trying to get back at me for the way I've treated him. We were together for a year before I told him I couldn't see him anymore.

That was it. I said I couldn't "do this" and stopped calling. There was very little explanation really—though I don't think he needed it. Nash knew why I couldn't see him anymore.

As if that would matter to him, though.

I twist my hair around my finger until it pulls at the scalp.

What am I going to do now? I give it another minute and then send him a message.

Penny:

where are you?

I stare at the screen, willing him to open the message and reply, to tell me that he's running late and is almost here.

What I get is nothing.

It's what I deserve.

The last thing he did before he slammed my door was snap at me.

I look up again, craning my neck to check every direction. The town is silent and cloaked in darkness. No cars on the road, no people—masked or otherwise—on the street. It's even colder now, and I shiver inside my coat.

He's not coming, and I have to get myself home.

It's ten minutes past midnight, officially the anniversary of the double murder. I don't want to be next.

If. If. If!

If it's happening again. This might not be a copycat killer. We're assuming here. I have to admit, it's a pretty massive coincidence *if* it's not.

Penny:

at least tell me if you're not coming.

He was last online twenty minutes ago. About the time he would need to leave his place to meet me. So why isn't he here now?

I'm watching for a reply from Nash when Zayn's name flashes on-screen.

Incoming call.

Crap.

With a last glance around, I answer the call and hold my phone to my ear.

He's talking before I can say hi. "Penny, what the hell are you doing in town at midnight?"

"How did you . . . Oh my god, are you *tracking* me?" My voice is the shoutiest whisper I can manage.

"Find My is still on, Penny."

"So you randomly decided at midnight to trace me?"

I'd forgotten it was still on, to be fair.

"Not randomly. Adi said you messaged Nash today and then you ran off before we got to hers. Then I remembered you two used to sneak out. Is he with you?"

With a sigh, I reply, "No, he didn't come. I'm worried."

"Why?"

If I tell Zayn about the masked person in the square, he will freak out worse than my parents. Okay, not worse. Our group of five survived the loss of Nash. The dynamic changed, but if anything, it made the rest of them stronger, tighter. *Ride or die,* that's what Zayn would say as we skated down the road. A joke between the five of us—we have each other's backs.

"Because he has no one."

"He has his weird sister."

Zayn only thinks she's weird because he had the biggest crush on her, and she barely acknowledged his existence. I think he asked her out once, but he'd never admit it and she was too nice to tell us what went down. She knew Omar would make fun of him.

When I don't reply, he asks, "Do you need me to come and get you?"

"My parents will hear your car."

"I'll drop you half a block from your house. You're alone and Noah was just murdered. I actually can't believe you snuck out tonight."

The wind sweeps behind the wall, sending an ice-cold chill down my spine. A little reminder that I'm alone and vulnerable.

"Yeah, okay," I relent. "Thanks, Zayn. I'm by Benji's theater."

But he knows that already.

"Stay there, keep down, and make sure your phone is on silent. I'll be, like, two minutes."

I had thought of all those things already.

As Zayn hangs up, I check my messages with Nash again.

He still hasn't read them.

That can't be good. I'm not sure who it's bad for, though. There's a strong possibility that he's just paying me back for ditching him. As if it was as simple as that.

I'm crouched down behind the low wall that runs to the entrance of the theater. The doors and windows are boarded up; no one has stepped foot in there in years. A large crack above one of the fire exits and multiple broken roof tiles show how unloved the building has been.

I watch over the top of the wall for Zayn's car, knowing the direction he will appear from. He should be here any second and then I can be sure to never do anything this dumb again.

But I'll still need to do *some* dumb stuff. Like going to see Nash again. I have to know why he stood me up.

Headlights flash in the distance. *Come on, please be Zayn.*

I don't want to stand up too soon in case it's not him and I can't recognize a car by its headlights—something that Omar can do . . . and he does it *all* the time.

The car slowly approaches. I lean forward, peering around the corner of the wall while also trying to remain hidden.

It's then that a loud scraping sound, like metal on metal, rings out from inside the building.

Gasping, I twist around and freeze. My butt hits the cold, damp floor as my legs slide out underneath me.

I'm not alone.

6

"Shit," I mutter, pushing myself back onto my feet as the abrasive noise rings through the building again.

I turn back to the road, shove my hands against the wall, spring off the brick, and fly down the steps. The headlights get brighter as I sprint toward the road.

The car pulls up outside the theater, and Zayn reaches across to open the passenger-side door.

I throw myself into the seat and slam the door shut. "Drive, Zayn!"

"Whoa! What happened? Are you okay? Jeez, Pen, you're making ghosts look tan."

"I heard something from inside the theater and it freaked me out. Why are you not driving?"

He looks past me to Benji's. "What did you hear?"

"Does it matter? Let's go! Can you lock the doors, please?"

Without looking, Zayn thumps the button and the doors

lock. I sink into the seat, finally able to breathe. The car sits idle, though, Zayn not responding to me.

His hazel eyes are boring holes into me, and I have no idea what he's thinking but it's probably about how crazy he believes I am. "Calm down. What did you hear, Penny?"

"Metal. Scraping. Seriously, can we *go*?"

He leans back against his seat, still staring at me like I'm a circus freak. His black brows are pulled together, and he pinches the bridge of his nose. "You weren't supposed to go near him. Your parents . . . What are you doing out here?"

"I swear I will answer every question you have if you could please drive! I really want to get out of here, okay? It's been a very bad day and we're only"—I check my watch—"twenty-three minutes into it."

Zayn puts the car into drive, and we finally pull away. I watch him for a second and my heart rate begins to slow. Zayn has always been safe. He has this magic calming effect that makes you want to spill all your secrets. He has the kindest hazel eyes, dark skin, and black hair that's recently been braided into a zigzag pattern that runs down his scalp to the nape of his neck. He must've had it done today—or rather, yesterday—because he was rocking an Afro on Friday at school.

"I like the hair," I say.

"Took hours. Tell me what's going on," he says, and he's never sounded more like my dad.

"Where do I even start?"

"Why were you meeting Nash?"

He says his name like it's something gross. I don't want to think about why. We were past that . . . I thought.

"He asked me to."

"Why?"

"To talk, I guess. He didn't say when I drove him home from the police station," I say.

"What?" His voice is so high-pitched it makes me laugh. "Penny!"

"Sorry. He was taken to the station to be interviewed. I saw him being taken away in a cop car and followed. I waited for him and gave him a ride after. It was weird, sure, but I thought we were getting along a bit better."

"Why couldn't you just talk while you took him home?"

"I had to get back before my parents got home. They were out of town when I found . . . the body. They wouldn't understand why I wanted to see Nash."

"Not sure I do either."

"Zayn, he was your friend for *years.*"

"I know, but so was Brodie."

Jackson's final victim.

"Nash didn't kill Brodie," I say quietly, being as gentle as I can with him. He lost a friend that night. But Brodie's blood isn't on Nash's hands.

His grip tightens on the steering wheel, and he steps a fraction harder on the gas pedal. His jaw is hard, eyes tight as if he's regretting picking me up already.

We haven't spoken about Nash since the night Zayn asked

me out—a month after Nash and I stopped talking—so this is real awkward.

"I'm sorry," I say. "But he needs us too."

"Do you think I don't know that?" he asks. "I've tried, Penny."

"What?"

"I've tried reaching out to him recently. I got nothing back."

I thought I was the only one who was struggling with not seeing Nash. The only one still trying, although I haven't been very good at it lately. Zayn hadn't been pro-Nash in a long time, especially after I told him I wasn't ready to date again, so it seems weird that he'd reached out to him.

"Why didn't you tell me this?" I ask.

"Because you always seem so sad whenever we mention him. Because . . . you know."

I wish I didn't know. Zayn has been a close friend for years and we're still not back to normal. Mostly we just pretend he never told me he wants more.

"No one talks about him because they think it will bother me?"

"That's pretty much why *I* don't talk about him. I can't speak for Omar or Adi."

Pretty much.

"It feels like Adi hates him. She was quick to blame him for the murder today."

Zayn pushes down harder on the gas, and we accelerate. "I've heard that crap all day too. No one knows him the way we do."

That is genuine, I'm sure of it.

"Man, it's so nice to talk to someone who doesn't hate him," I say. "I wish you'd opened up to me before."

Shrugging, he flies through a traffic light and turns down my road. "Look, I know things have been a bit odd with us, but we're cool, Pen. You can talk to me anytime you want."

"Yeah?"

He gives me a little smile. "Did you think I'd pine over you for the rest of my life?"

That insinuates that he's done at least *some* pining. "No, of course not! I just . . . You were one of my best friends."

"Still am." He laughs. "I can feel the awkward vibes radiating from you. Stop, okay? I'm fine. You're fine. Talk about Nash all you want."

"All right. Thanks. I'm worried about him," I say, my shoulders sinking with the relief of clearing the air.

We should've talked about it ages ago.

"I'll call him."

"Have you spoken to him at all?" I ask.

"A month ago was the last time. He stopped taking my calls."

I blink twice in shock. A month ago. I didn't even speak to him then.

"How was he?"

Zayn pulls over half a block from my house as promised. "He was the same. Angry. Hurt. Confused."

"I should've reached out to him sooner."

"Don't blame yourself. This whole situation is insanity."

I open the door. "Will you let me know when you've spoken to him?"

Zayn nods.

"Thanks for coming to get me."

"It's cool." He shrugs.

I close the door, but he doesn't drive off. He waits like the gentleman he is as I make my way along the sidewalk and back around my hedge. It's so good to have him back, as uncomfortable as addressing the elephant in the room was. It was a miracle we managed to keep it a secret too. Adi usually sniffs out things like that.

I hear the quiet rumble of his engine as I open the back door and let myself in.

The house is dark and silent. Kicking off my shoes, I go back upstairs and change into my pajamas. When I'm back in bed, and no longer able to get in trouble, I send another message to Nash. My previous one is still unread.

Penny:

please just let me know you're okay

I fall into a restless sleep with no answers.

I wake up what feels like a moment later. Rolling over, I check the time on my phone: 5:27 a.m. There's a message from Zayn that he sent a couple hours ago.

Zayn:

couldn't get hold of him, drove to the farm and his light was on. sorry, pen.

My heart drops. So he is just ignoring me. He made me think we were going to talk and sort things out, but he was just getting revenge. That's so unlike Nash. I hate how much this past year has changed him.

Penny:

he was chilling at home while i was hiding at Benji's???

I don't want to tell Zayn about the person I saw in the street because he was annoyed enough that I'd gone to meet Nash alone while there's a killer around.

Unless . . . the person in the street was . . .

No. It couldn't have been Nash. Even if he wanted to scare me like that, he wouldn't do it on the night we decided to meet. It would be too obvious.

Besides, Nash isn't a bad person.

Zayn:

i don't know. I'm going back there today. don't worry, i'll figure this out.

Penny:

can i come?

Zayn:

i don't think that's a good idea. he stood you up yesterday and i want him to talk.

Meaning if I'm there, he will tell us to leave.

I can't help the sinking feeling that thought gives me, even if it's exactly what I deserve.

Penny:

i need to see him.

Zayn:

let me do damage control first.

Penny:

okay, let me know.

Sighing, I throw my phone down onto my pillow and groan. What the hell am I supposed to do now? There isn't much besides trust that Zayn will be able to get through to him. We need to let him know that we're on his side, especially now there's been a copycat murder.

I take a quick shower and get ready to meet Adi, Zayn, and Omar for breakfast before we go to the Halloween fair in the town square. A fair I assumed would be canceled, but right now, the cops seem to think this is an isolated incident. On the news they said there was nothing to suggest this was going to go serial.

Nothing to suggest it wasn't either.

"I don't want you to go anywhere alone today," Mom says, frantically packing things she needs into her bag. She grabs her travel mug and a slice of toast.

"I won't. I promise."

I can't seem to keep those these days.

"I mean it, Penelope."

I've been full-named. She's not messing around.

"I get it, Mom. You still haven't done your hair," I say.

She gasps, putting her coffee and toast down to clip her hair up with the grip hanging from the hem of her jacket.

"I spoke to the neighbor today. Rumor has it the police have a person of interest, something to do with bad blood between Noah and some other kid, and they're going down that route already."

"Who?" I ask.

"She couldn't tell me that. Looks like it'll all be over soon."

"You're not to be alone, though, like your mom said," Dad tells me, sliding folders into his briefcase.

They're both working flat out for the next two days because they're trying to close a big deal in the city. Or something like that. They don't talk much about their boring jobs in insurance. I only know that they're gone *a lot* when large companies contact them.

"We need to leave, love," Dad says to Mom. "Penny, *never alone.* We'll be checking in and if you don't answer or reply every time, we'll be home."

I want to roll my eyes because I've heard that one so many times before. They just send the neighbor around. But there's never been a murder while they were away. Last year they were home over Halloween.

"Answer or reply," Mom repeats, kissing me on the forehead and grabbing handfuls of things they need.

"I will. See you tomorrow."

"And keep the doors locked at all times!" Dad calls, and hesitates.

"Always do, and I'll be fine. I promise!"

"The neighbors will be looking out for you."

I salute as he turns to leave the house.

There's no way they'd leave if they thought Noah's murderer was some guy about to go on a spree. Whichever neighbor told him the cops are close to an arrest must be right. My dad obviously trusts them.

The front door slams, and I'm finally alone. That should scare me, especially after last night, but my parents fussing makes me more anxious. I'll keep the house locked and park in the garage so I won't even have to walk between the car and the house.

All just in case this isn't an isolated incident.

I was never in Noah's circle. He was always kind of an asshole and had zero respect for his mom or anyone else, but I can't think who would have a grudge against him. Not one big enough to kill him, anyway.

Since I can't take Zayn's advice and leave Nash alone, I send another message to him. My self-control at this point is nonexistent.

Penny:

Are you okay? Zayn is worried too.

I dropped Zayn's name to take the heat off myself, hoping it'd make Nash reply. I don't know if Zayn told Nash he doesn't want me to know that they talk.

I'd give anything to know what they spoke about. I must've come up at some point, unless Nash refused to mention me. Though the last time they spoke, I had rejected Zayn's date request, so he probably didn't feel like discussing me either.

I don't think I could've made a bigger mess of things if I'd tried.

Getting up, I send a message to our group, letting them know I'm about to leave for the diner. I'm hungry and really need to eat. Gina's pancakes are the best; I just hope I can stop stressing long enough to actually eat.

I've had a new churning in my stomach since last night. This uneasy feeling that's gnawing away at my insides.

Another murder. The Jackson look-alike. The masked person in the street. Someone in the theater. Being lied to and ditched by Nash.

Benji's. What if Nash was the one making noise in there?

No, that doesn't make sense.

He's not evil or stupid.

Like Zayn said, he's hurt and angry.

I grab my phone and keys and head into the garage, needing a distraction from all this death.

The roller doors draw up and I reverse out. I watch as they close, something I never usually do. Feels like a good idea to make sure no one wearing a mask and brandishing a knife ducks in there to wait for my return.

The town square is busier than usual, even for the Halloween fair. Everyone is out to gossip. I find a space in the parking lot and cross the street. Hanging from streetlights are bats and two of the speakers hum creepy music.

People are everywhere, hanging out in groups outside stores and sitting on benches. So many are dressed up, more than usual. Most of them young and silently enjoying it.

News vans have parked in the street and reporters are circling like vultures, preying on the town's pain.

I step around a group dressed in gray overalls and creepy masks. A couple I recognize as juniors by their distinctive haircuts, but the others have masks that cover their entire heads. They laugh and shove each other.

Gritting my teeth, I pass them and a group of women around my mom's age gossiping about the Whitmores.

"Did you know his children own that house now?"

"All that land they can do what they want with."

"And we all know what they're doing."

"The boy was seen in the square yesterday."

I ball my hands into fists and stuff them into my hoodie pocket. One of them catches my eye as I walk past. She clears her throat and nudges her friend. Subtlety is obviously not one of her talents.

"Good morning," I say in a sickly sweet voice.

They all mutter a reply and avert their eyes, knowing they've been caught bad-mouthing the Whitmores by the son's girlfriend.

Ex-girlfriend. Can't keep forgetting that fun fact.

I push open the door to the diner and find Adi, Omar, and Zayn already seated. It's not like Omar to be early. Or even on time.

There's a Frankenstein head hanging from the wall near our table.

"Hey," I say, sitting down next to Zayn.

"You good now?" Adi asks.

"I'm great."

"You saw Noah. What was it like?" Omar asks, earning a thump on the arm from Adi.

"Not funny, asshole. It was awful!" she hisses. "I'll never forget it, and I wasn't even the one who discovered him."

Omar raises his hands. "All right, I'm sorry. I've spent almost the whole of yesterday looking around three different mosques for my sister's wedding and now I need to get caught up with what happened here."

"Can you do that sensitively?" Adi asks.

Omar looks between the three of us. "Since when do we not talk straight?"

Since last year.

"Let's forget it," I say. "It was horrific, Omar. So much blood and now the town thinks there's a copycat killer. Can we order now?"

I've left out a few details.

"Nah, I heard it was some bad blood with someone. It's driving me crazy trying to think who," Adi replies.

"He had a few enemies," Zayn says. "But I can't think of anyone who would . . . you know."

"Has anyone spoken to Nash or Grace?" Omar asks.

Omar, another boy who had a crush on Grace. I think he once got as far as pre-asking her out, laying the groundwork apparently. It wasn't smooth, and as far as I'm aware, he never tried again.

"I did," I say. It's not like it's a secret at this point. "You can't tell my parents."

"Right, because I have a habit of running to your parents," Omar says, deadpan. "What did Nash say?"

"That he's not responsible for the murder. As if we didn't know that."

"Well, duh." Omar scowls. "He and Grace might be . . . you know, all weird now, but that doesn't make 'em killers."

"All weird now?" Zayn asks. "No wonder you failed your verbal essay."

"Shut up, dude!"

"Stop." Adi hushes them as a server comes by to take our orders.

Pancakes all around. Looks like we all need comfort food this morning. I lean back against the padded chair, chewing on my lip, desperate to quiz Zayn on his plans to see Nash.

I have to get through breakfast and a morning at the Halloween fair first, hooking zombie-looking ducks and carving a pumpkin that I'm probably too old for.

It doesn't have the same effect since last year.

I look outside while we wait, not able to remember the last time there were so many people in the square. Of course, the fair is about to begin, but a lot of them just want to be where the drama is.

"The town has already condemned them," I say.

"Yeah, Ruby's been very vocal on TikTok," Adi says, showing us her latest video.

Ruby is a classmate of ours who went semiviral last year

covering Jackson's murders. I turn my nose up as she dances to "Monster Mash" along with captions like *Whitmore psycho 2.0* and *Daddy's boy.*

A rumbling groan above us makes us all jump. My nerves are completely frayed after last night but at least a couple other people at nearby tables scream too.

Omar laughs as he looks up at the Frankenstein that just scared a restaurant.

Placing my hand over my thumping heart, I sit back in my seat. "Someone take the batteries out of that!" I say.

"You all right?" Zayn asks, placing his hand on my knee under the table. He removes it just as quickly.

"Does she mention Grace too?" Omar asks, and I could kiss him for the distraction.

Zayn and I cleared the air, and today I feel weirder. I've hugged the guy hundreds of times and never thought anything of it.

Adi shakes her head in reply to Omar.

"She never liked Nash," Zayn adds.

She hated Nash because he hated her. She's rude and stuck-up. I bet she's loving being able to drag his name all over the internet again. Last year, when Jackson was arrested, she was queen of the Ostracize Nash and Grace Club.

"I heard something weird last night," Zayn says.

"Someone called you hot?" Omar asks, laughing and dodging Zayn's fist as he leans over the table. "Ah! All right, I'm sorry. What did you hear?"

"I was driving around town—late-night iced coffee run for

my mom," he says, avoiding my eye. I obviously know he's lying about that part. "I heard some scraping noises in Benji's."

I side-eye him. What the hell is he doing?

"That place is abandoned," Adi says.

"Not so much. I heard the noise more than once. I'm telling you someone was in there . . . and I think we should check it out."

7

"Have you lost your tiny mind?" I ask, kicking him under the table. At some point he's going to clue me in, right? Why the hell would we want to go back there?

Omar's eyes light up at the thought of the adrenaline rush. He's always encouraging Zayn's bad ideas. If Zayn suggests we make a ramp from the top of the theater steps to skate down, Omar says we should make one from the second-floor window.

"You want to stay here and play fair games and eat cotton candy?" he asks.

Adi throws a wadded napkin at him. "Hey, I like those games and cotton candy."

Our pancakes arrive, which pauses the breaking-and-entering conversation.

I dig into my blueberry stack as enthusiastically as I can, getting a few bites in and wishing I'd ordered a child's meal. As soon as all this is over, I better get my appetite back. I put the fork down and sip my drink.

"No one will notice we're missing while the fair is going on," Omar says.

"Isn't your mom out there?" I ask him. "She never misses town events."

He scoffs. "Aafiya put on three pounds and had a meltdown, so Mom's taken her to the gym. As if encouraging that kind of thinking is helpful. I can't wait until this wedding is over. If any of you ditch me that day . . ."

"We'll be there," I assure him. "Now, is this a good idea? We'd be breaking in."

Zayn nudges me. "What happened to your sense of adventure?"

I think he knows *exactly* what's happened to my sense of adventure when he picked me up in the early hours.

"It'll be fun," Adi says, shoving a fork loaded with chocolate chip pancake into her mouth. "I'm in."

"Same," Omar adds.

Well, I'm not letting them go alone or staying in the square by myself. Besides, I want to know what Zayn is up to. Does he want to see if there's any sign that Nash was in there?

It's not like Benji's isn't broken into often.

"You not hungry?" Zayn asks while Omar and Adi are distracted talking with Mae, who's stopped by the table.

"Not had much appetite since finding Noah . . ."

"Yeah. Sorry. Do you want to talk or anything?"

He looks so uncomfortable, like he thinks he's put his foot in his mouth. "I'm good," I say. "We're really going to Benji's?"

"We need to know what you heard."

"Are you thinking it could be Noah's killer hiding out? The cops are on to him . . . or her."

Or Nash.

"I don't know, that's why we're going."

Once we're done with breakfast, we all walk across the heaving square, dodging small children running around screaming, draped in dime-store costumes and loaded with sugar.

Spooky, ominous music still drifts from speakers on the square, playing as people run around and have fun, as if we're in a horror movie and about to reach the part where the scaring begins.

"Is it strange that this wasn't canceled?" Adi says.

"Why, you think the hanging skeletons and bloodstained sheets are in bad taste?" My voice drips with sarcasm. Last year nothing was canceled until the double murder on Devil's Night.

Adi laughs. "Do you think trick-or-treating will be called off again?"

I shrug. "It should be."

The mayor is in the middle of the square, drinking hot chocolate with marshmallows and talking with a reporter. She has on devil horns and a black cloak.

I listen hard as we get close.

"We are all devastated at the sad loss, but we want the children of our town to . . ."

We get too far away for me to hear the rest. What do they want us to do? Forget that now six teenagers have been *killed*? Have fun despite the undertone of fear and murder?

"Is she really using kids as a reason why we're still partying?" Adi asks.

Omar scoffs. "Sounds like it."

"She's a treat," Zayn replies, throwing his arm over my shoulder as we fall a bit behind Adi and Omar. "I need to know if it was him in there," he whispers.

"And what, you think he'd have left a clue behind, Scooby-Doo?"

Laughing, he shakes his head. "I don't know, but something's going on with him. Don't you want to figure out what?"

"Of course I do."

"Then this is where we start," he says, dodging a bunch of middle schoolers in traditional Halloween costumes. Dracula, mummy, skeleton, and two witches.

"I thought you were going to go by his place again?" I ask as we walk along the alleyway to the theater, leaving Halloween behind.

"I will."

"Have you tried calling him?"

"What do you think?"

"Zayn, I'm losing it a bit here. No one has heard from him since yesterday. Someone was in the theater last night, and now we both think it could be him."

"Ah, I knew you would stress over that." He drops his arm from my shoulders. Lowering his voice even further, he says, "I had something happen last night too."

"What?"

"When I got home, my lamp was on."

"Okay, that's . . . something, I guess," I say, frowning. Hardly a masked killer sighting.

"That's not the weird part, Pen, jeez. I didn't leave it on."

"Maybe your mom did."

"That was my first thought, but she got home *after* me. And my dad is still on the rigs until November. Who turned it on?"

I stop walking as we reach the bottom of the theater steps. Adi and Omar are at the top, trying to look through the windows between the boards.

Grabbing Zayn's wrist, I say, "You think it was Nash?"

"Dunno. It's possible. All I know is that it wasn't me. I've moved the spare key now so whoever it was can't get back in."

"Unless they copied the key. You should get the locks changed."

He laughs, shaking his head like I've suggested something outrageous. "Yeah, that'll be a great conversation with my mom."

"Zayn!"

"I'll think of something."

"I don't like this. When we're done here, we're both going to that farm."

He nods. "All right, but you wait in the car in case he doesn't want to see you."

Okay, ouch.

"Come on, you two!" Adi shouts over her shoulder.

Omar walks down the steps. "We'll have to go around the back. The doors are padlocked."

"Can you pick the lock?" Adi asks.

"Yeah, just give me a hairpin."

Her eyes widen. "Really, you can do that?"

"No!" Omar rolls his eyes. "Let's go around the back."

I look over my shoulder as we walk around the building.

Everyone is in the square and hardly anyone comes around here now that the stores are all empty. I can just about hear the faint sound of "Monster Mash" playing.

"Omar and Adi are too excited about this," I whisper to Zayn.

"Yeah, well, they don't know why we're doing it."

Because they blame Nash and Grace for what Jackson has done. Zayn is right to keep them in the dark. I trust them but if they think I'm in danger, they will go to my parents.

Life or death, we all would.

"Here!" Omar calls. "This door isn't locked."

I look down at the busted padlock on the floor. "It used to be."

The last party here was in the summer. I've not been back since last night, so I don't know when it was locked up again.

"See, someone managed to get in," Adi says to Omar.

"They didn't do that with a hairpin."

She narrows her eyes playfully as he opens the door. I go in next, followed by Adi and Zayn.

The foyer is dark. Thin layers of light streak between the boards over the windows, creating shadows from popcorn buckets and the odd plastic cup that litters the ground. A thick coating of dust covers everything in sight. The red walls are peeling and the air smells musty, stale, and grimy.

"Anyone home?" Omar calls out.

I slap his chest with the back of my hand. "Shut up!"

Adi pushes between us. "Are you trying to get us killed?"

"Whoa, who says there's a killer in here?" He looks over his shoulder at Zayn. "Are we searching for a murderer? Because that's the sort of thing you tell your friends *beforehand*. We'll still do it, but it would have been good to know. I'd have brought a weapon."

"Omar, keep walking. Why would a killer hide here?"

"Maybe this is just their lair?" I say, getting a scathing look from Zayn. "If you can't beat them . . ."

We walk through the foyer. Ahead of us is the ticket booth and along the two walls are doors for theaters one through four and upstairs are two more.

"What do we do now?" I ask, looking around for the source of the noise I heard last night.

"There are four theater rooms down here," Omar says.

"I swear if you even think about splitting up, I will kick you," Adi says.

"All right, Adi and Omar take one and two. Penny and I will do three and four," Zayn says. "Meet back here before we go upstairs."

I'd really rather not go upstairs.

Omar and Adi laugh as they rush off into their first room.

"Do you see the footprints?" I ask, shining the torch from my phone on the floor.

"Yep," he replies. "But that might not be Nash or the killer. We're not the first ones to be in here since it closed."

"True."

Plenty of our classmates have bragged about sneaking into here. We've even been to a few parties in screen room three, the only one that had most of the seats ripped out before work came to a sudden stop.

"Come on," Zayn says, grabbing my hand.

I'm glad he did because I really wanted to hold hands but don't want him to think I'm a massive baby. I hold on to him tight as he opens the door. Theater three. I remember the cheap beer we drank in here last summer.

The floor is still littered with Solo cups.

If we all had DNA on file and the cops tested those cups, half the school would be in trouble.

Zayn looks over his shoulder. "Good times, huh?"

"Easier times. I miss it so much."

"You think you and Nash will get back together?"

That came out of nowhere and it's not something I want to talk about.

I laugh but there's absolutely nothing funny about this situation or the fact that getting back together isn't even an option. "I'm sure my parents would love it."

"Would they have to know?" He drops my hand and walks down the first row of chairs. There are only four rows left at the top. I go to the other side.

"You think I should sneak around with Nash?" I ask.

"Not until the murderer is caught. Last night was the dumbest thing you could do. You trying to get killed?"

"All right, I get it." I watch the floor as I walk, shining the light in front of my feet. There's a jacket on the floor, slightly covered in dust, so it could've been left from a party. "Zayn, I might have something here."

His footsteps thud toward me. "What is it?"

"Dark, zip-up hoodie."

"Like the one Jackson wore."

"Like the one most people own. Look, it's dusty but not as dusty as the chairs."

"Is it Nash's?" he asks.

"How should I know?"

"Look at the label. Don't you know where he shops?"

"Not really," I say, nudging the neck of the hoodie with my toe. "Old Navy. I don't think he shopped there."

"No, but Grace does. I didn't know Jackson well, but I can't see him clothes shopping anywhere," Zayn says. "Dude definitely let Grace and Nash loose with his credit card."

"Yeah, maybe. I've never seen this one before and the thread is quite worn down."

"What does that mean?"

"It means that it looks older than a year, so I would've seen Nash with it."

In the darkness I can just about make out Zayn's frown. "Let's keep moving. This could belong to anyone, and it probably needs fumigating."

Gross.

He turns and goes back to his side of the room.

I step over the hoodie and continue my search for . . . something. "Gum wrappers, a shoe—who forgets their shoe!—and what looks like a bra strap. I so don't want to know. Anything on your side?" I call.

"Not much. Just litter. There are a few unopened bottles of water. No dust on them."

"Maybe someone's sleeping here."

"Homeless person?" he asks.

"Could be. Do you see a sleeping bag or anything?"

"Nah, no evidence that anyone is sleeping here."

Good, that would be kind of sad. It's cold and dirty in here.

"Zayn, what do you think is going on with Nash?"

He walks over to me and sighs. "Honestly? I don't know. He's been spiraling for a while."

"What? Spiraling how? You never told me that."

"He doesn't want you to know, Pen."

"Why?" I breathe.

"Come on, you know why. His dad had just tried to contact him again the last time we spoke. It messed him up a bit. Nash wants nothing to do with him, but he'll always be his dad."

"You talk to him more than you told me."

"We used to talk regularly. Until last month when he went quiet."

"Why didn't you tell me?"

"Why would I? He's my friend, too, and you weren't talking. Not everything has to go through you."

He was talking to Nash at the same time he told me he *liked* me.

I narrow my eyes. "I wasn't suggesting that it did."

"Then why are you acting like I'm shady? You never mentioned him to us either. It's fine if you want to pretend that you're not still totally hung up on him, but don't expect the rest of us to ignore him because of that."

"That's not what I was doing! What the hell, Zayn."

He steps closer and so do I. We walk toward each other, ready to meet in the middle, to fight our corners.

"When have I ever expected you to ignore him? I was the one who was pushing for us all to go see him," I say.

"Then what happened?"

I throw my hands up. "Everything got difficult. My parents . . ."

He shakes his head. "It doesn't matter now. It's done. He's spent at least the last four months thinking he's alone."

"What else don't I know?"

"What are you talking about?"

"You have secrets, Zayn."

"And you don't? Where were you last night again—"

His jaw snaps shut as we hear the same scraping sound from last night. I grab his wrist, my eyes widening as I try to sharpen my vision in the dark.

"Is that what you heard?" he asks.

"Uh-huh. Where did it come from?"

We hear it again, the sound of metal scraping on . . . concrete, I think.

Zayn and I look up at the same time.

"It came from up there," I whisper.

"Any chance it's Omar and Adi?" Zayn asks.

As if on cue, they burst into the room, gasping and shining their flashlight toward us. Adi has her arms wrapped around Omar and he's looking around, chest puffed out, like he's ready to take on whoever's up there.

"Did you hear that?" Adi says.

"Um, yeah, we heard that!" I hiss.

"That the noise from last night?" Omar asks.

"Yeah," I say at the same time as Zayn.

Right, he's the one who was supposed to have heard it. As far as anyone other than Zayn—and Nash—knows, I was tucked up in bed at midnight.

"What do we do?" I whisper.

Adi pulls on Omar. "I'm *not* going up there. Can we please leave?"

"We came here for this, Adi. What did you expect?" he asks her.

"I thought it was just a bit of fun for Halloween. I don't want to be here anymore. What if it's Noah's killer?"

Zayn gives her a look that makes her glare back at him. "There might be a draft up there. Most of the windows are smashed and badly boarded up."

There aren't too many windows, only a few in the foyer and hallways.

"You and Adi stay here; we'll go and look," Omar tells us.

"No way! I'm coming too," I say.

"We shouldn't split up," Adi says. "That's the first rule in situations like this."

The noise scrapes again, louder this time, and something thuds. The one person who would make this better, who would make me not feel so afraid, is the one person Zayn and I think might be doing this.

"Okay," Omar says, and clears his throat to hide the tremble in his voice. "We stick together."

Inside my head, I'm screaming, *Bad idea, bad idea.* But we have to know. Zayn said that Nash is having a hard time. Why would he lead me here for no reason? Maybe there's something that he wants me to see.

I follow Omar out, Adi clings to me, and Zayn sticks close behind. We follow the flashlight on Omar's phone out of the room and come to the large staircase.

"Ah, man, this is a dumb idea," Zayn mutters from the back.

Well, we're committed to stupidity now.

My heart thumps hard against my rib cage as I place my foot on the first step.

Are you leading me to something or just messing with me, Nash?

I really wish we'd gone to his house first.

"I hate this," Adi whispers, squeezing my hand and crushing my knuckles together. "For the record, I didn't want to come up here."

At the top of the stairs, we look around in the pitch black, barely making anything out. I've been up here dozens of times, but it's been at least four years.

I'm sure up here there are six doors. Two are theater rooms, there's two bathrooms, a fire escape, and a restricted room that states STAFF ONLY in such big letters I used to trace them with my finger while we waited for popcorn.

"Where do we think it came from?" I ask.

"It sounded directly above us, so I think in there," Zayn replies, pointing left. That's where the staff room is . . . was.

I strain my eyes, barely able to make out his hand up here. The few windows that're up here have been boarded more successfully than the ones in the foyer. No light has made it through at all.

The air is so thick I can feel dust in the back of my throat, and it's cold. So much colder than outside even.

If I could see, there would be vapors in front of my face.

"Shall we, then?" I ask, trying not to gag on the dirty air.

"No," Adi replies.

"I'll go first," Zayn says, walking ahead. I almost lose sight of him after a few steps.

I take a step in his direction and then the loudest crash booms through the theater. The sound of a door hitting the wall after it's been thrown open.

Adi screams. I scream. Omar shouts. Zayn swears. Someone falls, I think. I turn to run, not really knowing where I'm going, only that I need to get the hell away from here.

Nash can't be behind this.

Would he really take things this far?

8

Leaping forward, I bash into another person and scream again. "Who's that?"

"Run!" Zayn shouts from somewhere else in the building. I don't know which light is his. And who did I just bump into?

I shine my phone in front of me as a hand grips hold of my wrist. "Penny!" Adi says. Her terror-filled eyes bulge as her fingers dig into my skin.

"Oh my god, Adi!"

"I can't see, and my phone is in my bag," she says, huddling against me, trembling.

"Stop!" I yell. "Everyone stop. I can't hear anything."

"Why are you still up there?" Zayn calls. His voice is coming from the first floor now. The light from his phone shines up at us. He got down there fast.

"I don't think it's a person," I say. "It's the exact same noise over and over again, like a machine or a recording."

"Seriously, let's go, Penny. I don't care what's making the

noise." Adi pulls away from me and I hear her footsteps as she tries to make it down the stairs.

"Wait there, Penny. I'm coming back up," Omar says.

"Are you two crazy? Let's just *go*!" Adi hisses, her voice floating from below. She made it down to Zayn.

Omar touches my arm. "I respect the fact that you're all girl power—"

"Woman power."

"You're seventeen but sure, woman power, but can you please stay behind me when we go in there?"

"You're very sweet, and yes, I will stay behind you. My hero."

I just about see his dark eyes roll at my sarcasm.

I walk with him, half a step behind, as requested, and we move toward the staff room. Omar's heavy breathing syncs with mine.

"If we die, I just want to say that you're the best friend I could ask for."

Omar chuckles quietly. "Yeah, back atcha."

He reaches out and turns the handle. Shoving the door, he steps back, taking me stumbling with him.

Gasping, I right my steps before I fall on my ass. "What?" I snap, my heart leaping. "What is it?"

"Nothing, it's okay. Jumped back in case."

"Really? You scared me to death!"

"What's happening up there?" Zayn calls. "Adi's crushing my ribs, and I think I'd prefer hooking a zombie duck to this."

He's not the only one.

"We're going in," Omar replies, and steps forward.

I follow his lead as we shine light into the room.

We don't need it because there's a small window with a board that's half slipped down, allowing a triangle of natural light in.

We're alone.

"There's no one here," Omar says.

"Nope and look." I point to a broken metal shelving unit. It's against the wall behind us, wedged against the adjacent wall, slowly falling. Deep welts in the concrete show its path from where it used to sit.

A freezing gust of wind whistles through the broken glass. A folder falls off the shelf and the whole thing moves again, scraping another inch. On the floor are stacks of paperwork and boxes. They've been falling off for a while.

Omar shoots me a look and points to the shelves with his thumb. "This our killer?"

I laugh as my heart rate returns to normal. "I'm *so* stupid."

"We all were. Can you blame us, though? We've seen a lot of death here."

Every town experiences death. Not all of them experience murder. That's what we're known for now. Our pretty little rural town that farms corn is also home to a serial killer.

"Penny? Omar?" Zayn shouts. "Seriously, I have five broken ribs at this point."

"You're so dramatic, Zayn. We're coming now," Omar calls.

I snap a picture of the shelving unit to prove that the noise is nothing to worry about. As if we thought some murderer was up here, sharpening his ax on the walls.

Omar and I leave the room and walk down to the others.

I show them my screen. "It was this."

"Are you kidding me!" Adi shouts. "I'm going back to the square."

She lets go of Zayn, who rubs his chest and scowls.

Once we're outside, we fall silent. I don't know about them, but I'm rather embarrassed and wishing I hadn't overreacted.

Why would a killer make so much noise?

"It's not him," Zayn says as we drop back from Adi and Omar again.

"Yeah."

"That's a good thing, Penny. Why do you sound gutted?"

"No, I'm not. Obviously I'm glad he's not hiding in there plotting my death. But what *is* he doing?"

"Don't sweat it. We'll find out, okay?"

I nod, but I'm not at all confident because Nash doesn't want me in his life anymore. He could ask Zayn not to talk about him with me and Zayn would respect that.

We reach the square again and the air is filled with "Thriller," excitement, and apprehension.

"Where are all the reporters going?" Adi asks.

We watch the last two drive off as groups of residents grow.

The games in the square have stopped, the fair deserted for whatever's going on, but the music continues.

"Do you think something's happened?" Zayn asks.

Omar snorts and says with heavy sarcasm, "No, they just heard about a special on coffee at Jay's Mart."

Adi gasps. "Another murder?"

"Nothing like that," Ruby, queen of mean, says. She walks up behind us, arm in arm with her friends, every one of them dressed as cats, with fishnet tights and black skintight leotards. "Karter was just arrested. Can you believe it? 'Cause I can."

"What?"

Mrs. Vanderford's lazy son Karter? The one I sit next to in math? *That* Karter?

Ruby places her hands on her hips. "Karter killed Noah. I mean, it was *so* obvious. They hated each other and were fighting almost daily. I told the cops this yesterday, but it took them a whole day to realize that I'm right." She twirls her finger in a circle. "Let's go. I want one of those Squishmallow bats."

Omar and Zayn step in front of me and Adi. "Karter did this," Zayn says.

"That's what they think," I reply. "I mean, they *were* football rivals and Karter hated him for going out with Rebecca right after him. But would he really kill Noah over her? He dated most girls in school."

Omar shrugs. "Why would he be arrested if he didn't?"

"His parents own the costume store. It makes sense," Adi says.

I shake my head. "Not really. You think it makes sense that he would dump a body in the store his mom owns? Where he works? I would probably pick somewhere less suspicious."

"Again, I don't know how killers think," Adi replies, and walks off. She has had enough of murder and scary talk for one day. Omar runs after her, telling her he'll buy her a soft pretzel to cheer her up.

Zayn and I go a different way, not wanting any food.

"So, no copycat killer," Zayn says. "Nash is off the hook. That's a good thing, Pen. You should be happy."

"Yeah," I breathe, smiling. "It is, it's more than good. Do you think he knows about Karter yet?"

He tilts his head to the side and says, "You think it would take longer than ten minutes for news to spread in this town?"

"Good point."

"You should message him."

"I thought you were going to tell me you'd do it."

"I'm going there later. You message now. I'll meet you by the vampire darts stall."

"Okay," I mutter, sitting down on a freezing bench.

Penny:

have you heard that karter was arrested for noah's murder?

I don't really expect a reply, because clearly he's not a fan of mine anymore, but I still watch to see if he'll open the messages. He still hasn't read them from yesterday. He could be reading them when the notification pops up.

Penny:

everyone knows you didn't do this.

I should stop messaging him now. I'm looking desperate, and he's probably hating me.

That will be my last one.

Standing up, I slide my phone into my back pocket and go to meet Zayn.

"I take it from that thrilled expression he didn't reply," Zayn says as I join him in the line for the dart game.

"No. It's okay, I guess. He doesn't want anything to do with me and I have to respect that. I won't come with you today, and I won't contact him again."

He lifts a brow. "But?"

"Nope, no buts. We're over, so I'm moving on. I'm going to kick your ass at this game, you know?"

I'm not really there yet, but pretending is the first step, right?

"Oh, fighting talk, Pen, I like it."

Zayn and I play two games of darts and then move on to meet up with Adi and Omar.

The sense of shock and sadness doesn't leave, but there's definite relief in the air that we don't have another serial killer. Noah's family will get justice, and we're safe.

I check in with my parents, who are super relieved that Noah's murder was an isolated incident and has been solved. My mom sighed for, like, five whole seconds. They both feel better being away tonight, though they wouldn't agree to tell the neighbors to stand down, so I'll probably still have ten check-ins.

Bunches of flowers adorn the doorway to the costume store, lying in front of a stack of pumpkins, but fewer than this morning. What the . . . ?

"Is someone stealing those?" I ask, my jaw hitting the floor.

"No, look, they've been moved to the bench over there," Zayn says, pointing to a bench on the corner of the square.

"Because the son of the owners killed him. Makes sense, I guess. Noah's parents wouldn't want to see flowers outside the store."

Adi and Omar sit on a wall, eating a bag of candy.

"I'm splitting," Zayn says. "See you later."

"Where are you going?" Omar asks.

"Need to do something for my mom," he replies. "I'll catch up with you at school tomorrow. We still hitting Scream Fest after?"

"Hell yeah," Adi says.

"See you later, dude," Omar mutters around a mouthful of candy corn.

My stomach turns and I look away. Candy corn reminds me of rotting teeth so I can't even look at it. So gross.

Zayn gives me a nod before he walks away. He's not going to do anything for his mom; he's going to see Nash. I know I said that I would leave Nash alone, but I hope Zayn still calls me once he's been there. Just because I'm not calling him doesn't mean that I don't want to know he's okay.

I spend the next hour hanging with my friends and obsessively checking my phone. I try to be casual while I'm doing it, but Adi notices.

"Spill," she says when Omar has gone to the bathroom.

I lean against a giant fake spiderweb on the wall of the pharmacy. "Nothing, I just have to check in with my parents a lot or they'll be driving straight home."

"I was going to see if you wanted to sleep at mine tonight."

"Thanks, but Karter has been arrested now, so I'm good. I'm

going to take off. I still have calculus homework to do. I've been putting it off all weekend."

"Are you sure? We were going to get dinner and hit the movies."

"I'm tired," I tell her. "I'll be there for the *Scream* marathon on Wednesday, though."

"Okay, see you tomorrow."

I wave over my shoulder as I head to my car, suddenly exhausted. Once I've ordered pizza, showered, and finished my homework, I'll be able to get into bed and watch a movie.

All I want to do is lie down and forget the last two days ever happened.

I park in the garage, closing the roller door immediately, despite the danger now being over. Being home alone hits a bit different now. But I don't want to hate it. I've always loved a quiet house where I can do what I want and watch what I want.

Closing the car door, I walk into the house and vow to enjoy my one and only night alone. Maybe when I go up to bed to watch a movie, I'll take chocolate up too.

I grab a Coke from the fridge and finish my homework before going upstairs for a hot shower. I need to wash away the creepy old theater and the knowledge that Nash and I are *really* over.

Turning the shower off, I grab a towel and wrap myself up in it. Goose bumps scatter across my arms as I step out into the cold air. It's freezing in here now. I dry quickly and put on a pair of my coziest pajamas.

I grab the door handle, and at that same moment, something thuds outside the room. I startle, my heart leaping into my throat.

It takes me a second for my scalp to stop burning.

Don't be stupid.

I've done this once today.

Shaking my head at how ridiculous I am, I open the door and walk into the hallway. I can't worry that something is out to get me every single time I hear a noise.

This noise is probably someone putting decorations up outside—the Bravermans have a habit of hanging things terribly. Every morning I leave for school, I pick up some ghost or ghoul that's fallen.

I walk into my room, towel-drying my hair, when I hear another noise.

This isn't nothing.

Leaping back, I crouch behind my dresser as a dark figure walks across the landing. My heart pounds harder.

Who the hell is that?

I scan my room, panic ramping up as I look for something to use if they find me. Where's the pepper spray Dad bought me last year? I'm sure I threw it in a drawer somewhere.

"Penny?"

I let out a shriek, jumping up as Zayn walks into my room.

"Pen?"

I slam my hand over my heart and breathe. "What the hell is wrong with you?"

Frowning, he asks, "What were you doing down there?"

"I thought you were . . . I don't know, I heard a noise. What are you doing here? How did you get in?" I get up and run my hands through my hair.

Zayn raises his hands. “Sorry I scared you. I still have the spare key.” He holds it up as proof and then puts it down on my bedside table.

“How did you know I was here?”

“Group chat. Omar and Adi are at the movies. She said you’d gone home.”

“Oh.” I haven’t checked my phone since I got back. “Did you go to Nash’s?”

He drops down on my bed and puts his feet up. I love him but if he doesn’t leave soon, I will kick him out. I want my chill evening.

“Yeah.”

“And?”

“Grace told me to leave. Well, she used a lot of other words and screamed a bit.”

“You only saw her?”

“He was inside.”

“You know that for sure?”

“I heard him, Pen. He was in there, talking to someone else.”

The Jackson doppelgänger boyfriend? “Was there a new truck in the drive?”

“Yeah, why?”

I sit down on the bed. “Okay, you remember I told you that I followed Nash when he was taken to the station?” Zayn nods. “Well, I also saw that truck and, I’m not crazy, but someone who looked exactly like Jackson was in it.”

Zayn crosses his legs at the ankle and throws his hands behind his head, way too relaxed.

"What don't you understand?" I ask.

He smirks. "The part about Jackson Whitmore having a double."

"It looked like him."

"Did *you* get a good look?"

"No, just from the side but he had a blue baseball cap on like Jackson wore. It's not him, obviously—he's still locked up—but someone is there, and Nash lied when I asked. He said the truck is Grace's and she's selling hers."

"That might be true."

"Yeah. I think Grace might have a boyfriend, but we need to find out, right? I don't like that Nash lied about it."

"And you want to be sure so you don't go crazy."

"Precisely. So we go over there tomorrow. Into the house. At night."

"Why not tonight?"

"I'm about to collapse, Zayn, and Grace is home. She's still working at that diner by the interstate, right?"

Zayn nods. "My mom stopped there on the way home last week. Saw her serving. Apparently she works most evenings."

"Good. We'll go after dark once she's at work. There will be evidence of who the boyfriend is in there somewhere."

"He really looked like Jackson?"

"Tall with a blue baseball cap. He might not *look* anything like him." I smile. "We'll find out *tomorrow.*"

He rolls his eyes. "Right, I can take a hint. Lock up behind me. You don't know who's out there."

9

MONDAY, OCTOBER 25

I wait in the car at Scream Fest after a super slow day at school. We don't usually come so early but my parents are not allowing me out late, even though Karter is in custody.

The killer might've been caught but the fear lingers. It changes you, makes you more cautious, less trusting.

Mom and Dad will never again be the easygoing parents they once were.

Across the road is the pumpkin patch where Cait was found a year ago. The area where her body was stuffed into a trash barrel has been cordoned off. Trees were planted to replace the horror.

The three birch trees are the only ones in the massive field, so they stand out like a sore thumb. Like a leafy arrow pointing to the dump site.

I watch for a minute as the small trees blow in the wind. The leaves have turned yellow and orange. A colorful puddle lies beneath the trunk of each one as if it's trying to conceal the blood that seeped through the bottom of the cracked barrel.

Omar pulls up beside me with Zayn and Adi in the car since they all live within a block of each other.

I get out and we head across the field and toward the forest.

It's quieter than usual but we thought it would be. Some people still feel it's in bad taste to carry on as normal after what happened this weekend.

Selfishly, I'm just happy that Nash is in the clear and Karter is locked up.

Omar and Adi push each other playfully, arguing over who will pee their pants first. It'll be Adi for sure.

"Are you ready to be *terrified*?" Zayn asks in a deep, creepy voice. He slings his arm over my shoulder, and we can just about pretend that we're four normal teens with no worries and no darkness looming over our heads.

"In this town. Always," I reply.

"There's still some good here, Penny."

"Yeah, well, I can't wait for college. I'm getting out of here as soon as I can. There are too many memories."

"You can't let Nash drive you out of town," Zayn says.

"He's not."

"He's the reason you want to leave, isn't he?"

"Here I'll always be the girlfriend of Jackson's son."

Across the field from us is a carved sign, the letters painted red and dripping like blood.

Scream Fest.

Beyond the makeshift entrance is the forest. Acres of green

with webs of footpaths that we need to follow, all while having people jumping out at us and chasing us around. I shudder in anticipation. My frayed nerves probably aren't ready for tonight, but I don't want to stay in and wallow.

I've been coming since I was twelve and say never again each time. Even though the actors aren't allowed to touch us, it's still terrifying.

"Pre-warning," I say. "I'm going to cling to you like a spider monkey."

Zayn laughs. "Don't be a baby."

Not possible. The fear lingers in me, too, a part of me now.

"Welcome to Scream Fest," a tall guy with an electric-blue Mohawk and big smile says. He has a sick oozing scar painted on his face with jagged flesh that's so realistic it makes me queasy. "Feel free to record or take photos but no physical contact with the actors. Once you're in, you're in, so turn back now if you're chicken."

"Thanks, dude," Omar says.

We walk on and the group behind us stops for Mohawk's speech.

Omar bounces up and down, loving all things scary. He's a horror aficionado, the murders not putting him off watching scary movies. All I can think about when I see someone killed on-screen is how Mac, Cait, Kelsie, Brodie, and Jia must have felt. And now Noah.

The forest is too dark, with only enough lights hanging from trees or shining up them to be able to see where we're going. Bats and webs hang from branches everywhere.

"This way," Omar says, swinging left and leading us to . . . somewhere.

Last year we spent almost two hours in the forest. My throat hurt for days after, but it was a lot of fun. Well, it was fun once we reached the end. I'm determined to enjoy tonight.

The temperature drops about thirty degrees as we walk deeper into the forest. Twigs crunch under my feet. Somewhere in the distance, a muffled scream fills the air.

Omar laughs. "Where do you think our first scare will be?"

Adi shouts and grabs his back. "Here!"

He looks down at her deadpan. "You'll have to do better than that."

"Keep going," I say, laughing and pushing them both on.

Wind blows gently through the trees, sweeping my hair into my face. I tuck it behind my ear and follow Omar, sticking close to my friends because although the actors don't touch, they do get right in your face.

I almost smacked one the first time I came. It was instinct, but I thankfully managed to stop myself before I got kicked out.

The path bends and forks off in two different directions. Doesn't matter which path we take; we'll be scared along both.

"Which way?" Omar asks.

"Right," I reply. "We went left last time."

Omar immediately turns right, and we hear another round of screaming. It sounds like it's coming from somewhere up ahead, and I try to steel myself.

My pulse quickens as we move along the path. The anticipation is almost worse than the actual scare. I watch the trees, trying to see if I can make out any movement behind them.

I can see a vertical pallet. There are lots of those all over the forest, as well as huts and other places people can leap out from behind. Not all of them, though, because that would take away the element of surprise.

"You ready?" Zayn asks as we approach the first pallet.

"They're never behind the first one," Omar says.

"Shit, I'm scared already," Adi says, laughing and gripping Omar's sleeve.

I move closer to Zayn. "I'm using you as a human shield."

"Nice to know you care," he mutters sarcastically.

As we get closer, my heart thumps so hard that I feel dizzy. It's not a horrible feeling, being scared with the knowledge that you won't be hurt, and it makes me feel alive.

Probably more alive than I have all year.

"Zayn," I say, squealing as we come level with it.

"See, nothing there," Omar says.

At the same moment, someone drops down from a tree in front of us. He's dressed head to toe in camo gear and has fake blood dripping down his head and wild yellow lenses in his eyes.

I scream, jumping backward and almost pulling Zayn to the ground with me. He catches me as we stumble. His shout turns into a laugh and so does mine.

"Jeez, dude!" Zayn says.

"What the hell was that? Since when do you scale trees?" Omar asks, chuckling as the guy climbs the tree again for the next group.

Adi grabs my hand and pulls me along. "I need to keep moving," she says. "The faster we go, the faster we can leave and drink punch at the end. I'm getting the biggest corn dog and cotton candy they sell."

"Always thinking of your stomach, Adi, I like it," Omar says.

"Food settles my stomach," she argues.

We move on, following the sounds of screams echoing around the forest.

"What the hell is that?" I ask. I look up ahead and see shadows running around between trees.

"They'd never win a game of hide-and-seek," Zayn says.

"If it's a bunch of clowns, I am out of here," I tell them.

"Hello?" Omar calls like an absolute idiot.

"What are you doing?"

The horrible little creatures come more sharply into view as we get closer. And they're not little. They're fully grown men cloaked in black with white masks.

My stomach drops. "What the hell?"

"It's not the same mask," Zayn says, noticing the similarity to the one Jackson wore while on his killing spree.

"Still . . . talk about dancing close to the line," Adi says. "I hope none of the victims' families come here."

I look up at Zayn. He's got his poker face on. No way of telling if he's upset about this. But he does smile at me, making sure I'm okay, like always.

"Shall we keep going?" I ask.

"Yeah, we've already seen them. How scary can they be?" Adi says.

"Their movements are creepy," I say as we approach.

They walk with their knees slightly bent, fingers spread, jerking their heads and arms, and as we get even closer, I can hear hissing.

Goose bumps break out over my arms as another long hiss whistles from one of the figures in the trees. We're surrounded by them now. Dozens of creepy figures on either side of us.

We're almost past them when suddenly, they leap into the pathway and wail.

I scream, holding my hands over my face.

This is all pretend, this is all pretend.

Menacing laughter blasts from speakers in the trees.

The others shout and jump to the side as one runs right down the middle of us.

Looking up, I back against a tree and something catches my eye. It's just a flash and probably a trick of the light, since I'm still hyperventilating, but one of the masked freaks looked a little different, older than the rest . . . kind of like Jackson.

I gasp as two snap their necks to the side in front of me. I jump around them, trying to figure out where that other one went. Two more join the others staggering in front of me, arms moving in quick robotic movements.

Turning around, I search for *that* mask.

I feel dizzy as I try to see through trees to find out if I'm imagining things. I want to get the hell out of here right now.

Six people surround me, turning around and dipping between trees and jumping out again. Dull lighting flashes rapidly.

"Zayn!" I shout.

Squinting, I look over my shoulder and feel something clamp my wrist.

I spin around. Two of them stamp toward me, stopping inches from my face. Shouting out, I step back. I'm sure I see Jackson's mask again, this time by a pallet on the other side of the path. The side I'm on. The side where I was just grabbed.

I do a double take as Adi calls my name, but when I look back at the pallet, he's gone.

"Penny, come on, run!" Omar says, grabbing my hand and taking off.

He jerks my arm, and I run after him, through the creepy people, dodging a few. I keep my eyes down low and let Omar lead the way. Adi's and Zayn's footsteps thump behind us. Along with at least a few more that definitely aren't ours.

A stitch digs into my side as we run. It's not long before the other footsteps disappear and it's just the four of us again.

We slow to a walk once we're past the commotion.

"Okay, I didn't expect that," Adi says, laughing and bumping Omar's side.

I drop his hand. "Did you see that?"

"The fifteen masked men in black jumping in front of us? Yeah, I did." Zayn's voice drips with sarcasm. He smirks, pleased with himself.

I open my mouth to tell them what I saw—or rather what I *think* I saw—but quickly swallow my words. So far, the lead-up to Halloween has been all about what Jackson has done. My life has been consumed by the past.

No one needs to keep hearing about my issues.

"I don't care what anyone says, they were the scariest," Adi says. "Even if we did see them before they started creeping."

I'm with her there. I thought they were just going to be distantly eerie and add to the vibe. I didn't know they were going to do *that*.

"I can't wait to review this year's event," Omar says.

"You're such a dork," Zayn replies, thumping his arm.

Next, we come to a shed with a large barn door opening. Last year it was set up like a dungeon.

I groan.

"Come on, Pen, this will be fun."

There's a path you can take to avoid the shed but there's absolutely no fun in that. Plus, things will chase you either way.

Inside the hut is dark with low red lighting. This year's setting is an operating theater. Not a sterile one. Fake blood is splattered all over the walls. Two beds are against one wall and a set of cupboards are on the other.

We take another step, all of us laughing in preparation for what's coming. Whatever that will be. I manage, just, to push away the mask thing, desperate to be normal.

My guess is a blood-soaked surgeon is going to run at us.

"This is so sinister," I say, looking above us at the blinking strip light. There are two lumps in the beds, but I can't see movement, so I think it's probably nonliving props.

"Creepy as hell," Zayn adds. "I love it."

My pulse is skittish as we move closer to the middle of the room. Whoever is in here doesn't have long to make their move before we're out.

A scream echoes through speakers hidden in the room.

I startle, bumping into Adi and laughing.

The lighting flashes again and then the room goes dark.

I gasp as my eyes adjust to the dark. As I do, I see them again—the person in black wearing the Jackson look-alike mask.

"There," I say, pointing outside the barn doors.

"What is it?" Zayn asks at the same time our surgeon leaps out from behind the cupboard holding a chain saw.

He cackles menacingly, a shrill laugh that sends shivers down my spine.

We run out of the barn to the artificial sound of a chain saw gaining on us. I pant as we stop along the path, the shed way in the distance. I hear another scream as someone else goes inside.

We break into laughter.

"Why do we keep coming back every year?" Adi asks.

"Fun," Omar replies, slinging an arm over her shoulder and mine. "I think we're supposed to head this way."

He guides us to the left, through gnarly trees with branches that look like bony fingers, like they could reach out and grab us.

I cross my arms as we approach a bunker, a sign outside reading ENTER TWO BY TWO IF YOU DARE.

"Nope," I say. "Fours sound good to me."

"Come on, little chicken, I'll go with you," Omar says. "Zayn and Adi first."

"Ugh, you suck," Adi says, pushing Omar and laughing as Zayn holds the door open for her.

"A bunker."

"You're not usually a baby, Pen. What's going on?"

"Not the same after you've found a dead body."

"Noah's killer was caught. We're perfectly fine. Besides, the people here aren't allowed to touch you. Nothing is going to happen, so chill, girl."

Yeah, I know all that. But I'm still scared.

"You talk to anyone about finding Noah?"

I shake my head, jumping as Adi screams from inside the bunker. The sound echoes, bouncing off the walls. Then I hear a mechanical whirring noise. No idea what it could be.

"No, but my parents are pushing for therapy. I'll go soon. Is it quieter here this year?"

"Definitely. Not surprising. My parents were so close to not letting me come." He shudders. "They've gone overprotective; it's doing my head in. My parents said this town isn't as safe as it was now there's been another murder."

Yeah, well, they're not wrong.

"My dad got a gun last year. Do you have pepper spray?"

He rolls his eyes. "Left it in a drawer but they gave me some."

"Mine's in my pocket."

"Town's on edge. Cops are hiring more officers, mayor's having more cameras installed, brighter bulbs are going in streetlights. My parents can barely talk about anything else. Did you know house prices have fallen again? Heard my parents talking about it."

"Yeah, well, no one wants to live in Murderville," I mutter.

The door to the bunker flies opens and Adi tugs Zayn out.

"You are going to *pee* your pants, Penny," she says, laughing and flattening her hair, pulling a leaf out.

Great.

Omar takes my hand and I cling to him. The bunker doesn't look that big, about twenty square feet. Big enough for more than two at a time, so this has nothing to do with space.

Inside is pitch-black and so silent I can hear my breathing. Omar chuckles from beside me.

"Do not go anywhere," I tell him.

"This is creepy," he replies, wrapping an arm around me so we don't get separated.

Gasping, I curl into Omar's side as a bluster of air hits me like a ghost passing through my body.

Omar and I laugh after the shock and spin to the direction of the wind. "What was that?" I ask.

It felt like my dad's leaf blower when he's obsessed with cleaning the yard and irritating me.

"Listen," he whispers.

I hold my breath and look around the room, trying to see whatever it is he heard. My eyes adjust and I can see the outline of what appears to be trees. The room smells plastic and kind of musty, so I think they're artificial.

"Omar, is someone over there?" I whisper, pointing.

"Where?"

My heart thumps hard as Omar pulls me a step deeper into the bunker.

What are we supposed to do in here?

Just survive.

"There!" I shout at the same time white morphsuits leap up from every corner of the room.

Omar and I shout and grab each other harder. The suits disappear back into the ground as if they really are ghosts. They were real and not holograms . . . but where did they go?

"Ghosts," I say. "Do we just stand here and wait for them to jump again?"

My question is answered in the worst way. Gusts of wind hit us like an assault. I half scream and half laugh while Omar and I huddle in the middle of the bunker. The morphsuited people jump up again, leaping around the room in sideways crab-like jumps.

"They don't move like ghosts!" Omar says as gust after gust of air whacks into us.

I turn around, following as they move. Then the movements suddenly change. Instead of jumping sideways, they jump forward and land in front of us.

I scream and Omar leaps back, letting go of me and falling on his ass.

Although the creepy dancing morphsuits are about five feet in front of us, leaping and running in different directions, I still laugh at Omar on the ground. I reach out for him but two of them jump between us. Then they start moving in a circle again, one around me and the other around Omar.

He gets to his feet as I turn around, counting four people jumping around me. I see a break, a couple-second gap, and run through them. They run to the outside of the room again and that's when I think it's over.

I move to Omar so we can leave, slightly disappointed that it was just a bit of wind and morphsuits. Before I can reach him, a crackle echoes through the walls as if the concrete is cracking.

Omar and I look at each other in the dark. We didn't hear this when Zayn and Adi were in here.

"What was that?" I ask.

The morph people are nowhere to be seen. The tree line around the room disguises them perfectly.

"Let's just go, I'm done," I say. The anxiety of something happening again is making me want to get out.

"All right, this was kind of a bust anyway."

We turn and that's when the crack booms again. I jump as something hits us over and over, the wind carrying whatever it is and whipping it around the room like a tornado. Leaves? Fake leaves?

I bat my hands as they fly in my face. The morphsuits leap up from their hiding spots again, doing star jumps and disappearing back into the ground.

Through the leaves and my arms waving around, I see something in the corner of the room that sends ice trickling down my spine. I stumble sideways, trying to put as much distance between me and him, bumping into Omar as I go.

"There!" I shout.

"I see them, Pen!"

I open my mouth to tell him it's not the morphsuits, that it's the Jackson mask, when another crack explodes through the room.

Swinging my arms as the wind picks up, I reach for Omar to get us out of here. When I look back, the mask is gone.

Where the hell is he?

I don't ever want to see it again but if I know he's here and lose sight of him, we could die.

"Omar!" I shout, spinning around, my eyes picking out blurs of white as featherlight leaves blow into my face. My stomach turns upside down.

He tucks his head against my shoulder and laughs. "I love this room."

Well, I don't and we need to get out.

I push him toward the door . . . which turns out to be a wall. Over the other side of the room is another break in the tree line and that must be where the door is.

I look over my shoulder to the corner where the mask was and a scream dies in my throat as I see it again. It's a flash as he ducks down but he was there.

Grabbing Omar, I run forward, dragging him behind me. I don't look at anything but the outline of the door in front of us.

Running too fast, I trip and slam into the door. Omar laughs, saying, "Easy."

My hand trembles around the handle. I look back as I shove the door open, seeing the morphsuits duck down.

As soon as the door opens, the wind halts as if I'd pressed the off switch.

I stumble out, pressing my hand over my heart thudding against my rib cage. My pulse and breath too quick.

"That was insane," Omar says, brushing leaves from his silky hair.

"There was someone in the bunker with a white *mask,*" I say when I can breathe again. "Did anyone else see? Omar?"

He shrugs. "I saw all those creepy white *things.*"

"I was too busy being terrified by the white suits," Adi replies. "What even were they? Besides, there are people in masks all over."

"Right."

No one else has seen it, and I've seen it three times.

What if it's in my head? That's all I need.

After an hour and forty-five minutes of pure fear and screaming my head off and thinking I'm going insane, I'm relieved to be at the end where I can eat and wait for my heart rate to slow down.

"That was epic!" Adi says.

I head straight for the punch stall. "I need a drink so bad, my throat is burning."

The punch is the same every year, some sort of red fizzy concoction that tastes like cherry and something else indefinable.

The boys go straight for the food so we can get through the lines faster. The sign that says I SURVIVED SCREAM FEST is blocked with dozens of groups wanting pictures.

We always do ours at the end when we're no longer hungry or thirsty.

"Adi, did anyone grab you while we were in there?" I ask as we carry four cups of punch to a picnic table the boys have grabbed. They were clearly hungry because they have corn dogs, mac and cheese, cake, and white chocolate–dipped marshmallows with ghost faces on them.

"No, they're not allowed to do that. I did almost kick one of those creepy masked freaks dancing around, though."

"Yeah."

I hand Zayn a punch and sit down.

"Penny said someone grabbed her," Adi tells the boys.

Zayn's black brows rise. "Really? You want to talk to someone about that?"

"We should. They can't have people grabbing everyone," Omar adds.

"No, it's fine. Besides, we all kind of clung to each other out there—maybe that's all it was. I don't want to get actors in trouble for nothing."

Adi shrugs. "Maybe. I think I clawed Omar a few times."

He holds his hand up where there are three scratches. "You *think*!"

I sit, uneasy, listening to them buzzing.

I was definitely grabbed, and I wasn't imagining the Jackson look-alike.

Not this time or in the street the other night.

There might not be a copycat killer, but someone out there is running around dressed like him.

But why?

10

TUESDAY, OCTOBER 26

I spent nearly all of last night stressing and wondering whether it's a good idea to give Nash and Grace a heads-up that someone in their daddy's mask is wandering around town and joining in at Scream Fest.

Can't see them reacting too well to the news. Whoever it is, they're seriously shameless.

I've seen the Jackson look-alike twice now, so it's only a matter of time before someone else does. If that someone is a cop, whoever is playing dress-up is in big trouble.

There are about ten people in my class I can think of who would do something tasteless like that. Ruby's top of the list.

I drag myself through the hallway and open my locker. I'm half asleep still as I take my book to first period, wishing I was back in bed.

My legs are heavy, eyes blinking slow. If my parents were home, I would pretend I was sick and stay home. Since they're away, I can't. If school called them, they would come straight back.

Ruby and her group of friends are ahead of me in the hall. One of them does a double take and then the rest of them not so discreetly glance my way.

They make no effort to hide the fact that they're talking about me. About Nash and their latest accusation. Now they're saying Nash was in on it with Karter.

Those two were never even friends, so it makes no sense.

Idiots.

"I heard she faked an alibi for him."

"I bet she's still seeing him."

"Do you think they both knew what their dad was up to?"

"Probably. Nash is such a creep. He's so going down for this."

"Like father, like son."

My stomach burns as I listen to the nasty BS they're spewing.

"Hey!" I snap. "You have no idea what you're talking about, so shut the hell up."

"Ooh, we made her mad," Ruby teases, pushing her hair over her shoulder. "You should worry less about us and more about your sick boyfriend joining his daddy in jail."

I launch forward and shove her into the locker. She gasps and her coward friends take a big step back from her.

"You bitch!" she shrieks, and throws herself at me, but I'm ready and waiting.

I push her before she collides with me.

"Cut it out! Penny and Ruby, my office, now!" Principal Farman bellows from down the hall.

Ruby straightens her hair, pulling out a stringy fake cobweb that was stuck on the locker. "*She* attacked *me.*"

"You'll both have the opportunity to explain when you get into my office. The rest of you, get to class!"

I turn around and follow Principal Farman as he leads us to his office. On the way I pass Zayn, who's watching with pride in his eyes.

He mouths, *You okay?* as I pass. Giving him a quick nod, I walk into the principal's office and take a seat. Ruby huffs and drops herself down next to me.

The only sign of Halloween in this office is a spider in the corner of the room, but I don't think that's decoration.

"I want to know what happened out there. Penny, you can start. Not a word, Ruby."

"She was talking crap, as usual. Telling her minions that Nash is just like his dad, that I probably knew what Jackson was up to, and that Nash is going down."

Principal Farman nods, his expression impartial. "And then?"

I clench my hands by my knees. "I was angry, and I pushed her."

"Ruby?"

"Yep, she went postal. I wonder why—"

"Enough, Ruby," Principal Farman says. "If I see this from either of you again, it will be a week of after-school detention. Am I clear?"

We both nod our understanding.

"Ruby, you can go to class. Penny, please wait behind a moment."

Ruby smirks as she leaves, and I wish I'd gotten a slap in back there. She's such a witch. I hate her.

Once the door is shut behind Ruby, Principal Farman clears his throat. "Penny, what's going on? This isn't like you."

"Everyone talks about him like this is his fault. *He didn't do anything.*"

I pushed her twice; it was hardly a fight.

He nods. "I understand."

"He can't even come to school."

"He hasn't been expelled from school."

"That doesn't mean he's welcome here."

Principal Farman sighs. "I think it would be a good idea for you to see the guidance counselor."

"What? I don't need to talk to anyone. I need people to stop talking trash about my . . ." My what? "About Nash."

"I've been keeping an eye on you for a while now, Penny, and it appears that you're struggling."

"My grades haven't slipped."

"It's not your grades I'm worried about. You no longer take part in drama, and you've dropped your music lessons."

"I have music lessons outside school."

Which I've also stopped attending, but he doesn't need to know that.

"You no longer work on the paper, and you've quit track."

"I had too many activities," I say, and sound defensive even to my own ears.

"We always advise students to only take on what they can manage, of course. But you used to do all of those extracurricular activities and still maintain high grades. In the last six months, you've slowly dropped them all."

Since shortly before Nash and I stopped talking altogether, I've been struggling and I knew my friends noticed, but I didn't think the damn principal did too.

"I don't want to talk to anyone."

"All right. You know where Ms. Chen is if you need her. Please ask for help when you're ready."

I chew on my lip, wishing I could make a run for the door and not get in trouble.

"I will. Are you going to tell my parents about the thing with Ruby?"

"No, I believe it's been adequately dealt with, and it won't happen again," he replies, his voice stern—a promise that he will absolutely not do me any favors again.

"It won't. I can't believe I let her get to me."

He smiles sympathetically and it's slightly condescending. He might as well say that he thinks I let Ruby get to me because I'm not coping well . . . and should take his offer of seeing the guidance counselor.

"Can I go to class now?"

"Of course. My door is always open, Penny."

I duck my head as I get up and mutter, "Thanks."

Outside his office, I take a breath and try to stop myself from hyperventilating. I thought I was managing things better than that. I thought I was on top of it. Giving up drama club was such a mistake.

I'm late to my first class but Mr. Williams knows why. All through his lesson I feel him watching me. How have I not noticed the teachers keeping an eye on me before?

Zayn, sitting beside me, tries to get my attention as we pretend to read the biology book in front of us, making notes about cell structure. I can't think of anything but how I'm going to get the teachers off my back, pretend to my friends that I'm okay, deal with the anniversary of the murders, and figure out what's going on with Nash.

"You're going to talk to me soon, right?" Zayn whispers.

"No."

"Pen!"

Smirking, I say, "After class."

I can't afford to be anything other than a perfect student right now or I'll be forced into Ms. Chen's chair and asked to talk about my feelings.

But that won't help me.

I manage to avoid Zayn and Omar until lunchbreak. Adi, currently serving a detention for back talking a teacher, seemed extra agitated that she wouldn't be getting the gossip until after school.

We're in the cafeteria. I'm nibbling on a slice of pizza while trying to pretend I can't see two pairs of eyes staring intently at me.

"Penny, will you tell us what's going on? I wish I'd seen it, by the way. Slammed right into the locker. I love a chick fight." Omar reconstructs the shove, his hands flying out in front of him. "Bam!"

"I'm seconds from slapping you, Omar," I say.

"Then tell us what's going on."

Zayn slides a wedge of cake toward me. I'm not sure if it's a peace offering or a bribe but it's chocolate, so I give in to it.

"Ruby was being her usual hateful self and I'd had enough."

"What was she doing?" Omar asks. "Was it about Nash?"

Here we go. Omar and I never talk about him. "Yeah, it was."

"You're still hung up on him."

"I don't care if you don't understand. I'm so tired of pretending. Nash was . . . *is* our friend and he's alone, Omar."

"This bothered you so much you got in a . . . you fought with Ruby. *You.* The girl who's perfect, who's never even missed a homework assignment."

"I'm not perfect."

He raises his dark brows. "You are, Pen. I wish you'd talked to us before. I don't hate Nash. It's just that my parents would lose their minds if I started hanging out with him. He didn't want us around much, either."

"Can you blame him? His whole world had just been crushed."

Omar holds his palms up. "No one's saying we blame him. What do you need us to do?"

"Stand up for him. He only has Grace."

Laughter erupts in the cafeteria, stealing our attention. Two students run between tables wearing Momo masks with the creepy smile and bulging eyes.

I shrug, arching my back as one of them brushes my hair on their way past.

"Ew, don't touch me!"

Another one throws their arms up in front of Mae and shouts.

Omar stands and shoves him. "Leave her alone, dude."

I don't know if he recognizes them but with full masks on and generic clothing, it's impossible for me to tell.

They run off, laughing as two teachers try to get them to stop.

"You okay?" Omar asks Mae.

"Yeah, thanks, Omar. See you in class, Penny."

"Very chivalrous, I'm so proud of you," Zayn says, pinching Omar's cheek.

"Shut up." He turns to me. "We've got your back on the Nash thing, Pen," Omar says.

"Thanks." I take a sip of water. "You're being real quiet, Zayn."

"I think we've been over it enough."

Omar whacks Zayn's arm. "Wait, you two talk about this stuff?"

Zayn dodges his arm. "He's a friend."

"But?" I ask, sensing a new hesitation in Zayn.

"But he stood you up and left you alone outside the theater in the middle of the night, and he was in town when Noah was discovered."

"Whoa, what the hell is this?" Omar asks, and shoos away someone trying to sit at our table. "He stood you up? Damn, girl, you're still sneaking out with him?"

"No, not in about five months. This was the first time we were supposed to meet at Benji's, and he didn't show."

"So, Zayn isn't the one who heard the noise there?"

"No, that was me," I admit. "Zayn gave me a ride home."

"You called him and not me. Ouch."

"I didn't call him. He stalked me."

"I did not stalk you! I knew you were probably doing something stupid, so I checked your location. *And I was right.*"

Omar looks between us with an open mouth, trying to keep up. I think he's also a bit irritated that we didn't tell him sooner. "Jeez, guys, I need you to catch me up."

So I do. For the next thirty minutes, we fill Omar in on everything that's happened, and we discuss how to help Nash. Then we draw breadsticks that Omar was supposed to have for lunch to see who gets the short one. Zayn gets to fill Adi in.

"Hey," Zayn says, nudging my arm as I stare into space. I'm sitting on a bench in the school's parking lot, bundled up against the brisk air. The day dragged despite everything that went on.

"Hi."

"You coming? It's pumpkin patch time."

"Just waiting for Adi. She is talking to Mr. Kelty about her lunchtime detention. He wanted an apology for how she spoke to him, apparently."

He rolls his eyes. "All right, I'm going to run home quickly first, so I'll meet you all there."

"Where's Omar?"

"Trying to flirt with Mae again. He thinks she was giving him *the eyes* after he defended her at lunch."

"The eyes?"

Laughing, he shakes his head. "No idea. She was probably trying to figure out why he keeps staring at her. See you later."

Adi comes stomping toward me five minutes later with a scowl. "He's the most boring man on the planet. The monotone voice. The 'where is your respect for authority' bullshit."

"Pumpkin patch?" I ask, ignoring her.

"Yes, please. I'm going to carve one that looks like his face and then smash it."

"You keep taking that high road."

We drive from school to the pumpkin patch and join a short queue of cars pulling onto the field. Gray clouds clump together in the sky. I don't think there has been one year I've come here and it hasn't rained.

The whole car ride, Adi quizzed me on the almost-fight with Ruby, telling me how proud she is and how gutted she feels to have missed it.

"Are you carving or painting this year?" Adi asks.

"Painting."

"Slicing into something doesn't feel the same anymore?"

"Subtle, Adi."

I park in the massive muddy field and take a breath. Last year my car got stuck and Nash had to tow me out. We had no idea how much things would change just two days later.

There are people in costume walking around and selecting pumpkins. My stomach lurches at the thought of seeing Jackson's mask again. I don't think whoever it is would bother. It would be stupid to even try.

Hay bales are stacked and covered in giant spiders. Halloween character mannequins with masks—clowns, ghosts, vampires—stand randomly in the field. I count ten at first glance.

"Did you watch Ruby's TikToks last night?" Adi asks. "They were insane. She was going off on Karter *and* Nash."

"Why Nash?" I ask, getting out of the car. "He's innocent."

My boots sink into squelchy mud.

Adi slams my door. "Who knows. She also mentioned Grace, said she was probably working with Karter since they dated."

"They dated for about a week, like, two years ago."

I think about Grace's mysterious boyfriend. Maybe she and Karter rekindled their relationship . . .

"That's what a bunch of people said in the comments. She got so mad that she deleted the whole thing." She links my arm. "I hate Tuesdays. We have no classes together and lunch detention without you was dull."

"Well, think about that the next time you tell a teacher he's an idiot."

"He *is* an idiot. Hey, hot chocolate?"

"Yeah, I'm frozen." I rub my gloved hands together.

The line is short, but it still takes almost ten minutes to get a hot chocolate. We huddle together and order two large cups. Periodically a speaker near the food carts lets out a scream. Adi and I laugh every time it makes someone jump as they walk past.

"Let's head into the maze first. The boys will find us eventually."

"Sure."

I don't want to hang around in case it rains anyway. I want to do the maze, paint a pumpkin, get fresh doughnuts, and go home. Although Noah's killer has been caught, I'm not feeling very festive. There was still a death. Noah won't get to carve a pumpkin or eat a bunch of candy.

"*Ohmygod,* Penny, look!" Adi says.

I follow her gaze. Billy, Adi's crush.

She gasps as he looks our way and quickly turns so her back is to him. "Is he coming over? I'm going to die, Pen. Is he coming?"

"That's real smooth, and yeah, he's coming over. Want me to leave?"

Her eyes widen. "Don't you dare!"

"Hey, Adi. And Penny."

I'm an afterthought.

Adi turns to him, and I can feel her nerves. "Hi, Billy."

"So . . . are you going into the maze?" he asks.

"Adi was about to, but I'm waiting for someone," I say.

She gives me a look that could strike me to the ground, but I know they're both super shy when it comes to each other. That means she really likes him because she is not a reserved person usually.

"Yeah? Want to head in now?" Billy asks.

Her cheeks turn as red as her hair as she nods in agreement.

"Have fun," I say, smiling.

She'll kill me later if they spend the whole time in awkward silence.

I watch them go in and wait two minutes before going in myself. Corn stretches high above my head as I walk. The maze is always huge, hundreds of people can be in it, but you might only see a couple.

Ignoring the lonely feeling of doing this by myself, I take a right and jump as I come face to face with a clown mannequin. Not cool. I've hit a dead end. This is definitely not as fun without my friends. We'd be chatting, laughing, and messing around. Omar would lead, pretending that he knew where to go. Adi and Zayn would tease him relentlessly each time we took a wrong turn, and Nash and I would follow them, flirting and not caring how long it took to get out.

I turn around, leaving the hideous Pennywise behind, and immediately hit another dead end. As I follow another little track, I hear a rustling behind me. Some of the corn is snapped and leaning over where others have cheated.

Looking over my shoulder, I watch for a second to see if I can catch the cheat. No one emerges after a few seconds, so I carry on.

Corn dances above me in a strong gust of wind. The weather is cooler than usual for October, like it knows we've had another death in town.

Fall doesn't look the same this year.

The rustling, this time up ahead, startles me. That can't be the wind.

I hear footsteps.

Craning my neck, I look around a corner to see who's there. I can hear voices from all directions, but I can't locate the source of the footsteps near me.

"Hello," I call out, patting the mannequin beside me. "It's a dead end this way . . . only me and a Dracula here."

They're not replying.

Crap.

My heart thuds louder as footsteps crunch and corn bends down in front of me as if someone's pushing it.

I jump back just as Nash walks through the makeshift wall.

Oh my god.

His eyes lock on mine and he freezes for a second. He's not here to see me, then; the look of surprise on his face tells me everything I need to know. He wishes he'd taken another route. Or not come at all.

My jaw falls open, and I look around. "Nash, what are you doing?"

"Walking the maze. Like every year."

Nothing is the same this year. We at least had a little bit of Halloween last year; now we have nothing.

I rush to ask him all my questions before he can run the other way. "Are you okay? You didn't meet me. Zayn and I were worried."

He scowls, eyes narrowing, and throws his hands behind his back. I take a second to try to think what happened between me driving him home and him standing me up.

"Were you?" he asks.

"Yes!" I step closer and he visibly stiffens, not wanting me near him.

It's night and day compared to when he willingly climbed into my car.

"What's going on? I'm *so* lost here. I know things are weird between us, but I thought we were going to talk about that. I was waiting outside Benji's that night. Why didn't you show?"

"Why didn't I show? Are you serious, Penny?"

"Yes, I'm serious. What's going on? I have no idea what you're talking about."

He goes to turn away, but I block him and try to ignore the sting as he takes a step back like I could shock him if I got too close.

"Nash, please. Tell me what's going on. Why didn't you meet me?"

Blinking twice, he tilts his head. "You really don't know . . ."

"Know what?" I throw my hands up. "Can you please explain before my brain is fried!"

Attempting to hide his amusement at my outburst, he says, "I thought it was you. I was about to leave to meet you when the cops turned up again."

"What? Why?"

He rolls his eyes. "Someone had reported seeing me in town again. Said I was hanging around the Halloween store. Looked like I was revisiting the crime scene . . . or dump site."

"Someone saw you?"

"No, they didn't. I was home."

"I can't believe you thought I would call the cops on you."

"The second I was about to walk out the door to meet you, the cops turn up."

"Why would I do that?"

Sighing, he shrugs. "I don't know anymore, Penny. It's hard to trust anyone in this goddamn town."

"You can trust me."

"Can I?"

"Yes," I breathe.

There's a second where we don't say anything at all. We stand in the cold and watch each other like we're trying to figure out how the hell we ended up here and if it's possible to go back. I hear the rustling of the wind between the corn and the faint sound of conversations and laughter.

I'm the one to pop the bubble. "Who else did you notice in town that day?"

"Zayn."

"He wouldn't call the cops."

Nash scratches his neck. "Someone did, Penny. Most people in town hate me, so it could be anyone."

"Ruby was doing these TikToks," I tell him.

"Yeah, I was tagged."

I wince. What kind of asshole tags someone in a video hating on them?

"Ugh, I hate her."

Shrugging it off as if nothing bothers him, he looks up at the sky. "It's going to rain."

"Nash, how are you really?"

"You should get going."

"No, not yet. Talk to me."

He looks back at me and asks, "What do you want, Penny? With me."

"I wish things were the way they used to be."

"Yeah, you think your parents would invite me over again?" He sounds as bitter as I feel. "Do you care what everyone else thinks?"

"Not one bit."

He laughs and the sound feels like sandpaper on my skin. It's a harsh laugh that's more of an accusation. If I didn't care, I wouldn't stay away. That's what he's thinking.

"Nash, I don't. Things were . . . complicated. My parents and, well, everything. I wasn't allowed to see you." I glance down at my feet, the shame of leaving him to deal with everything alone almost taking my breath away. "I'm sorry I wasn't stronger."

"Hey," he says, stepping closer and lifting my chin. "I don't want to keep having this conversation. Okay? I'm over it, Penny. What the town did to me, they also did to you. I know what everyone said about you being the girlfriend of the killer's son. I know the pressure was hell for you. I know that your parents wanted you out of it all, and I can't blame them for that. The only asshole here is my dad."

"I can think of a few more."

"Ruby and her TikToks?" he guesses.

"Yep."

"I should go, and you should find Adi, Omar, and . . . Zayn."

The way he said Zayn's name bothers me. Nash believes that his friend, possibly his last remaining friend, called the cops on him. Or maybe Nash knows that Zayn asked me out.

"What about you? Why don't you join us?"

He laughs again. "I'm not sure that's a good idea. I should go before the gossip starts."

"Why did you come?" I ask as he turns to leave through the corn wall again.

He turns back just before he disappears and replies, "I wanted a normal moment."

Then he's gone and I'm stuck watching the corn sway back into place and wondering what the hell I'm supposed to do next.

How can I go against my parents' wishes and tell them I don't care what anyone thinks of Nash?

Thirty minutes later, I'm out of the maze. I head over to the field to find Adi and pick a pumpkin. I'm not feeling it at all after running into Nash, but my friends will be suspicious if I duck out now.

I find Zayn sitting on a large pumpkin in a field, his head in his phone.

"What's up," I say, nudging his foot with my own.

He jumps and looks up. Shoving his phone in his pocket as he stands, he says, "Where did you come from?"

"Maze. You seen Adi or Omar?"

"Omar's around. Adi's with Billy and I'm not going anywhere near that." He rolls his eyes. "If I have to listen to one more *Billy is so funny, Billy is so hot,* I'm going to kill someone."

Bad choice of words there.

"They're cute."

"If you say so."

"Um," I say. "I saw Nash in the maze."

Zayn looks over to the corn and frowns. "He came?"

"He's gone now."

He doesn't seem very surprised by this.

"What did he say?"

"He told me the cops came to his house again right before he was going to meet me."

Zayn nods. "Why?"

"Apparently someone called and told them he was hanging around the costume store again. Obviously, he wasn't."

"People in this town need more hobbies. Want to get a hot chocolate?"

"Sure," I reply. I don't have a big appetite, but I can drink hot chocolate all day. "Did he tell you the same thing?"

We walk to the cart and wait in line.

"He didn't tell me anything. Refused to talk about it. I guess he didn't want me getting involved. He knew I would tell you he suspected you called them."

Do I tell Zayn Nash now suspects him? But his frosty response to Zayn could be because of me.

My head is dizzy trying to figure out who to trust. Honestly, I don't believe either one of them would lie.

"I wish he would open up a bit more."

"Pen, you haven't agreed to meet him again, have you? It didn't exactly go well last time."

"No."

"But?"

I hesitate before admitting, "I want to. What do you think about inviting him out with us?"

Zayn's brows shoot up. "Do you think that's a good idea?"

"No, I think it's a terrible idea. People will talk. My parents will *freak,* but I'm so past caring about that. You were right—he's drowning. He looked *so* unhappy. He came here today, hiding in the corn, just to do something normal. He's lonely."

Zayn blows out a long breath. "Just me and you at first. I don't know how comfortable Adi will be. I'll talk to Omar."

"Thanks," I say, and order two hot chocolates when we reach the front of the line.

"Ugh, I need the bathroom before we find Omar," I tell him, handing him both drinks.

"Enjoy the portable toilets," he says, sitting on a bench to wait for me.

"I'll disinfect myself when I get home."

I go to open the door, but it's stuck, despite being vacant. It feels like there's something heavy against it. The others bathrooms are taken, so I tug harder, and finally the door flies open.

A scream rips from my throat as Ruby tumbles out like a rag doll, landing at my feet with blood on her chest and her vacant eyes staring up at me.

Zayn shouts my name as I jump back, bashing into him and then a plastic skeleton dog. Our hot chocolates fall to the ground and spill everywhere. I grab Zayn and my gaze drifts back to Ruby on the ground, lying lifeless in the muddy grass.

"Oh my god, is that Ruby Mountford?" a bystander says.

"Someone needs to help her."

"Help her? She's dead."

"This couldn't have been Karter."

People around us close in fast with their observations.

Mr. and Mrs. O'Neil, the owners of the patch, take charge. He kneels and places his hand on Ruby's neck, checking for a pulse.

I turn away to retch.

"Move away," Mrs. O'Neil says, physically moving us back. She's so pale I'd be surprised if she doesn't pass out. "Everyone, move away. Now. Back up."

I shiver, holding my queasy stomach, and lean against Zayn as we're shuffled farther away from Ruby.

My hands tremble, the shock of seeing another body, this one falling right in front of me, makes me weak as wet paper. I could tear apart in an instant.

"Oh my god, it's Ruby. Ruby," Zayn says. "She's . . . dead. Jesus, Pen. She's dead."

Zayn holds me up, but I can feel the tenseness in his body. His arms are rock solid around me, and I'm afraid I'll snap him if I move.

"I saw," I mutter, my voice hollow like someone else is speaking for me. "I saw."

Two people have now been murdered.

"She just . . . fell out. Someone put her in there like she was nothing. Zayn, she was posting TikToks last night, attending school just this morning, and now she's gone," I mutter.

"Back up, you two. Sit here. You've had a shock," Mrs. O'Neil says, still ushering us backward. "I'll get you something hot to drink in a moment."

I look up at her mottled face and whisper, "Are you okay?"

This is the second year in a row her property has been used to dispose of a body.

She pats my shoulder. "You stay here. The police will want to speak with you both. I'll sort those drinks."

I shiver against the chilly breeze as she mentions hot drinks. Our hot chocolates lie in puddles close to Ruby's body, mixing with her blood.

"Zayn," I say. When he doesn't reply, I look up at him and he's staring off into space. I'm not sure if he can hear me.

The staff have cordoned off the area around the body, creating a barrier, and I assume they've called the cops.

"Hey?"

He snaps out of it, shaking his head and rubbing his palm over his face roughly. "This is really bad, Pen."

"Yes," I agree. "Because Ruby's dead, Karter didn't murder Noah, and the real killer is still out there."

His hollow eyes finally meet mine. "And this is victim number two, found at the pumpkin patch, just like last year. Which means we *do* have a copycat."

11

Zayn and I sit perfectly still on our bench while the world around us spins at a million miles an hour. Or that's how it feels. I have a new hot chocolate in hand, as promised by Mrs. O'Neil, but it's quickly getting cold.

I take another sip, but it does little to warm me up. I'm frozen to the bone.

That's the shock, according to Mrs. O'Neil.

There's a large crowd now, standing at the makeshift barrier created with hay bales. Zayn and I are on the inside of it. We're not spectators. We're a part of it. The only ones left out in the field are the mannequins. A few people have been yelled at for recording and taking pictures. The first thing people think to do in a tragedy is get their phone out.

The afternoon has turned bright, despite the chilly wind. Vivid orange pumpkins are dotted around but there are no young children running in between them anymore. They've been taken home, far away from the horror.

Cops are on the scene now, arriving just after we were given hot chocolates. They spoke to the O'Neils first and then they all looked over at us. They were obviously told we—*I*—found her. But they haven't come over to get our statements.

"Pen?" Zayn says, breaking what feels like a very long silence as we watch the cops work.

"Yeah."

"Did anyone else see Nash?"

"I . . ." My teeth snap together, and I turn ice cold. "I don't know." I turn to him and grab his wrist. "Zayn, if anyone did, they're going to think that he was behind this. He was there, in the background, *both* times."

It will look like he wants to stick around and witness the reaction to his handiwork.

"So were you. Adi, too, she's around here. There were a lot of people out the day Noah was found, and I bet some of them are here now."

Yeah, but he's the only one whose dad was the original killer.

Adi's being kept back with the rest of the *spectators.* Billy is with her, so at least she's not alone.

"I found them both," I say, my eyes widening. I grip his arm. "Will the cops think *I* did this?"

"No one would ever think you're behind this. You belong on the top of a Christmas tree, Pen. You're nice to everyone."

"Everyone but the people who've been horrible to my boyfriend." *Ex!* "I just had a fight with Ruby."

"That wasn't a fight. You didn't even get a punch in."

"Do you think that's going to matter? The principal had to stop us. I think I'm going to throw up."

He puts his arm around me. The cops glance our way. "Hey, breathe. You're getting ahead of yourself. You have an alibi for Ruby's murder."

"How do you know?"

"Well, we've been together for a while, and she looks . . . fresh."

I stare at him, open-mouthed. "Zayn, what?"

He covers his mouth with his fist and pales. "You saw her too. The blood. It was new. She couldn't have been there long."

"Maybe it was before opening," I whisper. "Two on weekdays."

Nodding, he rubs my arm. "See, you were at school."

I shake my head, trying to expel the images of Ruby tumbling out of the toilet. Zayn's right, she didn't look like she'd been there long. Not like Noah. The blood on him had already dried dark red.

"How long does it take for blood to dry?" I ask.

"How the hell would I know?"

"School has been out for an hour and forty-five minutes."

"No one is going to think you killed Ruby. Even if you had time to. Besides, you've been here and there are plenty of people around."

Nash is my only alibi for most of my time in the maze. I didn't see many others until I got out.

"Yeah, but what makes you think someone didn't do it here with plenty of people around?"

"No way. They must've dumped her before it opened. You would've been seen leaving school and been seen by at least one person the entire time you've been here."

"But for a while that one person was Nash in the maze."

"Shh." He looks around to make sure no one's listening to us. "Don't tell a soul that."

"You're unsure about Nash. Have you ever considered it could be me?"

I watch his reaction carefully and there isn't one.

"Not really the time to joke, Penelope."

He's full-named me now too.

"I'm not joking. How can you be so sure I'm innocent but doubt him?"

"You . . ." He rakes his hands through his hair. "Are you seriously comparing yourself to Nash? It's a totally different situation."

"Well, yeah, it is. But we're both your friends."

"Penny, I'm saying this as your friend. We're not having this conversation again. Stop overthinking everything or keep it to yourself. You won't make things easier for him like this."

"Penny and Zayn."

We both look over as an officer I recognize as a classmate's mom kneels in front of us. She came just at the right moment because things were getting uncomfortable.

"How are you doing?"

"Not great, Mrs. Barone. Sorry, I mean Officer Barone," Zayn says.

She smiles warmly. "Either is fine, Zayn. Don't worry about that. Can you tell me, in your own words, what happened?"

Her eyes are on me.

"Um. Yeah. I needed the bathroom. I had to pull the handle pretty hard because it was stuck. And when I got it open, you know, Ruby . . ." I take a moment to swallow a lump that's swelled in my throat.

"It's okay, Penny, you're doing really well."

"She fell out. She just . . . fell out and rolled in front of me. Someone stuffed her in that toilet."

Mrs. Barone nods. "Okay. What time did you arrive at the pumpkin patch?"

"We came straight from school. I don't know exactly because I didn't look but it would have been around three o'clock."

"My Jemima likes to come from school too."

"I . . . I haven't seen her today."

"Home with the flu, I'm afraid. Penny, did you notice anyone hanging around the toilets? Maybe watching them or anyone coming out of that one?"

I shake my head. "No, nothing."

Beside me, Zayn's body stiffens. He'll snap if he does that any more.

"Okay, you're doing great. And, Zayn, where were you when Penny opened the door?"

Zayn gives his account, and we go over once more that we didn't see anyone hanging around. There are lots of people here, more now that there's been another murder.

The vultures are back and this time they get to legitimately talk about another Halloween serial killer.

Mrs. Barone has noted our statement and told us that our parents are on the way. She stands, moving away from us while speaking to another officer privately. Zayn and I are left alone.

"You didn't tell her about Nash," he says, raising a brow.

"Neither did you."

It's a petty comeback but it's true. He was the one to tell me to keep it to myself, not that I was going to spill anyway.

I search his eyes for any sign that he's mad at me or thinks that we've done the wrong thing. He's poker-faced at the moment, the way he was for ages after I told him I only wanted to be friends.

"It wouldn't look good for him if we did, Penny, but what if it *was* him?"

"I don't know how you can say that. It wasn't."

"His dad was the original killer, haunting our town. What's to say that he's not angrier than we could ever imagine? He's home most of the time, cut off from everyone, thinking about everything he's lost, seething that he's paying for his dad's actions. Do you trust him with your life, Pen?"

I'm not sure how to respond. His words wind me. I try to take a breath but there's nothing there. Do I trust him with my life?

"Don't," I finally mutter. "Don't try to make me doubt him."

"That's not what I'm doing. I just don't want you to do something stupid and get yourself hurt."

"If you truly believe he could be behind this, why didn't you tell Jemima's mom that?"

"I'm not sure anymore. Something's going on with him, and he's shutting me out of it." Zayn stands and walks off.

It takes a second to register where he goes. In the direction of two cops.

My heart stutters. I hold my breath and sit taller on the bench, but he doesn't seem to be name dropping Nash. There are a thousand other questions he could be asking. If he does tell them Nash was here, I won't have time to warn him.

With trembling hands, I call him, getting up so that I can walk about and avoid having anyone overhear.

The phone rings and rings. *Come on, Nash. Please pick up.* I don't think he will know what's happened yet; he left ages ago.

"You need to stop contacting me," he says as he picks up.

No pleasantries. Straight to telling me to stay out of his life. Nice.

"D-don't hang up. Please, Nash, you need to hear this."

"Penny . . . What's wrong?" he asks, picking up the urgency and fear in my voice.

"Um."

"You don't sound good. What's happened?" he asks again.

"I'm not good. Ruby's dead. I just found her."

"What?" he breathes down the phone. "What happened? Are you okay? Where are you?"

"The pumpkin patch still. My parents are on their way, but I really need to see you soon, okay?" I say, my voice all over the place. I sniff, wipe tears from my cheeks, and look around.

"She's dead. God."

"She was in a portable toilet. I opened the door."

"I'm sorry."

"Did anyone else see you?" I ask.

"No, I don't think so. I came in from the field that backs onto the maze. Did you tell anyone I was there?"

"Only Zayn and he won't say anything."

He's silent for a moment, and I want to fill the space, but I can't think of anything to say.

"Are you sure he won't?" he asks, and I can tell that he's worried now.

"You should know, Nash. You've been in contact with him this whole time."

"Wow, babe, you sound bitter."

I've not heard him call me that in months. *Babe,* not *bitter,* obviously.

"There's something else. Something that I'm going to have to tell the cops before the principal does."

"The principal?"

"This morning Ruby and I kinda had a fight. Well, we pushed each other."

"You got into a fight?"

I can hear the smile in his tone.

"Zayn said it didn't count as a fight. She was being . . . herself and I shoved her. The principal saw and called us both in."

"So, now you're stressing because this doesn't look good for *you.*"

"Well, it doesn't, does it?"

"No one would ever think you'd hurt anyone."

"That's what everyone keeps telling me."

"Why did you push her?"

I wrap one arm around my waist. "She was talking about you."

He's silent for a second. Then says, "When you tell the cops, they're going to ask about your relationship with her. Don't mention anything that she's done to you before. None of the bitchy stuff, you got it? Don't give them the chance to build a picture that Ruby was bullying you."

"She wasn't. It was the odd comment, not unusual for her, but she does that to *everyone*."

"I know that. The cops don't. Seriously, Penny, don't give them a reason to believe you don't like her."

"Okay," I reply. "I'm going to tell them now."

"Call me later. I've got to go speak with Grace. It's only a matter of time before I get a visit, and it looks like I'm going to need an alibi."

He hangs up. I lower my phone and that's when I notice Zayn watching me.

12

Officer Barone smiles as I walk over to her. "Penny."

"I missed something earlier," I tell her, wringing my hands.

"Okay," she says, gesturing for me to follow her, and we sit on a bench out of the way. "What is it?"

"Okay. This morning me and Ruby had this thing."

Her back straightens the way Adi's does when there's gossip incoming. "What *thing* is this?"

"It was at school. She was talking about Nash Whitmore."

She tilts her head like she didn't need his surname to understand who I'm talking about.

"What happened, Penny?"

"She's been quite vocal about him since Noah was killed and was saying this horrible stuff when he's done nothing wrong. I pushed her."

"You pushed her."

"Yeah. I'm not exactly proud of it, but it's so unfair that he's dragged into everything just because of something his dad has done."

Nodding, she asks, "What did Ruby do?"

"She pushed me back and then the principal called us into his office."

"What time was this?"

"First thing, just before eight."

"Have you had any other issues with Ruby before?"

This is what Nash was talking about. Here's where she starts to paint her own picture, control the narrative.

"No. We don't hang with the same people, so I don't have much to do with her. Um, I mean, I didn't, I guess. I wanted to tell you myself."

"You've done the right thing. When was the last time you saw Ruby today?"

Frowning, I try to remember if she was in the cafeteria at lunch. "We don't have any classes together, and I don't remember seeing her at lunch. A couple students ran around the cafeteria in masks, so there was a lot going on. Like I said, we don't hang out."

She nods. "It's been brought to my attention that Ruby has made a number of TikToks about Nash and his family. Have you watched those?"

They'll be able to tell that if they take my phone.

"I don't follow her, but Adi has shown me some. I think Adi sent me a couple links, so I would've watched a couple from my phone."

"Okay. Are you aware of anyone who has a grudge against Ruby?"

And here is where she's trying to add Nash to her little painting.

"It's no secret that she's not always nice to people. But to hate her enough to kill her? No, I don't know anyone who could do this."

"Have you had any recent contact with Nash Whitmore?"

They'll also be able to check this.

"Yeah. We spoke after Noah was found . . . and I gave him a ride home from the station that afternoon."

There's no point in lying about taking him home because if anyone did notice, it'll look bad on us both, just like I had to tell her about my fight with Ruby. I have to be as transparent as I can.

She nods, knowing that Nash was brought in for questioning. She might've been there.

"Does he know about Ruby's TikToks?"

"I don't know. We don't send them to him."

I do know the answer to this, but I don't know if he'll deny it. If I say nothing, I can't lead him into a lie.

She nods again but it's stiff like she doesn't believe me. I'm starting to regret telling her this stuff, but she'll find out soon enough anyway.

"What time did you leave school today?"

She's asked this before.

"Straight from school, just before three. I came with Adi."

"Is this Adeline?"

"Yeah."

"Where was she when you found Ruby?"

"We split up. She went off into the maze with Billy. She's behind the hay bales now."

"Did you leave campus at any point today?"

"No, I was late to first period because I was talking to the principal, but I went to every class afterward. I didn't hurt Ruby," I add.

"I'm not suggesting that you did. I'm just trying to put together a timeline."

Yeah, I'm not buying that one.

"Is there anything else you want to add? Even if you don't think it's helpful or relevant," she asks.

"Nope. That was it."

"All right. You're free to go now, Penny. Your parents have arrived." She dips her head toward my parents, who are arguing with an officer by the hay bales. There's now police tape in front of the bales. A double wall to keep people out.

"Thanks," I say, walking away from her and shuddering.

"What are you doing to protect my daughter?" Mom asks.

"Mrs. Langley, Penelope is quite safe," the young, flustered officer says. He looks like he wants to run away.

"Mom," I say, ducking under the tape, then stepping over the bale.

"Penny!"

"Come on, we're leaving," Dad says as I'm squished to death by my mother.

They usher me to my car, and Mom drives while Dad follows

behind. The drive is silent, but I can tell she has a lot to say. We thought it was over. An isolated incident. It can't be a coincidence.

When we get inside, I curl up on the sofa, watching my phone in case Nash texts me.

"The mayor is calling a town meeting tonight. There are a lot of people who want answers. I'll be taking some time off and will drive you to school and pick you up."

"Dad!"

"This is nonnegotiable, Penny. If there's somewhere you want to go, I will be taking you. Do you still have your pepper spray?"

Well, this is just great.

"Yes."

"Make sure you have it with you at all times."

"All right," I breathe, my stomach tightening in knots. Since last year, everyone is hypervigilant. Dad's never taken his gun out of the safe, but it's still there. Neighbors were getting alarms and cameras installed on their houses. We have an app to view the house.

"I want to go to the town meeting too," I tell them. "Please."

"We'll all go," Mom replies. "We need answers."

The town hall is a large wood-paneled room, painted off-white, with a thin dark blue carpet. Rows and rows of metal chairs have been set out, and I notice right away that the Halloween decorations have been partially taken down, but a few stray bat cutouts remain on the bulletin boards around the room.

We sit near Adi and her parents. A few rows in front of us are Omar, his parents, sister, and future brother-in-law. I can't see Zayn, but he messaged and said his mom is bringing him.

Everyone wants to know what the cops are doing and how the mayor is going to handle this.

I nudge Adi as the mayor walks in with a bunch of cops and four new faces. Two are dressed in suits—no ties—and the other two have FBI jackets on.

"They're back," I whisper.

When they were called in last year, it only took them two days to find Jackson.

I want to message Nash, but my mom is sitting right beside me. It's going to be so hard to get away from them now that Dad is staying home and escorting me everywhere. They're going to lock me down like last year. It was suffocating but I understood.

"Good evening," the mayor says. "Before we start the meeting, I want us to take a minute of silence to reflect on the lives of Noah Smith and Ruby Mountford."

I bow my head as silence falls over the room. The feds do the same, paying respects to the two kids who are no doubt pinned to a whiteboard at the station.

I wonder if I'm up there too. On the board for suspects or at least people of interest. Along with Nash and Karter. With Ruby's murder, they'll surely have to let Karter go. He hasn't been released but being in police custody feels like a pretty solid alibi.

Mine will be iron-clad when I'm seen all over school CCTV, I hope.

I wonder what Nash's will be. Or Grace's, for that matter. Her name has been brought into this too.

After the moment of silence for the victims and their families, the mayor stands to the side, handing it over to a woman in a navy suit. She steps up to the microphone and pushes her graying hair behind her ears.

"Hello. I'm Agent Rosenthal with the FBI. We're here to help with the ongoing investigation into Noah's and Ruby's murders."

There's a rumble in the room as muttered questions fill the air.

"Do you have any suspects?"

"Are you releasing Karter?"

"The Whitmore kids are behind this!"

I ball my hands into fists. Dad notices and lifts a brow.

"Who else has to die before you stop this guy?"

Agent Rosenthal holds up one hand. "Please, I will take some questions but one at a time."

"What are you doing to protect our children?" Dad asks, standing up and making the whole room turn.

I shrink back in my seat.

The agent standing near Rosenthal does a double take. They must recognize me from last year—I was interviewed a bunch then, since I'd been such a frequent guest at the Whitmore house.

I vaguely recognize two of the agents here, but not Rosenthal or the one currently staring me down.

"The local police department will have officers on the streets. We're urging young people not to go out alone—"

There's a collective groan from every teen, myself included. We were shut away last year, too, listening to adults discuss the case and what the cops should be doing. It was all anyone could talk about, and we couldn't get away from it.

Makes sense, though, obviously.

"No freaking way," Adi hisses beside me.

"As of yet, no other town event has been canceled—that will be up to the mayor—but I urge you to exercise extreme caution if you decide to go out. I would recommend staying in groups of three or more and, wherever possible, an adult should be present."

Groups of three or more because of Kelsie's and Brodie's double murder on Devil's Night. The anniversary of that atrocity is in four days.

"Karter was in custody, so do you have any more suspects?" Zayn's mom asks.

"We are looking into that, but I cannot divulge any information."

"Are you closing the school?" The question comes from the back of the room. I don't recognize the voice.

"At present there are no plans to close the schools. Officers will be present across the middle and high school campus to ensure the students are safe. I recommend carpooling or taking the bus. If you have to walk, stick to larger groups."

She addresses the teenagers for the last part.

We're the ones being hunted here.

"Does this person wear a mask like Jackson? It's a copycat, right?"

Good question.

"No mask has been spotted, so we're keeping an open mind and investigating all lines of inquiry."

I bite my lip. I've seen someone in a mask twice now. The

exact same mask. I could tell them, but then I'd have to admit I snuck out.

Still, it might help narrow their investigation if they know for certain that they're looking for a copycat.

"Yeah, but it's obvious this freak is copying Whitmore!" someone in the front row spits.

"We cannot speculate."

Rosenthal gives information about what to do if anyone sees anything suspicious and tells us to grab a leaflet on our way out with information about the hotline they've set up.

"Unbelievable," Dad rages. "They don't know anything."

As people start to disperse, my parents and Adi's start talking. All four of them are animated in their discussion about how the cops are handling the case. Or not handling it. Adi and I slip out of the row and find Omar and Zayn.

"Can you believe this? My mom's already talking about homeschooling me until the killer is caught," Zayn says, shuddering.

"I'm not allowed anywhere on my own. Dad's working from home now and has to take me everywhere. I'm going to lose my mind," I tell them.

"How are we going to get to the *Scream* marathon tomorrow?" Omar asks.

I tilt my head. "Omar . . ."

"Right. I'm at yours, you're at Adi's, Adi's at Zayn's, and Zayn's at mine."

Something like that. Last year we were only allowed to see

each other at school or each other's houses. We can use that to our advantage.

"My parents are freaking out too," Adi says. "Almost banned me from going out."

Omar snorts. "My dad wanted to move me to another school. Even talked about that all-boys private school." He shudders. "I'd rather the killer got me."

"Omar!" I gasp.

Adi slaps his chest.

"All right. Too soon."

"Did you see that agent looking at you?" Adi says, nudging my arm. "Because he's doing it again. Don't look!"

My back is to the agents. Or where they were standing when Rosenthal was talking anyway.

"Can't wait until I get to speak with them again," I murmur sarcastically.

"You have to admit, the girlfriend of the OG killer's son finds both bodies—it's suspicious," Zayn says with zero tact.

"Yeah, thanks for that."

"Hello."

We turn to see Rosenthal smiling down at us. Up close she looks younger. She either has a crazy good night cream or her hair is prematurely gray. It's hard to figure out even a ballpark age.

"Penelope Langley?" she asks, as if she's unsure, but she's looking directly at me.

"That's me."

"Are your parents here?"

She knows they are.

"Yeah, they're over there," I reply, pointing to where my parents were. Now they're heading toward us.

"Can we help you?" Dad says, wrapping an arm around my shoulders.

"Hello, Mr. Langley. I would love it if I could speak with your daughter."

"In what capacity?"

"We have some questions, that's all."

"I already told the cops everything I know," I say.

Rosenthal nods, smiling warmly and trying to look like she doesn't suspect me at all. Despite being innocent, it's really freaking scary having police and the FBI asking you stuff. I've done nothing wrong, but they make me feel like I'm guilty.

My friends watch with wide eyes. Adi was with me when I found Noah, and Zayn was with me when I found Ruby. Shouldn't the feds talk to them as well?

"I appreciate that, but it's helpful for us to hear it from you too, Penelope."

"Penny," I correct. People use my full name when I'm in trouble, so when the freaking FBI agent uses it, it makes me nervous as hell.

"Penny," she says. "Would you prefer if we talk here, once everyone has gone, or I can come to your home?"

"Here," Dad says. "We can wait."

Rosenthal nods. "I appreciate that."

As she walks off, Zayn scowls. "She could read your statement."

I shrug. "It's fine."

As people filter out of the hall, I stay behind stressing internally with my parents. I'm trying to pretend that this is no big deal. So the feds want to talk to me; doesn't mean anything.

Right?

My fingers drum on the edge of the chair I'm sitting on.

"You should do that on your piano," Mom says. "You've not practiced for a little while."

Since my first music instructor told my parents that I have a natural talent for the piano, they have really pushed it.

Piano used to be the thing that grounded me if I was having a bad day. All of my worries and anxieties would disappear with the first touch of the keys.

That doesn't work anymore. Nothing does.

Rosenthal catches my eye across the room. She moves in my direction, and I'm glad that she's interrupting. We don't need to have this music conversation right now.

"Penny, can I ask you again what happened on the morning of Sunday the twenty-fourth?"

I answer her questions methodically as she goes over the discovery of both bodies, seeing it in my head like my personal horror movie.

When she asks about contact with Nash, I feel my parents glare at the side of my head as I tell her that I have spoken to him, giving her the same account that I gave the cop at the pumpkin patch.

"And how did he seem?"

"Shocked, same as the rest of us."

Dad clears his throat but doesn't say a single word. Mom and

Dad loved Nash. He was over at my house as much as I was at his. Jackson's murders scared the crap out of them—I'd spent so much time with a serial killer—and they suddenly didn't want me near Nash.

"And you were the one to tell him about both murders?"

"Definitely Ruby today, but as you know, he was in town the morning I found Noah. He must've known something serious was going on."

"Do you speak to Nash much anymore?"

She sounds like she's asking as a friend's mom now and not as a cop.

"Nash and I don't really talk anymore," I say, looking down at the ground. "I gave him a lift home from the police station the day he was questioned about Noah, but that's it."

"Why is that?"

"Because no one seems to understand that he's not his dad! He and Grace were shunned. They lost their mom, have no other family, and then their dad turned out to be a total psycho, and the town's answer was to cast them aside. They can't get the pitchforks out over Jackson now he's in prison, so his kids will do."

I bite my lip. Crap. I've said *way* too much.

"Penny," Mom breathes. "That's not . . ."

But she has no argument because I'm right. That is exactly what happened. We should all be ashamed.

"What part of what I just said is untrue?" I ask her.

"I'm sorry, Penny has had an awful shock," Mom says to Rosenthal.

"Not at all. Thank you for being so honest with me, Penny."

The way she looks at me, pointed gaze, no-nonsense expression, makes me think that she knows I've not been totally honest.

Well, I can cover that with this . . . "I saw someone in the same mask Jackson used to wear at the Scream Fest."

Rosenthal's back straightens. Mom and Dad gasp at the same time.

"Penny, you never told us that!" Mom is furious; her jaw is tight like she's trying not to show her anger in public. If we were at home, she'd shout and ground me.

Whatever.

"Is that opposite the pumpkin patch?" Rosenthal asks.

"Yep."

"Why didn't you mention this before now?"

"I wasn't sure. There was this bit in the forest where, like, twenty masked people do this creepy, robotic dance thing around you. They were all dressed in black and had white masks. Their masks all had black rings around the eyes and were slightly longer, a bit like Ghostface. Then I saw this other one, plain white, just like Jackson's. But no one else saw it and it might've just been what they were supposed to wear."

"So, it was similar to Jackson Whitmore's?"

"No, not similar. It was the same one. I mean, maybe not his since those were taken, but you get it."

That mask isn't one I will ever be able to forget. Nash and I found one in Jackson's workshop, down the back of a loose drywall board. Nash was getting rid of his dad's tools, and I knocked a bunch of wood over that was stacked.

Nash burned it and barely spoke for the rest of the night.

I wish he was able to get out of that house. It's sucking the life out of him.

"Are you certain?"

"I'm certain."

"Okay, thank you, Penny. Is there anything else you can think of that would be helpful for us to know?"

Yeah, lots.

"No."

"All right. We'll stay in touch but for now, I'm sure you want to get home."

With the way my parents are looking at me right now, no, I do not want to get home.

13

WEDNESDAY, OCTOBER 27

Dad drops me off at school in the morning. I give him a half-wave over my shoulder, still burning in anger over the big argument we had last night.

I'm "untrustworthy" and "reckless."

Those are facts; I can't deny them, but they have no clue how hard it is when you miss someone the rest of the world hates. When you have to stay away from someone whose only crime was being born to a killer.

Adi sprints over to me the second I get through the door, eager for gossip.

"I tried calling, like, literally a million times!" she says. "Are you okay? What happened?"

"*Literally* a million times?"

"Penny! What happened?"

"Ugh. My dad confiscated my phone. I've got it back now because he needs to be able to contact me at all times. I'm *so* annoyed, Adi."

"Man, that sucks. What did the FBI woman say?"

"Same thing as the cop did. Listen, this will come out soon, so I might as well tell you now. At Scream Fest, I saw someone in Jackson's mask. More than once, actually."

"What?" she shouts. Her voice bounces off the walls and rattles against lockers. Everyone in the hall turns and looks at us.

"Subtle."

"You *saw* him?"

"Not Jackson, obviously."

The doppelgänger, my mind screams. The boyfriend, whoever he is. One I hope only resembles Jackson in my paranoid mind.

I should've told Rosenthal about seeing someone at Nash's farm. I also should've told her about the other sighting of the mask, and the fact that Nash was at the pumpkin patch too.

But I'm a "reckless liar," so there we go.

I explain to Adi what I saw and tell her that I kept it to myself because I wasn't sure. Also, I didn't know if I was going crazy. She listens silently, for the first time in her life, with her jaw almost touching her chin.

"Oh my god," she whispers over and over as we walk along the corridor.

The decorations are still up in school. Bats everywhere. Cobwebs spread across every bulletin board.

"This is really happening, Penny. When do you think the cops will say this is an official copycat?"

I shrug. "She didn't exactly give me the inside scoop. I don't think she likes me much. I got bad vibes. She thinks I'm hiding stuff."

"What stuff?"

Lowering my voice, I say, "The driving Nash home and arranging to meet him stuff. Zayn was supposed to tell you but then Ruby . . . Slipped his mind, I guess."

I'm so flippant.

Totally over everything.

Adi blinks heavily three times. Her pale eyes full of so many questions that I know she will make me answer.

"I don't even know what to say or where to start. What the hell, Penny? Why haven't you told me all of this? I can't believe you've seen Nash."

"You talk a lot for someone who doesn't know what to say."

"Penny!" She grabs my arm and drags me closer to her. "How was Nash?"

"Hurt, scared, lonely."

Her eyes drift, the look of guilt. I know it well. "Does he have an alibi for the murders?"

"He was home with Grace," I tell her. "I just hope that's enough."

"I hope so too but . . ."

But Grace is his sister and would cover.

"When did you arrange to meet him? I want to come," she says.

"It already happened but he didn't show."

"When? Why didn't he show?"

"Night before we snuck into Benji's. The cops came to his house right before we were meant to meet."

Adi frowns. "That's when you were meant to be at my house with Zayn and Omar?"

"Yeah, why?"

She shakes her head, frown deepening.

"Adi, what?"

For, like, five agonizing seconds, she says nothing. Her mind putting things together like a puzzle. "I don't know. This could be a coincidence, and it probably is, but Zayn was on his phone the whole time he was at my house, then kind of rushed off. But he wouldn't call the cops on Nash, right?"

The shrill bell rings loud above us, making us both jump.

"He turned up that night to pick me up. Said he figured I would be meeting Nash so tracked my phone. Turn Find My off if you want some privacy, by the way. It doesn't make sense that he would call the cops on him."

"Well . . . you did reject him because you're still totally hung up on Nash."

"No, he's over that. We spoke."

"Oh my god, you don't tell me anything anymore!"

"Sorry," I say as we both take steps back, needing to go separate ways for class but also needing to figure out what's going on.

"Should we ask Zayn if he dropped Nash in it?"

I shake my head and step back again. "No, not yet. I don't want him to think that we're accusing him of anything."

"Ugh, I hate class. I still have *so* many questions."

"Later, Adi."

"Okay, talk to you at lunch," she says, turning to run to her first-period class.

The day drags on and on. No work gets done, everyone who turned up for school is talking about Karter's release, Noah's and

Ruby's murders, and "this year's serial killer" as if it's going to be an annual thing now.

That thought makes me want to throw up.

During lunch, Zayn is with us the entire time, so Adi and I can't talk.

By the end of the day, I'm crawling out of my skin to get away.

I'm so tired of Nash and Zayn being evasive. I'm tired of seeing dead bodies and being questioned.

I rub the stinging from my eyes and try to focus. My stomach is queasy. I skipped breakfast, barely ate at lunch, and picked at dinner last night. I'm hungry but I can't eat.

"Penny, is everything all right?" Miss Byers asks, her hands on my desk as she looks at me like she thinks I'm going to drop down. She's wearing a purple dress with black witch hats all over it.

"I didn't sleep well and feel kinda sick."

"You're very pale. I think you should see the nurse and go home," she says.

My car isn't here but the walk to Nash's will only take me ten minutes if I cut through the cornfield next to the pumpkin patch.

It's something I've done a hundred times before.

I just have to make sure I'm back at school by the time my dad arrives to pick me up. No problem. Hopefully.

"Thanks, I will," I say, grabbing my stuff and getting out of that class like the room's on fire.

The hallway is empty as I head to the nurse's office, so I don't have to pretend to anyone else. In fairness, I don't feel great and should go home.

It takes one look from the nurse for her to decide that I shouldn't be at school. Clearly, I look even worse than I feel. As I walk out of her office, I pretend to call my mom, hoping that's enough to convince the nurse not to do it.

I leave school and, running on adrenaline alone, head straight to Nash's house. The last block before cornfields take over has spooky scarecrows along the sidewalks.

Scarecrow row is the place we used to kick off Halloween. The scarecrow "ghost" tour. This year includes a straw-filled Ghost-face, Chucky, ghosts, and ghouls.

It's only when I reach the edge of the field that I hesitate. Walking down scarecrow row used to mark the beginning of trick-or-treating; this year it might lead to my death.

Town is behind me, hundreds of pretty houses, and cute yards. A picture-perfect square and independent stores. Ahead is miles and miles of cornfields and farmhouses. All of them are spread out and with plenty of privacy.

Nash's land is probably the biggest, though they don't use it much.

I should be smart and head back to safety.

The corn is taller than me. I know where I'm going; it's across the field on a slight diagonal, and the rows of corn make it easy to see the way.

I'll only have to push through two deep rows to hop the fence, cross the next field, and reach the Whitmore farm. I clench my hands a few times. If I want to make it back to school in time, I'll have to take the shortest route.

Ruby was found in the toilet at the pumpkin patch just beside this field. The killer could've come through the corn to avoid being seen but that's a long way to carry a body.

I don't even want to think about how that links the murder right to Nash. He could easily use the two fields between his property and the pumpkin patch to avoid being seen. He's strong, but I'm not sure he could carry a body across an acre field, then another acre through corn.

Once I'm in there, I won't be seen.

That's either a good thing if the killer is on the prowl . . . or a very, very bad thing.

After looking around to make sure I'm alone, I swallow my fear and take a step into the corn. I disappear between the long leaves in a heartbeat.

I push through, separating stalks and brushing away cobwebs that stick to my clothes, until I come to the first opening. A long track leading to the end of the field. It'll be safer to walk that to the end and then push my way through the corn until I come to the corner of the field.

Since I can't see anything but corn and mud, I rely on my hearing a lot more. Along the far side of this field is the old part of town.

My breath catches as something scutters on the ground. I jump up, doing high knees like I'm working out. Something small and gray darts past me.

I hate mice!

How many more of those are around? There could be hundreds right near me. Let's not dwell on that.

Ignoring the fact that I could be sharing the field with all sorts of critters, I move on toward Nash's house. It's still a dot in the distance but a bigger one now. He'd better be in. I'd call but I don't want to give him the chance to ask me to stay away.

The air deeper in the field is thick and hot despite how cool it's been recently. I don't know if it's that or the sense of claustrophobia, like the field could retract and swallow me whole, that makes me feel faint.

My steps falter for a second when I realize that other noise I hear isn't the tiny scurry of a tiny mouse. It's *footsteps.*

That's a person.

In here with me.

I crouch down, even though I'm shorter than the corn, and listen, my eyes trained on any of the crop moving in a different way than the breeze.

Did whoever's out there also hear my footsteps? Have they stopped, like me, to hear better?

I take a step back lightly and hit the edge of the corn. Somehow I have to get deep into that without being noticed or heard.

My heart pumps far too hard, making it difficult to hear anything other than my pulse screaming in my ears, warning me to get away. I breathe quietly, slowly, and try to keep any noise I make to a minimum while also focusing on not hyperventilating.

Another crunch floats through the wind and slaps me in the face.

I'm not imagining that. Someone else is out here. I scan the corn and find where it parts differently. The rest of it is uniform.

They're coming toward me.

I turn back and crawl on the ground, hoping the lower I am the less it will affect the top of the corn. Turning my head, I look back to see how much farther I need to go. I can still see the opening for the track so I'm not deep enough.

If I can see him, he might be able to see me.

This can't be happening.

I'm so grateful that I'm wearing dark jeans and my black coat today.

I push on, slowly making my way through stalks, gently pushing them and praying he won't notice. I turn and a scream dies in my throat as something black stands in front of me.

The bottom of their cloak is level with my face, taunting me.

Craning my neck, I look up with my hand over my mouth and swallow a sob of relief. It's just a scarecrow.

The footsteps get closer, coming right for me. I shuffle back again, around the scarecrow, and my hands sink into mud. I don't know whether I should move left or right. Will he go toward the old part of town or the road?

Corn dust floats in the air, sitting heavy in my throat with each breath.

My stomach clenches as the rustling and footsteps get closer. I want to reach for my pepper spray, but it's zipped in my backpack. He might hear my zip if I try.

Please don't find me. Please, please, please.

My dumbass instinct is to close my eyes and wish myself home, but I have to be ready to run.

Fumbling in my pocket, I flick my phone to silent with shaky fingers. Maybe I should call Nash, but I don't want to risk being heard.

Where should I go? I don't have a car here. If I run, I can make it to Nash's place in five minutes but that's through the corn and over a fence.

Pushing myself onto my hands and knees, I dig my feet into the ground and prepare to run. The road is the obvious choice but if no cars come, it's a long stretch to town. The closest house is Nash's. Those next closest is the O'Neils', but in the opposite direction.

Running to Nash has always been my instinct.

My stomach turns over as the person steps out of the corn and into the clearing. I can just about see between tall stalks, but barely. Not well enough to bet my life on running, but I have to get out of here somehow.

I don't need good sight to notice this . . . the dark clothes and the plain white mask.

The killer is here.

With me.

Alone in a cornfield.

Could I be any more typical horror right now?

Heat prickles at the back of my neck and I see black dots dance in front of my face. Pressing my lips together, I stifle a scream. I want to be as far away from here as possible, but I don't know how to do that without alerting the killer.

If they see me, I'm dead.

The masked figure walks along the track and quickly disappears. I can't tell from here where they are anymore but I can't hear rustling, so they must be on the track still.

That means they're going to the road.

Surely he wouldn't be so stupid. He must have a backpack to put the mask in. It's not a crime to wear dark clothing.

I wait another minute, until I can't hear anything, and then I stand up halfway. Bent low, I gently move corn, being careful not to make too much noise.

With trembling hands, I part the last stalks and poke my head into the track.

Nothing.

The field is still, silent, and peaceful. No sign that there has ever been a murderer in here.

Breathing deeply, I take another step and my heart stops.

The corn ahead parts and the masked man steps into the clearing.

Knife in hand, he faces me.

14

A scream rips from my throat as the killer tilts his head, considering what to do. He takes his first step toward me.

I'm not letting him get another one in while I stand still, so I spin around and sprint along the opening, my heart pounding harder and faster with each stride.

Clouds above me clump together and the sky turns an angry shade of gray, setting up the perfect murder scene.

I'm still as strong and quick as I was when I was on the track team. I push myself, flying through the whipping wind, running for my life. My breathing is labored, lights dance in front of my face, my body desperate for oxygen, but I can't slow down.

Big fat raindrops begin to fall from the sky, splashing onto my face, blasting on the corn around me like bullets. He's not far behind; his footsteps sound right on top of me, but I can't be sure if I'm losing him or if he's gaining on me. We're both sprinting for survival.

If he catches me, I'm dead. If I get away, he's at risk of being caught.

Who is it? I already can't remember much, their form well hidden under dark baggy clothing. But tall. That much I got.

Obviously athletic.

I come toward the end of the track and leap to the side, shoving myself through the corn, throwing it out of the way in an effort to not let it slow me down. My arms whip at stalks and leaves; corn thumps against my body, bouncing back as I go.

Everything aches, every muscle is torn to shreds, my body spent, and what little energy I have left is quickly evaporating.

"Nash!" I scream, slamming into the fence. I climb the two rails and leap over as a hand brushes my hair.

Another scream bursts from my lips at the close call. The field to Nash's has a slight decline, so I'll be faster. My feet slam into the wet ground, slipping a little on the mud beneath them.

I don't slow, not for a second. If I were timing this, it'd be a personal best. I'm doing this for my life, pushing harder than I ever have before. Adrenaline stronger than any kind of performance enhancer.

"Nash!"

I think I see people outside Nash's house in the distance. Two or three, I can't tell because they're moving, a blur in my weakening vision, and I can barely breathe properly to take much in.

"Nash!" I scream again. My shins and thighs are on fire as I push myself harder than I ever have before.

The edge of the field comes close. I leap, clearing the stream, and land awkwardly on the other side.

Pain shoots through my ankle but I ignore the burn.

"Nash!"

Where did everyone go?

I gasp a mouthful of air and wonder if anyone was even there in the first place.

Sprinting around the side of the first barn—Jackson's old workshop—I look for Nash or Grace. She's not my biggest fan, but I think she would still help me in matters of life or death.

"Penny?" Nash says, walking out of the workshop and frowning at me.

I run straight into him, slamming into his chest, and my legs give way, my bag sliding off my arms and onto the ground.

"Shit!" he says, catching me before I hit the grass.

Relief uncoils my tense shoulders now that I am with someone safe. Nash holds me tight, looking in the direction I was running from.

"H-he was there. He was in the field. Following me! In the corn. I ran," I say between sobs and gasps of air, gripping fistfuls of Nash's hoodie. "He's here!"

"What?"

Nash holds me up by the elbows, keeping me at arm's length so he can look at me.

"Pen, you're not making sense," he says. "Breathe. Who's where?"

He looks behind me again, and I turn around. I gasp, seeing the corn still and the fields empty. There is no one there.

No one at all.

"No! He was there, I swear. We have to get out of here, Nash. We have to!"

I'm too hot, my body a furnace. I press down on my chest, willing my lungs to work properly.

"Who was here? There's no one."

"The killer! He was in the same mask as . . ." I blink hard as my vision blurs, white fuzz in my periphery.

Nash drops his hands. "Same mask as my dad."

"Yeah. He almost got me."

A fact that I need to immediately forget, or I won't be able to function.

"There's no one there, Pen. You're safe."

"Not now but there *was*. In the cornfield. He touched my hair as I hopped the fence. I didn't look back again but I thought he was behind me. He must've stopped."

"What the hell were you doing alone in the cornfield?"

All right, that *was* super stupid.

"I ditched school. They think I'm ill. I have to get back before the end of the day because my dad is picking me up and he can't know I'm gone. I was coming to see you."

Why the hell is it so hot?

"Why?"

"I'm sure I had a reason but right now I can't think of anything other than the fact that I was almost victim number three. Where's Grace?" I shudder.

He shrugs, and I stand straight, holding the stitch in my side. "You don't know?"

"She's gone shopping. I didn't ask which stores."

Nash's car is the only one in the drive. But they have lots of buildings, so they could hide anything. Though I don't know why she would hide her car.

"No one else is here?" I ask, my hands trembling.

"No."

He maintains eye contact. I can't see him clearly, but I still feel like there's something he's hiding.

"I thought I saw, like, three people when I was running."

"I was carrying some planks to the workshop."

Could that be what I saw? It's possible, I wasn't in a position to take much in.

"I don't know what to do," I tell him.

"About what?"

"About anything. It's all falling apart. I feel like I'm going crazy."

He scratches the side of his head. "Welcome to the club."

"The feds are here again."

He startles, looking behind him.

"No, not *here.* In town."

"Oh. Yeah, I've had a visit. They probably stopped by here before going to the station."

I squeeze my eyes shut for a second trying to clear the fuzziness, my body still in a pressure cooker. "I told them I gave you a ride home after you were questioned at the station."

He smiles and it's the first glimpse of the old Nash. "Yeah, I did too. I figured they might have CCTV."

"We're still thinking alike."

His eyes drift and he chews on his lip.

"I didn't tell them you were at the pumpkin patch," I say.

"I figured."

"Adi said something today," I tell him, and curl my trembling fingers into fists. My whole body feels like it's about to implode. Now I really don't feel well.

"Adi says something every second of every day."

"She told me that Zayn was acting weird the night we were supposed to meet up. He was on his phone a lot and left abruptly. Then, as you know, he picked me up from the old movie theater." I'm speaking fast but he's keeping up.

Nash frowns.

"I'm not sure if it was him who called the cops. I don't know why he would."

"To protect you," Nash says.

"From what?"

"Me," he replies, deadpan.

"I don't need protecting from you."

"Tell that to the town, Penny. I already know you don't."

"I don't have long."

"You came here to say that? You could've sent a message."

I take a ragged breath and pull on the neck of my top, trying to cool myself down. "Everything feels weird. Like there are bugs all over my skin and in my stomach. I can't eat or sleep properly. I either get these dots in my vision or it goes blurry. I don't know how to make it stop."

And I'm far too hot.

He sighs like he's in pain. "Let me get you a Coke. You're pale and in shock. I'll drive you as close to school as I can so your dad doesn't know you've skipped."

"Okay," I whisper.

"Come in a minute."

I blink in surprise at the offer.

"What?" he says, the hint of a smile on his lips.

"I didn't think I would be allowed in."

"You're not the one banned from people's houses."

"Well, actually . . ."

He nods once. "Right. You're banned from my house."

"I'm also banned from going anywhere alone."

"You're so badass now," he says, gesturing for me to walk ahead.

I get two steps in before the world goes black.

• • •

I groan, tilting my head to the side. The movement sends pain slicing through my skull. I reach up to touch the sore spot.

What happened?

One minute I was walking and the next I'm on the floor with a killer headache.

But I no longer feel like every nerve in my body is on fire.

"Penny! Hey, don't move." The voice sounds so far away, floaty, pretty.

I blink twice to clear my blurry vision and look up.

Nash is leaning over me, eyes wide, dark hair spilling in his face. "Are you okay?"

"What happened?" I ask, wincing as my fingers find the source of the pain.

"You fainted. Is your head okay? I wasn't quick enough to catch you before you fell."

Groaning again, I try to push myself up. Nash's arm scoops behind my back and he helps me to sit. "I have a wicked headache, but I'll be fine."

"Are you sure? You were only out for a second, but you might need to get your head checked."

"I just fainted. I'm fine."

"Fainting isn't fine, babe. When did you last eat?" he asks.

Yeah, me and food haven't been on the best terms lately.

"Um, I can't remember my last proper meal. I've been picking where I can," I say. Nash is the first person I've told that. I haven't been able to talk about him to my family or friends. There was no one to discuss how missing someone and drowning in guilt can physically affect you.

"PB and J with your Coke?" he asks.

I don't dare look him in the eye because the worry in his voice is enough; there's no need to see it too. I haven't been taking care of myself, but I've had no appetite.

Gasping, I reach for my phone. "What's the time?"

"It's okay, you really were only down for seconds. I can feed you quick and get you back before school ends. We have time."

I check the time. Thirty-five minutes until the end of the day.

We do have time. Not as much as I want but we can't do anything about that.

"I have missed your PB and Js."

"I don't do anything special."

He helps me to my feet and takes me to their kitchen.

It's completely different. The cabinets have been painted a pale gray and the walls are now white. It used to be quite dark. Grace has worked her magic. She even has dried flowers in tiny vases and pretty artwork on the walls.

There's a new table and chairs and a massive coffee machine.

A picture of their mom sits on the kitchen counter. Tanned skin, silky black hair that falls in waves, and the most beautiful green eyes that look like lenses but are natural. She's smiling in the picture, pregnant with Grace and cradling a tiny bump. Happy.

Nash and Grace look more like her. They share her full lips, darker skin tone, and dazzling smile. But they have their dad's hair and eye color.

There are no pictures of Jackson anymore.

"I like the new look," I tell him, sitting as he points to the table.

"The old house was too Jackson. We can't move, so this was all we could do. It's a bit girlie for me, but Grace loves it."

"Right. Well, it looks better. No Halloween decorations?"

"Gone off it a bit," he replies. "I assume you don't want me to call the cops and tell them about the killer in the cornfield?"

He sounds like he half believes me.

"You assume right."

I can't even imagine how long I will be grounded if my parents find out.

"Are you sure, Penny?"

Sure it happened or sure I don't want him to call?

"I will never be allowed outside my house again if anyone finds out about this. You can't say anything."

"Who am I going to tell?"

"Grace. Zayn."

He lifts an eyebrow. "You don't want to tell Zayn? I thought you'd tell your friends."

They used to be *our* friends.

"Well, we don't know if he has the police on speed dial."

Nash places a sandwich and a can of Coke in front of me. He sits down at the table. "You're almost translucent."

"It's a good look, huh?"

He's the third person today who's said I look unwell. It's not something I can deny. When I looked in the mirror this morning, I could see it too. My skin looks the same color as my gray eyes.

"Eat."

He watches me closely, probably trying to figure out if I'm going to faint again.

"I'm fine," I tell him.

"Are you certain your head's okay? You hit it pretty hard on the ground."

"It's pounding, but I'm all right."

Sighing again, he gets up and grabs a box of Tylenol. "If the headache doesn't go, you should see a doctor. Tell them you tripped, make up what you like, but get help."

Translation: *Don't let anyone know you were with me.*

Because I will get in trouble, or because he thinks I don't want to be seen with him.

"Are you coming to the *Scream* movie marathon?" I ask after swallowing the last bite of sandwich. That's probably the most I've eaten in one meal for weeks.

He laughs. "You must've hit your head harder than I thought."

"I'm serious."

"No, you're not."

"I know people gossip but no one will say anything to your face." Not now that Ruby is dead. "Come. It used to be one of our favorite things at Halloween."

"You were chased by . . . *whoever* just now and you want to go out tonight? How are you even going? I'd have thought your dad would have you on lockdown."

"He thinks Zayn and I are going to Adi's."

"Right. Hey, maybe he'll let me pick you up and we'll both go."

I laugh at his sarcasm and take a sip of Coke. My trembling hands have settled, and I don't feel dizzy anymore. I swallow two Tylenol with it.

"Please come."

"Bad idea, Penny."

"There will be no pitchforks."

He shakes his head.

"Please."

"Don't do the eyes."

Gotcha.

I smile. "Yay! It'll be good to have the gang back together again. But as much as I want to see my dad's face when you knock on the door, I think we should probably drive separately."

With a resigned sigh, he says, "I guess I can meet you there."

"Will Grace come?"

He laughs and shakes his head. "She would rather burn the town to the ground."

"She's angry."

"Hurt mostly. She's angry with our dad, can't forgive him but tries to understand. It's his fault that our lives are like this now."

"Do you go out much?"

"Outside, yes. Outside of our land, no." He leans back in the chair. "I should take you back to school soon."

I glance up at the clock on the kitchen wall. The hands have frozen on 7:53. "You need to replace the batteries in that."

"I'll get right on it. Come on, Penny. We'll be cutting it close if we don't leave now."

"I don't want to go."

He stands. "How long before your dad turns up here?"

"Five minutes after I don't show at school."

Smiling sadly, he grabs his keys off the table. "Penny . . ."

"Fine." I stand and, feeling a hundred times better, follow him out of the house.

I notice the bumper of a red truck peeking out of the barn.

Grace hasn't gone shopping in what is supposed to be her new car.

I get into Nash's truck and buckle in. "Will you tell Grace that I came by? Or that you're coming to the movies?"

"No and no."

"She hates me."

"She doesn't hate you. She misses you. We both do."

Well, I think that makes me feel worse than if they just hated me. "I want to see her too."

He drives quickly toward school, taking the back road. It takes a few more minutes but we're less likely to be seen. He speeds past the cornfield, his knuckles turning white around the steering wheel.

"He almost got you."

"I'm signing back up for track again," I joke.

"You quit?"

"I quit a lot of things. Doesn't hit right anymore."

Nash exhales. "Because of my dad."

"Because I didn't stand up to everyone when they told me to stay away from you."

Nash chews on his lip, his brows knitting together as he thinks about what he wants to say.

"There!" I shout, pointing to the back of the old movie theater and derelict dance studio.

"What?"

A shadow moves between the buildings. I catch a glimpse of dark clothing and a flash of white. Then he's gone, ducking into the door of Benji's.

Hell. No.

The scraping was definitely the metal shelves, but the killer could have been in there too.

We were so reckless when we went inside.

Nash swerves the car, pulling over at the side of the road.

"What are you doing?" I shriek. "Drive!"

Why does everyone want to hang around when the masked dude is out?

"Stay in the car, and lock the door."

Gasping, I grab his arm and yank him back as he goes to get out. "You can't be serious!"

"Whoever that freak is, he's pretending to be my dad, or he worships him. I don't know which one is worse. I have to know who it is."

"Nash, no. If you get out, I'll follow you."

His eyes narrow. "Penny."

"Drive to the pay phone on Second Street. It still works and we can make an anonymous call to the cops. There's no CCTV near there," I tell him.

Nash takes seconds to decide.

"I will follow you if you leave this car," I repeat.

Growling, he pulls back out onto the road.

"Nash, we have, like, five minutes before my dad will be at school."

"Damn it! I'll drop you, then go to the pay phone. The one on the corner of Third is still there, right?"

"Yeah. Do you have quarters?"

He laughs, turning past the library and toward school.

"What?"

"I don't know, weird thing to ask."

He pulls over on the side of the road, and I get out. "Thanks, Nash. For everything today."

"I'll see you at the movies, Pen. Don't forget to eat."

I close the door and Nash peels away as fast as he can, heading to report the masked man sighting.

At least now that I've seen the killer and Nash at the same time, I can be sure that he's innocent.

I look up, my heart lighter than it's been in months, and find Zayn staring at me.

15

Groaning internally, I walk over to my best friend, ready for his disapproval. "Okay, say whatever you're going to say, but say it quickly because I'm meeting my dad."

Cars have already begun to arrive.

"What are you doing?"

"I pretended to be ill so I could leave early and go to Nash's. On the way there, I was chased through the cornfield by the killer. When I reached Nash's house, I passed out and hit my head. The killer was gone. Nash made me something to eat. Then as he was dropping me off, we saw the masked dude going into the movie theater. Nash is going to the pay phone on Third to report it now."

Zayn's mouth falls lower and lower with each sentence.

"Penny . . ."

"Where are you going anyway?"

"You can't change the subject after telling me all of that."

"You're leaving early?"

"Five minutes, Pen. I can't listen to the gossip any longer. It's doing my head in."

The gossip has never bothered him before. Would he have been able to get from the old movie theater to here in the time it took us to drive?

If he ran and went through the town square, maybe. But he's not out of breath.

"Why did you go to Nash's?" he asks as we walk back to school, stopping before the gate so that we're not seen. To my dad, it will look like I'm waiting for him. The bell rings and seconds later, my classmates run out like the building is on fire.

"I don't know. I couldn't focus. I just . . . wanted to."

I lean back against the brick wall. Zayn leans on the metal gate.

"And he's coming to the movies," I add. He won't have to lie about where he's going. Unless Grace asks him, I guess.

"What?"

"He likes horror, too, and I'm so done pretending that I don't want him in my life. I want things to go back to how they were before."

"Before his dad brutally murdered five of our classmates?"

"Yes," I say through gritted teeth, anxiety unfurling in my stomach. I don't want him to get this reception from everyone. "Zayn, you said you wanted to help him. What, did you suddenly change your mind?"

He blows out a breath. "No, you're right. It's just now there's a second murder and it's clearly not Karter . . . All I'm saying is people aren't going to be as forgiving, but I've got your back, Pen, you know that. Can I be there when you tell Omar and Adi?"

Laughing, I nudge his side and reply, "Sure. And when has anyone been forgiving when it comes to Nash and Grace?"

"The gossip died down over the summer."

That was because neither one of them came into town anymore.

"You're okay." He looks me over like he's searching for wounds. "What went down with the killer?"

"You can't tell anyone. He chased me but I got away. Clearly. I'm fine, I promise. Well, I'm shaking still—look." I hold up my trembling hands.

"I think that's normal. It's the adrenaline. You'll eat before the movies, right?"

"Not planning on going anywhere near a killer again, but I will."

He scratches the back of his neck and clears his throat. I know instantly that this is going to be awkward. "Did I have a part in all the anxiety?"

"No, Zayn, this isn't your fault."

"I shouldn't have said anything. I knew you still liked Nash, so I should've kept it to myself."

"You shouldn't have to keep anything to yourself. I'm sorry, Zayn."

He smiles. "Me too. We're much better off as friends. I just wish I'd realized that before getting rejected."

"Besties," I say, nudging his arm at the same time Dad pulls up. The car window slides down. “Ready, honey?” he says. “Hello, Zayn.”

“Hey, Mr. Langley.”

“See you later,” I tell Zayn.

Dad drives me home and retreats into his office. I order a pizza and plan to do some homework before Omar picks me up.

Alone in my room, I send a message to Nash.

Penny:

Did you speak to the cops?

Nash:

called them yeah.

Penny:

And?????

Nash:

I didn’t hang around to chat, Penny.

His messages are snippy. Or at least that’s how I’m reading them. We were okay today, so what’s changed?

Penny:

Are you okay?

Nash:

I’m fine. I’ll see you tonight.

I throw my phone down on the bed, irritated at his attitude. It's hard to know where I stand when he's so standoffish.

Not sure what the hell I expected, though.

Flicking the TV on, I find a local news station and watch for the latest on the case.

The reporter, standing on the square between a pile of pumpkins and a scarecrow witch, tells us that the FBI have taken over and released a statement. In the corner of the screen a photo of Jackson's mask pops up.

A shiver runs the length of my spine. I could go the rest of my life without ever seeing that again.

We're told nothing new. Stay in groups, don't go out unless you absolutely have to, most town events will be canceled, yada, yada, yada.

I wish I could go to Benji's and see what's going on. But there is another way to find out. I reach back for my phone and scroll through the town Facebook group.

It was going off when Jackson was around. Adi and I spent ages scrolling it and seeing what our parents were discussing.

Then there was the panic when the adults wanted to push for a 7:00 p.m. curfew for everyone under the age of twenty-one. That would have been horrific. I love my parents, but I don't think I would cope well being stuck inside with them every night.

I log in and go straight to the group. There are so many notifications, most from that group.

I'm probably not going to enjoy this.

And there it is. A post from a few minutes ago saying the FBI was spotted going along the alleyway toward the old part of town.

I swear most people must stand at their window with a pair of binoculars.

Nash called it in and now the feds are chasing the killer.

Penny:

Have you checked the FB group?

Nash:

No. Why?

Penny:

The FBI are going to the old theater.

Nash:

That's their job, Pen.

Penny:

You've not lost your sense of humor. i'm getting zayn to pick me up.

Nash:

Good for you.

Penny:

Jackass, you can drop me off.

Nash:

you got it

Good.

Idiot.

I get up and walk to my closet to find something to wear. It's dark outside, the sky covered with clouds, hiding the stars. It has to be nice but casual enough that my dad won't suspect anything.

As I walk past my window, I glance out and do a double take. Did one of those vampires in the neighbor's yard just move?

I move closer to the glass and strain my eyes. They have five vampires stuck into the grass but . . . weren't there four before?

Sucking in a breath, I watch, frozen, trying to see if one of them moves. How many was it? Four or five? I can't remember. Vampire or killer.

After the cornfield, I'm so paranoid.

My heart thuds hard in my chest as I wait. If that's a person, how long will they be able to play statue for?

"Penny, the pizza's here," Dad calls.

Jolting, my head slams against the window, and I steady myself on the glass. I stumble back and rub the spot. "Coming."

That's all I need, another knock to the head. I'm feeling much better now, though, no headache.

Whatever's outside didn't move even slightly. It was decoration. The killer isn't watching me.

• • •

"Zayn will pick you up and drop you off," Dad says, going over the plan for the tenth time.

"Yes, Dad, and Omar. He'll park in Adi's driveway, and we'll walk into the house together. He'll drop us all off later. I remember the drill from last year."

Only that's not what we're doing at all. He'd go mad if he found out I was off to the movies.

"This is serious, Penelope."

"Believe me, I know that. We're being careful."

Or they are anyway. I've not been great at that.

"The FBI has a lead anyway," he replies. "They caught Jackson quickly, so it's only a matter of time before they make an arrest."

"Oh, really?"

He nods, flicking through a web page of local self-defense classes. Looks like I'll be signed up for one of those soon. There was talk about the whole school doing it, but the principal hasn't mentioned anything.

"A person was spotted by the old theater. The FBI and the police haven't made statements, but they might even have someone in custody. Still, you're not to be on the streets until they've caught him. Your pepper spray packed?"

"I'm going to Adi's but yeah, it's in my bag."

Lying feels horrible.

Dad looks up as we hear a car pull up.

"That's Zayn. See you later."

"Message when you get there and when you are about to leave."

"Will do," I call over my shoulder as I run out of the house so I can stop lying to my dad.

I get into Zayn's car and Adi grabs my hand from where

she's bent down. If my Dad looks out the window, he can't see that she's with us since she's supposed to be waiting for us at her house. "You invited Nash and he agreed?"

"Yes."

Omar chuckles. "Your dad will kill you if he finds out. I'd be more scared of him than Whitmore 2.0."

Adi sits up as we leave my house behind.

"Let's use Jackson's first name, shall we?" I say. Some people have used Whitmore 2.0 specifically to reference Nash.

"Penny, are you sure this is a good idea?" Adi asks.

"Depends on your perspective, I guess."

"Penny!"

We park in the movie theater lot and head to the doors. I look over my shoulder as people file into the theater. Knowing Nash, he will be purposefully late to avoid the stares and whispers. Once everyone is seated, we have a chance of getting him inside with less fuss.

I don't think many people will care. Save for Ruby's group, it's really the adults in town who dislike him.

My friends wait with me as I watch for Nash. Omar is indifferent. Adi nervous. Zayn . . . I'm not sure. His eyes are everywhere, scanning for Nash or someone who shouldn't see us together. But he hasn't objected to him coming and he's the one who's had the most recent contact with Nash.

And me? Well, I have butterflies and just *really* want tonight to go well.

Two cops pass us. One heads inside and the other hangs around by the entrance. I'm sure an agent from the FBI is in the lobby, too, watching each group. Everyone is being very good, no singles or couples. Lots of them are dressed up but they're being asked to remove masks as soon as they're inside.

We've listened to the FBI's advice.

The theater is covered in *Scream* posters, Ghostface masks, and plastic knives. A display of cult classic serial killers is along the biggest wall.

"The reason these events are still going on is so they can catch the killer," I say, looking through the large, glazed doors at the agent who's walking the lobby and muttering to whoever's listening in his ear.

"Human bait. Nice," Omar replies. "Think he'll turn up?"

"Nash or the killer?" Adi asks.

I side-eye her and she smirks.

"No, I don't think he's the killer, Pen."

"Didn't know you still cared, Adi."

We all jolt at Nash's voice.

"Erm, hi," she says, her cheeks turning red.

I turn around. "You made it."

"Remembered the way," Nash says, catching my eye.

"Well," Zayn says, cutting through the slightly awkward atmosphere. "Shall we go inside? Ghostface waits for no one."

"Sure," I reply.

As we walk inside and move through the lobby, the FBI agent does a double take. He mutters something under his breath.

Nash arches a brow. "That was subtle."

I'm not sure if the double take was for me or Nash.

"Ignore everyone," I tell him.

"Everyone?"

Wincing, I push him through to Theater Six. Only a few people were in the lobby still, getting popcorn, oversized cups of soda, and candy, but they did still look over.

Nash hasn't been seen with us in almost a year.

"You don't want popcorn?" Nash asks.

"They're getting the snacks. We'll find the seats."

He blocks me with his arm as I try to pass to find our seats. The lights have dimmed but not gone out yet. A trailer for some new thriller is showing.

"Are you keeping me out of eyesight by getting me in here quick?"

"No."

"Come on, that's exactly what this is about."

"Nash, we're not invisible. In fact, the entire theater is watching us right now."

He looks up and, slowly, returns his attention to me. "Do you want me to leave?"

"They'll get over it in a minute," I say, stepping down to our row. Lots of people have put their masks back on.

"What if one of them tells your dad?"

"I can't see why they would. Our seats are here."

I lead him to the very end where we have five seats by the wall. Crap seats but we booked late and that's what you get.

Nash sits next to me, and we pretend to be very interested in a new trailer about the latest movie in a horror franchise. In front of us is a group all dressed like Grim Reapers. Next to them is Mae and her friends. None of them have dressed up but they didn't have time to buy cheerleader outfits before I discovered a murder.

Lots of people turn to look at me and Nash. No one raises a phone to take a picture, so I figure we're fine. Mae smiles, the only one to do so.

"Ever feel like a zoo attraction?" he asks.

"Right now."

Two minutes later and, mercifully, the popcorn arrives with my friends. It gives us something else to do. Zayn sits on the other side of Nash.

They make small talk, and it flows more naturally than mine and Nash's. But I can tell from the way that Nash is wringing his hands that he's not totally comfortable with Zayn. I mean, he wouldn't be if he suspects that Zayn is the one who called the cops on him.

I don't know if they've spoken about it. Zayn has been kinda shady with me, and Nash doesn't trust me anymore.

Neither of them are confiding in me much.

The movie starts and we spend the first forty-five minutes engrossed in *Scream.*

I'm finally relaxing, because Nash has leaned back in his seat and we're sharing an armrest. As I'm about to say something witty about the film, something catches my eye.

At first I think it's a person getting up to go to the bathroom or getting more food . . . but they came from behind the screen and out the fire exit.

I grab Nash's wrist. "Someone just went out the fire exit."

He leans in closer. "What?"

I repeat what I saw, and he looks at me like I've grown another head. Okay, it's not exactly news that will rock the world.

"Wearing a *mask* . . ." I emphasize.

"Look around, Penny. Almost everyone is wearing a mask."

Right. Sinking a bit lower in my seat, I turn back to the screen and shake my head. I'm a suspicious idiot. An embarrassed one. Thank God it's dark in here or Nash would notice my burning cheeks.

Nash goes back to watching the movie after a minute, and I'm just glad it's one that I've seen a hundred times before because I'm not paying any attention.

My head is filled with murder, dead bodies, Nash, the Jackson doppelgänger boyfriend, and stress over Zayn's motives. If I have a few honest conversations, maybe I would be able to figure it out.

Or if I did the right thing and told the feds everything, they could.

As the credits roll, the lights gently turn on.

Nash and Zayn discuss the number of times they've watched the movie. Every year we have a *Scream* franchise binge—among other horror films—but this is the first year that we've all been able to get into the cinema to watch it. I'm so glad that Nash was here for it too.

I stand as the room slowly empties. The rest of my friends are already on their feet. Omar and Zayn laugh and whack each other. It's like Nash was never away from us. The boys walk ahead, wanting to get more candy before the second movie begins in twenty minutes. Adi and I step outside with what must be half the theater.

"So," Adi says, wiggling her eyebrows. "How are things with Nash?"

"We're friends again. I think. He accepted my invitation to come here. That has to count for something. Wait, do you think that counts?"

"Friends. Sure."

"Adi!"

I nudge her when Zayn and Nash head over to us.

"Where'd Omar go?" I ask.

Nash hands me a box of Sour Patch Kids. "He was with us a second ago."

My face falls. "He disappeared?"

"Paranoid much, Pen?" Zayn teases. "He went outside."

"I didn't see him."

"No, you wouldn't, because he's behind you talking to my sister," Nash says, a deep frown on his face.

The rest of us swing our heads in the least subtle way possible. On the sidewalk outside are Omar and Grace. Teens hyped on sugar run around in full costumes. Neither Grace nor Omar even glance up.

"What's that about?" I ask.

Nash walks past us toward his sister.

"Er, do we follow?" Zayn asks. "What's the protocol for this situation?"

"Grace isn't a fan of ours."

"Of *you.* The rest of us didn't break her brother's heart." Zayn smiles and I know he wasn't being nasty, but what a low blow.

Adi slaps him. "You're not as funny as you think you are, jackass."

"She knows I'm kidding. Grace will come around. They're not the only ones affected by what Jackson did. We've all needed time."

Feels a bit pathetic to lump us in with Jackson's children. What we've been through hardly compares.

Ignoring Zayn and Adi, I focus on the three up ahead. I wish I could lip read. Grace doesn't appear angry. I can't tell what Omar is saying but he's scowling, and Nash has his back to me.

"This is so weird," Adi breathes. "Is she going to join us?"

"I hope so," Zayn replies. "She's still as hot as ever."

"And she's as uninterested in you as ever," I reply.

"Ouch, Pen. I'm impressed," he says.

"Thanks."

After another minute of them talking, Grace turns around and walks away. But not before she takes a very pointed look at me. Deep blue eyes send me a warning: *Don't mess with Nash again.*

It's as if she thinks I'd planned the whole thing. Jackson's murder fest, the whole town turning on them, my parents forbidding me to go near the Whitmores.

I stayed away because I had no other choice.

"Grace okay?" I ask Nash when he and Omar return.

"She's fine."

"What was she doing?"

"Making sure we were legit," Omar says, grinning at Nash. "Didn't want tonight to be some elaborate prank. *Carrie* style."

"She thinks we're going to dump pig's blood on him?" Zayn asks.

I roll my eyes. "What?"

"Forget it, Penny. She's gone now," Nash says.

"She thought we'd invited you to ditch you?"

He shrugs. "Who cares what she thought?"

I do. I probably care too much, actually. But one step at a time. Nash first and then Grace.

"Where is she going now?"

"Meeting up with a friend," Nash replies.

A boyfriend maybe. I really want to meet him, see if he has a blue cap like Jackson's.

"We should get back in there soon. I hate it when people turn up late and walk in front of the screen. Inconsiderate asses," Adi says.

Omar laughs. "We know. We've been there plenty of times when you've yelled."

"They should be on time! I don't want to see anything other than the movie."

"Did anyone else see a person walk from behind the screen and go out the fire exit?" I ask, hoping one of them would have.

"No, why?" Omar asks.

"It was, like, halfway through the movie. I just thought it was kind of weird. You know, for them to hide behind the screen for that long."

"Staff use those doors, Pen," Zayn tells me. "You can get from screen room to screen room back there. Another way of getting out if you need to. I used to use it all the time when I worked here."

"Come on, I'm not going to be late!" Adi says, grabbing Omar's arm. He grabs Zayn and tugs him along with them.

Zayn looks back but does nothing. No one is making me or Nash follow.

"Hey, what are you worried about?" Nash asks, taking my hand to stop me leaving. "I can see you stressing."

"I don't know," I say, looking around for . . . the masked man. Let's face it. I see him *everywhere.* Only a handful of times he's actually been there.

"You're pale again. Not as bad as earlier but are you eating properly?"

"I'm fine, Nash."

"You're not fine."

I'm about to argue my case but we're both cut off by a shrill scream coming from inside the cinema.

16

We run toward the source of the scream, and Nash pushes me behind him. An agent and two cops run past us and into the ADA accessible bathroom where someone from my school is pointing.

"Do you think it's . . . ?" I mutter behind Nash, looking around his shoulder.

Another murder.

"I don't know. Where's Adi, Omar, Zayn?"

I scan the lobby for my friends, my stomach churning because I don't have a clue where they are and that scares the hell out of me. "They'll still be in the theater. Right? Nash, that wouldn't be one of them in there?" My heart skips and I try to push past him, frantic to find them. "We need to find them!"

His arm scoops me up a second later. "Stop. Don't go anywhere yet."

"Let go! Where are they? Why can't we find them?"

"Calm down. Hey, it's okay." He sets me back on the ground but doesn't let go. "Look, there are two cops outside the theater door stopping anyone getting in or out. See? They'll be in there. None of them use the accessible toilet."

"Adi does if there's a queue in the ladies! Nash!"

"Shhh, they're fine."

Fumbling, I reach for my phone, but it slips through my fingers. Nash catches it, letting his box of M&M's fall instead. He uses my phone to call . . . I don't know, one of them.

I look up with my heart in my mouth as the call goes through, desperately trying to hear over the commotion in the lobby.

Nash's crystal eyes slide to mine, and he smiles. "Adi, it's Nash . . . Are Omar and Zayn with you?" He nods, telling me that they're all together. "Good."

Oh, thank the Lord!

"I don't know. Yeah, we're in the lobby . . . No, we're not allowed to move either. Cops are blocking every exit."

"All right, I need everyone to please leave your phones alone and move into screen room two. This way, please," a female agent says. She ushers us along, while another agent heads outside, presumably to get everyone out there to either come in or stay where they are.

"What happened?" I ask.

She looks from me to Nash, who is now off the phone, and holds her palm up. Someone recognizes us. Nodding to another agent, she gestures for us to follow her to the side. "Did you two see anything?"

"No, we were outside," Nash says.

"Is there any way staff can get from the back of the screens out to the lobby?" I ask.

The bathrooms are along the hall just past the counter and ticket booth. So, if they can get from the screens to past the bathrooms without going through the theater rooms . . .

Nash's eyes flick to me.

"I'm not sure. Why do you ask that?"

"I saw someone during the movie," I tell her.

"Who?"

I explain everything, telling her that I have no idea who it was, but they were masked and moved behind the screen.

Nash confirms that I told him but that he didn't see anyone. The room was dark, and it was only because I happened to look around that I noticed. A fact that makes the agent's brow twitch.

All I'm doing is incriminating myself. I should stop telling them things I've seen. It's not like I've been an open book. But the killer might still be in the building, hiding in hidden passageways.

"Were you both seated for the entirety of the movie?" she asks.

"Yes."

"Yeah."

"There is a theater full of people who can confirm that, Agent. As well as CCTV," Nash says tightly. He's not a fan of the feds.

The agent turns toward him. "Nash, have you spoken to your father since the first murder?"

He visibly tenses. "No, Agent, he's staying at your place now."

I bump his arm inconspicuously. I'm not a massive fan of the constant suspicion either, but I at least try to tone down the sarcasm . . . or say it in my head.

"What's happened?" I ask. "Has there been another murder?"

"A body has been found, yes."

Oh god. "Who is it?" I breathe.

"I'm afraid I can't say right now."

"Was it someone who was watching the movie?"

"Penelope, I cannot release any information right now, I'm sorry. Thank you for your statement. We should join the others," she says.

Nash ushers me into the theater and we hang around at the back. The agent questioning us moves on. Together, she and her colleague move around to different groups of people. This time, no one seems to accuse Nash. No one I can hear anyway.

"This is crazy," I whisper. "I didn't think the killer was supposed to strike in public. There's a crowd here. This isn't like your da—Jackson."

He shakes his head. His cheeks are pale from the shock. "You're right. Why?"

"Copycat going off script or someone else?"

"Two murderers."

Raising a palm, I say, "Forget that. I can't even think about there being more than one killer on the loose."

"But it could be a team," he says.

Looks like we're discussing this. "Yeah, I guess. It would make sense. How else would they transport bodies so easily? One must be the driver while the other moves the body. But they'd be working together on each murder, right? Not two independents, and can we *please* not do this?"

"No one can say he did it now," someone whispers behind us.

My eyes narrow and it makes Nash laugh.

He shrugs. "At least I'm off the hook, I guess."

"Or you're working as a team, and this is a ruse to make it appear like you're innocent."

"I'll sharpen my blade for the big finale." He winces as soon as he says it, and I realize how insensitive we're being.

"We shouldn't joke."

"I think we've both earned a pass for a few inappropriate jokes . . . but you're right, we shouldn't. Three people are dead. Let's move on, like you wanted. Are you okay, Pen?"

"Sure, just another day in our creepy, murder-infested town." My stomach clenches tight.

Nash and I hang around on our own while everyone around us mingles and talks about carrying weapons. I think the majority of us have pepper spray, but I've heard talk of guns and knives too.

"Thank you for staying behind and answering our questions," the male agent says, walking up to us. "We have your details and will be in contact if we need anything, so you're free to go now."

I groan. "If my dad finds out I was here . . ." If word has gotten out, I'm in *so* much trouble, it's unreal.

"Cops and feds were already here, so there's a chance it's not out yet," Nash says.

"This is the end of me going anywhere but school until the killer is caught."

"You're good at sneaking out, Pen."

"That's true, but it's not a good idea. Besides, my parents will hear my car, and I'm not walking anywhere ever again."

"I'll pick you up from down the road."

We filter out through the door and look for Adi, Omar, and Zayn. Nash seems pretty eager to hang out again, so it looks like I'm sneaking out after my parents go to sleep.

"They must be outside," Nash says. "Come on."

Their screening room was probably let go first.

We step outside and the first thing I notice is the lack of reporters and people wanting all the gossip.

"No one is here," I say.

"See. Cops and feds were on the scene. Reporters had no one to follow. Residents had no cop cars to spot from their windows.

That's why no one knows.

All I have to do is get dropped off at home and my parents will never know I was here.

I do another sweep and every person I see is now on their phone. It won't be long before the news is out. I should message my dad and tell him I'm coming home soon.

"There they are," Nash says, pointing up the street. The crowd is lined up on the sidewalk. Not many people seem to have gone home yet. They probably need selfies with the crime scene.

Nash and I make our way through the crowd until we reach our friends.

"I heard it's Mae," Zayn says, his face ashen.

"No! Who told you that?"

"Freddy heard it from Dulcie, who was behind Millie and Gunner when they found her," Adi says, not taking a breath.

Zayn nods in her direction. "What she said."

"Mae." I shake my head. "It can't be her. She was... my friend."

"Might not be her," Nash says, putting his hand on my back at the same time my phone starts to ring.

I groan as my dad's name illuminates the screen. It causes Nash to step back as if Dad can see him through the phone.

"Dad," I say.

"Penny, I've just heard. Are you okay?"

I step away, hold the phone tight to my ear, and say, "Yeah, I'm fine, Dad. We've just heard so we're about to get in Zayn's car and come home."

"I can pick you up, Penny."

"Yeah, but we're literally about to walk out of the door." I wave my hands at my friends, who are all smirking at the massive lie I'm telling my dad. Adi is on her phone, probably messaging her mom.

"He'll drop you right outside the house."

"You know he will, Dad."

"Your mom and I will be waiting on the drive."

"See you in ten," I tell him, and hang up.

I hang up and Omar shakes his head at me. "Tut-tut, lying to Daddy."

"Shut up. Do you plan on telling your parents where you were tonight?"

"That info dies with us. Come on, Zayn, you need to get us all home before we're in any pictures."

"I should take off too," Nash says. "See you guys later."

My heart does this squeeze thing that makes me feel like a total asshole.

"Wait." I grab his hand and pull him back as he takes a step in the opposite direction. "How are you getting home?"

He winces. "Grace dropped me off before she went to a friend's house."

Then she came back here, spoke to Omar and Nash, and left again.

She really doesn't trust us with her brother.

"You'll all fit in my car. Come on," Zayn says.

"You don't have time to take me home first. Penny's dad's expecting her."

"He'll get over it. I don't care if he sees you."

He arches a brow. "Really?"

"Yeah, really, because that dude was mad the last time you spoke to Nash," Omar says, slapping Nash on the shoulder.

Nash thumps him back, shaking his head and laughing.

"I'm all for not filming in the theater out of respect for Mae but there is nothing you guys can say or do to stop me recording Penny's dad reacting to Nash in the car. He's not going to be happy." Adi's animated, bright eyed, hands gesturing everywhere and teeth gleaming as she smiles.

"You're sick, you know that?" I tell her.

"Let's go!" Zayn says again, throwing his arms up.

We pile into his car and my nerves turn into something physical. Bile hits the back of my throat and, disgustingly, I have to swallow it. Mae is dead. I spoke to her at school today and waved to her in the theater. Now she's gone.

Zayn turns down my road, and I suck in a breath.

Nash side-eyes me like he knows what I'm thinking. "I can duck down," he says.

I place my hand on his forearm. "Don't."

Adi is, in fact, spot on about my dad not being happy.

The second my parents spot him, their faces turn furious. The vein on Dad's forehead pops.

"Here we go," Zayn mutters under his breath, stopping the car.

"Penelope!" he snaps as I get out of the car.

"Dad, please don't—"

"What are you doing with *him*?" He can barely look at Nash.

I clench my hands as red-hot anger burns my stomach. "Don't talk about him like that. We're not doing anything wrong. *He* hasn't done anything wrong!"

"Get in the house."

I fold my arms over my chest. "No."

My mom cuts in. "Penelope, listen to your dad."

"I'm done ignoring him. You had no right to make me do that."

"We're here to keep you safe, so you'll do what we say."

"Whatever." I turn to my friends. To Nash. "I'll see you later, okay."

"The hell you will," Dad snaps under his breath.

Oh, I will.

17

THURSDAY, OCTOBER 28

I yawn into my palm as I watch the news at four in the morning in my bedroom. Mae. One of the sweetest people on the planet is gone. Left in a bathroom like she was nothing. Karter has been released.

I'm exhausted, my eyes heavy and body needing rest, but my mind won't switch off. Never again will I sit near Mae in class. She won't smile or laugh or pretend that she doesn't have a crush on Omar.

I've been in my room since I got home, after a brief argument with my parents. They were so mad that Nash had been hanging out with us but at least they don't know where we were.

If the feds want to talk to me again, I'm in so much more trouble.

I've spent the last thirty minutes messaging back and forth with Nash. He's worried about Grace because she was briefly at the movie theater. What does that look like? Same as him showing up in the square and at the pumpkin patch. The Whitmore kids continuing Daddy's handiwork makes a great story.

There were other people outside, so someone, in addition to us, could have seen her. Omar, Adi, and Zayn couldn't have said anything because Nash hasn't had another visit from the cops.

Penny:

Where is grace now?

Nash:

locked herself in her room with her music on

Penny:

have you seen her since you got home?

Nash:

I know not to go in if she's blasting her music

Penny:

omg you need to check on her!

I get that Grace can't sleep. I've only managed a few broken hours myself, but to be "blasting" music all night and into the early hours . . . That doesn't seem right to me.

Nash:

Why? I can hear her. She's doing the angry thing and I don't want to get involved with that!

Penny:

she might be in trouble

Is he serious? Three dead bodies and he doesn't think it's necessary to check on his sister. I want to scream at him but all I can do is wait for him to reply. My attention is spread evenly between my phone and the TV, where a reporter is explaining that another body was found "dumped" in a bathroom.

She hasn't been named yet, but it's Mae. Her friend saw her. I can't imagine that. It's traumatic enough finding someone dead but for it to be a friend must be horrifying.

Mae was found at the theater, a place where Jackson never struck, and no one's sure what that means. Is the new killer doing their own thing now? The reporter said it'll be harder to catch them if they're no longer copying Jackson.

She also reports that the feds are still investigating and won't be making a statement at this point.

The killer is doing their own thing now. That's all I can think, and obsess, about.

We thought we'd be somewhat safe at the movies because Jackson never went near there. I'm not going out again, unless it's to meet Nash and sit in his car for a while.

That could mean the double murder on Devil's Night won't happen. It could mean the new killer is enjoying this a bit too much. There could be more bodies.

God, anything could happen now.

It's a chilling thought.

The few Halloween decorations that I have in my room are now in a box on the floor. I don't want any of it.

One thing's for sure, I need to ask Zayn if he called the cops on Nash and ask Nash who's been in his house. Who's the driver of the new truck, the one who looks just like his dad?

An uncle is my guess. There must have been things his dad didn't tell him. I mean, there was *a lot* his dad didn't tell him.

Nash:

she's not answering

Oh, come on! I want to whack him.

Penny:

Just go in!

My heart thuds harder as I wait for a response. No one has actually seen Grace since she left the movie theater. She could've been taken. We didn't check that her car was gone from the movie theater lot, if that's even where she parked.

Nash:

she's not here

Penny:

I'm coming over

Nash:

Don't. Your dad will kill you! I'll find her.

But I don't reply because I'm grabbing my hoodie and keys.

Fear creeps up my neck, squeezing as if it's trying to choke me. Grace can't be dead. I can't lose her. Nash can't lose her.

I sneak downstairs, tiptoeing with a quiet urgency, trying not to wake my parents but also needing to get to Nash's house as soon as I can. I sneak out the back door and close it quietly, gritting my teeth as it clicks shut.

My car is in the drive, which would be quicker, but it's a big risk, as it could wake my parents. Time isn't on my side this morning, though, so I have no choice.

My parents are heavy sleepers. I just have to hope that's enough.

They usually wake around six, which gives me a couple hours before I need to be home, pretending to be passed out in bed. Maybe I'll get lucky and actually fall asleep when I get back.

I press the engine button gently as if that will have any effect on how loud the car is when it fires up.

Wincing, I put it into drive and pull onto the road, keeping an eye on my rearview mirror for a light switching on in their bedroom, but when I turn the corner, it's still dark.

I'm okay.

My phone rings through my car. Nash.

I hit answer and ask, "Did you find her?"

"Why are you driving? Penny, don't be stupid. Go back home. Your parents. The killer. It's not safe."

"It's fine, I'll be back before they wake. Where could she have gone?"

"There's a killer out there. I don't want to risk you."

"I'm fine. Where is she?" I repeat.

"I have no idea. She hasn't left a note. You shouldn't come here."

"Maybe you should call the cops. Something bad could've happened to her."

He blows out a long breath. "I can't think about that."

"We have to, Nash."

"She's probably gone to her boyfriend's house."

"Does she definitely have one?"

"She's spending a lot of time with someone from work."

That was my guess. The guy she had a crush on.

"You think she's with him?"

"Maybe. I don't know. I hope so. This asshole is copying my dad, so he wouldn't hurt Grace, right?"

"We can't count on that but hopefully."

I turn into town and drive past the road the movie theater is on. It's quiet now. The sun is still hours away from rising, but I can see the yellow tape cordoning off the building.

"I'm almost out of town. I'll be at your house in a few minutes."

"I don't think it's a good idea that you're out alone."

"I'm in my car."

I hear him open the front door and grin to myself.

"Are you waiting for me?"

"Hurry up," he says in lieu of a reply.

"Go call her again. See you in two."

I shouldn't be smiling right now, but I can't help it. This is like the old days. There's not even a hint that he's frustrated or angry at me. I want to dive straight into what that means but I can't. Grace is our focus.

Nash is outside when I pull up at his farm. He opens my door and says, "I'm getting really worried now."

"You didn't find out where she is?"

"She isn't answering. I even tried Omar because they were talking earlier but he's not picking up."

Groaning, I say, "Zayn? He seems to know a lot of things."

"I don't think Grace talks to him."

"No, but he looked back at her when she walked away."

"That's what you're basing this off of?" he asks, stopping a second to look up from his phone.

"It was the way he looked at her, Nash, like he has so much to say. We don't know where she is or who the boyfriend is, so it's worth a shot. Call him."

"All right, but this would be best coming from you."

"Fine." I take my phone and call Zayn. He picks up on the third ring.

"Penny, what the hell kind of time is this? You better have a good reason for waking me up at the crack—"

"Is Grace with you?"

Nash's eyes widen. He gives me a look that says, *What the hell?* But I'm not playing around now; we don't have time to waste.

"What? No, it's . . . damn it, four-thirty in the morning. Why would she be with me?"

"Nash can't find her."

He groans sleepily. "Pen, you need to go back to bed and give it a minute before you obsess over Nash again."

Twisting around, I wince. There is no way Nash didn't hear that.

"Zayn, have you seen her or not?"

"No." He groans again. "I was asleep, like you should be. I haven't seen anyone. Where are you anyway . . . and what're you doing?"

"Nothing. He messaged me."

Zayn won't be able to check where I am because I've turned off Find My. The moment Nash mentioned to me that Zayn was weird with him, I removed it.

"Go back to sleep. She's probably with a guy."

Yeah, but that guy could be the killer.

"Bye," I say, and hang up. "That was no help."

"Safe to assume she's not with him."

"Is there anyone else here?" I ask.

"Just me and you, Pen."

Really?

"The day you were taken to the station—"

We both swing around as a thudding noise from one of the barns makes us jump.

"What was that?" I ask, grabbing hold of his arm. "Nash?"

They don't have any animals on the farm.

"Stay behind me. Grace?" he calls out.

I press my lips together to keep from hyperventilating. The farm is cloaked in darkness, and it's way cooler than I prepared for. Cold seeps through the thin hoodie I quickly grabbed.

"It's not Grace," I whisper.

"I think it came from my dad's old workshop."

"Hell no! I'm not going in there."

"Damn straight you're not. Get back in your car and lock the doors."

"No."

He sighs sharply. "For once will you not argue with me?"

I cling to him harder. "I'm not letting you get hacked to death alone."

"This isn't some Romeo and Juliet BS."

"Yeah, I know. They weren't murdered."

Shaking his head, he steps forward. I go with him, slowly, and we inch closer to the large barn door.

Nash looks around. We only have the light from inside his house. One small kitchen window with blinds half open. Not enough. There's not enough light in the world for this.

"Stay behind me. *No* arguments."

I stay beside him, clawing at his arm, but he doesn't say anything else. His posture changes; he's tense and his forehead creases in a frown. I understand instantly that he's preparing to see his sister's dead body.

It's not likely. No one's been discovered near their home. But I can understand how he got there. I don't know what I'll do if I see Grace dead.

Nash reaches out for the barn door handle. His fingers shake as he slides the wooden door to the side, and I hold my breath until I feel like I'm going to faint again.

"I can't see anyone," he whispers.

I release the breath I'm holding and press my forehead to his arm.

"I need to go in and check properly."

"Where's the switch?" I ask. "I think I'm going to pass out."

He flicks the switch, and I squint as my eyes get used to the light.

"Really pass out or . . . ?" he asks.

"No, I'm fine." The last time I was here, I dropped to the floor. That's the last thing Nash needs while we're searching for his sister.

I shudder as I take in our surroundings and realize that Jackson's classic Corvette is a yard from my feet. I spent two months over spring last year helping him and Nash work on it.

We're in a serial killer's workshop.

Nash moves deeper into the room, leaving me standing by a car that I helped rebuild. Jackson bought it in ruins. Only months after he finished it, he was locked up.

"There's no one here."

I look up and notice something odd. "Did you leave that side door open?"

He turns and frowns. "No, I didn't."

Outside, I hear the rumble of an engine, and a bolt of adrenaline sends my heart sprinting.

"Shit!" Nash hisses, and rushes out the door with absolutely no sense of self-preservation. "Grace?"

I run after him, around the car and two workbenches, then outside into the dark again. My least favorite place to be.

"Nash?" I call, my body freezing as I realize I'm alone. "Nash?"

I turn around, searching for him in the darkness, only able to see the outline of trees and cornfields in the direction he ran.

"Nash?" Wrapping my arms around myself, I strain to listen for footsteps. A rustling startles me, and I leap back against the workshop wall behind me as a flock of birds swoop from a tree.

"Penny?"

I scream at the new voice and spin around. "Grace!" Placing my hand on my heart, I try not to hit the floor. "Oh my god, you scared me."

"What the hell are you doing here?"

"Penny!" Nash's footsteps thunder back toward us. He stops dead, looking between me and his sister. "Where were you?" he snaps.

"I was with a friend. What is she doing here?"

"With who?"

"A guy from work, Nash. I do have friends, ones who don't turn their back on me for something Dad did. With this crap all happening again, I needed him more than ever."

"Who is this guy? You've never mentioned him before."

"I have, but you haven't been listening! His name's Brant, and he doesn't care what my surname is. He listens to me without judgment. Now, what is *she* doing here?"

"I came to help Nash find you," I snap. "We were worried, especially after Mae was killed today."

Grace gasps, her hand flying to her heart. "Mae Winstone?" Nash nods. "Oh my god. I used to be on the volleyball team with her. She was one of the only people who still talked to me when Dad . . ."

"I'm sorry," I rasp. "She was my friend too."

She takes a breath and the scowl on her face disappears. "You should go home, Penny. Clearly it isn't safe to be out alone, and I assume your parents don't know you're here."

Wow, it's the first time in a year that she's mentioned my safety.

"Nash?"

"It's fine. Thanks for coming over but you really should get back before they wake. They realize you're with me, they'll probably move you across the state."

Across the country.

"Okay," I reply, chewing on my lip. I'm still on edge and don't really want to be alone but he's right.

"And . . . you should message us when you're home," Grace says, averting her eyes and kicking rocks at her feet.

Nash smiles at me, surprised but pleased by his sister's concern. It's a good first step. Maybe she'll even let me in the house next time. I just hope that she doesn't view me as an enemy anymore. After all, I came out here because I was scared for her.

"See you later, Grace."

She nods and walks off toward the house. Nash and I are a few steps behind and he stops with me by my car.

"Call me when you get home," Nash says, opening my door for me.

"I will."

He steps back, and I set off along his drive.

A cloud of dust obstructs my view, but I see him go inside his house as I turn from the driveway onto the road.

The town is still and peaceful. Soon the sky will lighten, and we'll have to face another day of mourning and fear.

Cornfields are about to yield to buildings in town when a bright flash shines through the window, and I'm knocked sideways.

I scream, trying to cling to the steering wheel. I'm slammed against the door, my head hitting the window. The seat belt locks, trapping me painfully against the seat.

I'm flipped but it takes me a second to realize what's going on, that I'm upside down and back again.

My arms fly out in front of me, and my chin hits my chest as I go over again.

A deafening silence rings through my ears. I hear the sound of metal and glass denting and smashing, but it feels far away, as if I'm trying to listen underwater.

I'm slammed into the door again, this time getting the air knocked out of my lungs, and the car comes to an abrupt stop, nose down in a ditch.

Darkness drenches my vision for a while. Seconds? I'm not sure exactly. It takes a heartbeat to put it together. The headlights. I wasn't just in a car accident; I was hit, run off the road.

Groaning, I blink but the world begins to blur in color, like I'm seeing it through a kaleidoscope. I'm dazed, expecting this to be a dream but knowing it's not.

It's okay. You're fine. Get out of the car.

My hand reaches for the door handle and drops to the seat, having no energy to move at all. I turn my head to the side and in the distance, I see headlights again. This time they're not moving.

The car that hit me has stopped.

I open my mouth to call for help, but the white mask in the rearview mirror steals my breath.

18

My vision suddenly comes into focus. The ringing in my ears subsides, leaving behind a sharp pain radiating through my skull. With my senses returning, I hear the footsteps outside the car, getting much closer.

He's coming.

I need to get out of here, but I can't move at all. My body is so heavy, I sink into my seat as if I'm weighted in a pool.

Adrenaline pumps through my veins. The killer is outside, somewhere around my car, and I can barely lift my hand.

Panting, I try desperately to get my arms to wake up. If I don't get out of here, I'm dead. Clenching my fingers, I will myself to get it together. I can't see my phone; it was on the passenger seat so must have been thrown somewhere in the car during the crash.

Is this how Mae felt when she knew he was coming for her?

Come on.

I scramble for the door handle again, but my fingers just thud against the door and fall back onto my lap. *Move!* I can't let him get me. This can't be how I die.

"No," I mutter as my eyes sting with unshed tears. I refuse to give in and cry, to sit back and let him win.

I can't get my body to respond the way I need it to. There's no pain in my arms or legs, so I don't think they're injured. Unless it's masked by the shock.

You're fine, so *get up*!

Whimpering, I push myself up off the back of the seat and slump against the half-smashed window. Every muscle in my body screams with the effort it takes to move even a little. The jagged edge of glass is inches from my face, ready and waiting to cut me to ribbons. I can already feel blood trickling down my cheek from the earlier impact, so what would it matter at this point?

Breathing deeply, I focus on my hand and raise it to the metal handle.

Footsteps thump behind me as he circles the back of the car.

Hurry!

What is he waiting for? Why not just kill me now?

The door yields and I push with every ounce of energy I have, ignoring the pain pulsing through my body. I only get it open about five inches but that'll do.

Boots pound on asphalt outside the back passenger door. He's playing with me, making his way slowly to my door. The front of the car is in the ditch, on grass. I won't be able to hear him if he moves closer.

I twist to get out, but I'm stuck.

The seat belt!

A sob bursts from my mouth as I realize that he's going to make it to me before I get out. I'm pinned to the seat. Frantically, I fumble with the belt and my hands hit the buckle until I hear the click. At the same time, he crouches down and his mask fills the passenger side window.

A scream rips from my throat and I throw myself to the side, sliding out of the car and landing on damp grass. My wrist is in agony as I push myself onto my hands and knees, gasping for oxygen that seems to have been sucked from the air.

The cold, damp air hits my face, and I feel more awake.

The fog is clearing and it's now that I feel how bad the pain in my head and arm are. It brings bile to the back of my throat.

A prelude to the agony that's coming. Slamming my good palm on the side of the car, I shove myself to my feet. My weak legs tremble, and I nearly fall again.

A slither of light peeks over the horizon above the corn. "Help," I shout, stumbling sideways, stomach lurching.

Blood runs cold in my veins when I come face to face with the mask over the top of the car. He's on the other side, watching me. It's too dark to see his eyes, and I'm not exactly thinking straight, but he's tall and broad, fit.

Gasping, I press on, my knees almost buckling again as I move as quickly as my body will allow.

I don't know what my chances are, but I *have* to try. Town is closer to me now, but it'll still be a good five minutes of solid running before I reach the first house . . . and at my pace, I'm not sure I'll make it.

I slip going up the ditch, crying out as my feet slide out from under me. With a sob, I claw my nails into the dirt and heave myself up the slope.

He's right behind me. I feel icy air surround him, the aura of pure evil, and it makes me shudder. Is he already thinking about stabbing me? Does it excite him the way I used to get excited about playing the piano or acting in a play?

I don't stop or look back; I launch off the ground and run. Cold wind stings my cheeks and my entire body aches and screams in pain, a warning that it won't be able to do this for long. I think I've done something to my wrist and the fuzziness in my head and the nausea tell me that I probably have a concussion.

The focus that I had a minute ago slowly fades and the world in front of me glazes over like I've been pulled back underwater.

I stumble to the side again, my legs like those of a newborn horse, and I'm not sure where I'm going because everything has turned fuzzy. Black dots dance in front of my face.

No, stay awake!

I take another step and gasp.

The ground shoots toward my face, and for the second time this week, I'm out.

• • •

I blink heavily, but all I can see is the foggy outline of faces. Human faces. No masks. There's an irritating flashing in the background, and a ringing that I'm sure only I can hear. The ground is hard and cold, and I think I'm shaking.

And suddenly it's loud, like hundreds of voices have just

started shouting at the same time. I can't make out any word that is spoken. My eyes drift to the side, and I'm sure I see Nash and Grace.

Or maybe I just want to, I don't know.

Pain radiates through my entire body as if every bone was broken in the crash. I try to tell them, but I can't speak.

I go to open my mouth, to ask what's going on and where the killer is, but I'm mercifully pulled back under.

The next time I wake, my back is against something soft and warm. The pain is there but it's background noise now. I look around the room and see pale walls and hear an annoying beep.

The hospital.

Groaning, I try to sit, but I don't have the energy.

"Lie still, Penelope."

My eyes fly to the source of the voice.

Rosenthal.

"Where is he?" I rasp, looking around, panicked.

I'm no longer in the road, but I don't know who he is or where he is. The killer isn't here. I'm safe.

Another agent walks out of the room, presumably to get a doctor now that I'm awake.

"Where is who, Penny? Can you tell me what happened?"

"Was I stabbed? Where is he? Did you get him?"

Frowning, she shakes her head. "No, no one is here. You were in an accident. Your parents are here, gone to get a coffee. We'll get them back. You don't remember being run off the road?"

"I remember it all. Why are you here?"

"We're here to make sure you're safe."

"From the killer? He was there. He's the one who crashed into me."

She frowns. "We didn't see evidence of another car."

I catch sight of the clock on the wall behind her. It's a little after seven in the morning. I'm assuming morning. Bright daylight streams through the window into my room.

"Then why are you here?"

"To find out why you were out alone at night. Who were you meeting?"

That's . . . weird.

"Well, there was another car there. I was running from the *masked* killer. Nash. Did I see Nash?"

She leans forward. "Nash was there when the crash happened? He was wearing a mask?"

"No! Not then. After I collapsed, I woke up and there were flashing lights and people . . . I saw Nash. Where is he now?"

She looks like she wished someone else had the job of questioning me. "You don't need to worry about Nash or his sister."

"Grace? She was there too. Yeah, I saw them both. Wait, where are they? Are they okay?"

"They're at the station."

"What? No!" I try to push myself up but get nowhere, my body letting me down again. "You have to let them go!"

"Rest, Penny. You have a concussion."

"No! They didn't do this. It wasn't them. It couldn't have been. I'd just left their house, like, two minutes before. The car came from the crossroads in the opposite direction. They wouldn't have had time to take that road."

Frowning, she stands. "Are you sure of the timing?"

"I'm *positive.* It couldn't have been them. They probably heard the crash or the sirens. You have to let them go. Please."

She holds her hands up, looking pretty worried that I'm getting stressed. "They were questioned and gave a statement, that's it. Rest. We'll get your parents and take a statement when you're up for it."

"I'm up for it now," I say. It's a total lie. I'm exhausted and fighting the growing urge to close my eyes. "You have to find the killer."

"I'll be right back."

If ever there's an expression for someone who thinks you've gone crazy, she's wearing it.

A nurse comes in as Rosenthal leaves. I'm poked and prodded as she checks my vitals and administers pain medication for the wicked headache I have. I'm given water for the driest throat ever and instantly feel much better. The queasiness in my stomach hasn't gone anywhere but I can ignore it.

My wrist is in a cast but it's not causing me issues right now. The pain from my head is too bad to feel anything else. Though nothing compared to right after the crash. The meds are taking the edge off it.

My worry for Nash and Grace overtakes everything else. Why were they at the station if the feds only wanted a statement? Are they just being cautious and questioning everything even slightly outside the norm or is there more to it?

Does this mean they don't have a lot to go on so are covering it all?

I go out of my mind as I wait for Rosenthal to come back.

When the door opens, I'm half happy to see my parents and half disappointed that it's not Rosenthal. I need to know what's happening with Nash and Grace.

"Penny!" Mom sobs.

I assure my parents that I'm okay when they ask a hundred times, their panic temporarily overshadowing their anger.

"What were you doing?" Dad asks. He's only calm on the surface, his fear that I could've been killed tempering his anger at me sneaking out and putting myself in danger. I can tell by the control in his voice that he has a lot more to say.

"Nash couldn't find Grace."

Mom takes my hand and squeezes as if she never wants to let go. "*Why* did you go, honey?"

"I was worried something bad had happened to her. He could hardly call the cops, could he? Most of the time, they suspect him. But he *didn't* do any of this. He and Grace were taken to the station. I don't know why or what happened to them."

Dad clears his throat. "Forget them for now. You were in an accident."

"I was leaving their house when a car slammed into me coming from the opposite direction. They wouldn't have had time."

"Are you certain?" Mom asks, glancing at Dad.

"No doubt. This wasn't them, and I didn't make up the other car. I know the cops said there was no evidence of anyone else but there was."

Even through the fuzziness of getting out of the car and running, I can see everything so clearly; every detail is imprinted in my mind.

"All right, darling."

"I wanted to see who it was," I tell them. "To look into his eyes and figure out if I know who it is. But it was too dark . . . and I was so scared. There was no time."

"You did the right thing by running," Dad says. His voice is low and unsure, like he's humoring me.

"I didn't make it up, and I didn't crash on my own," I repeat.

Mom brushes her hand over my hair. "The police and FBI are investigating. Don't worry."

I close my eyes and do nothing but worry.

My parents stay in my room all day; they're there each time I wake. In the evening, I'm so relieved when they have to go home. Tomorrow I can be released if my doctor is happy with my progress. I want to leave now but that was out of the question, apparently.

I finish a hot chocolate that a nurse brought me. The sugar and pain meds have taken the headache down to a minor annoyance. After some food, too, I feel pretty okay.

I'd feel better in my own bed.

There's a knock on my door and Rosenthal smiles at me. "Can I come in?" she asks.

"Sure."

She steps inside. "How are you feeling?"

"Better, thanks. How's Nash?"

"He and Grace were only giving a statement."

"Why did they have to go to the station?"

"Nash's choice."

He didn't want them in his house.

I sigh in relief. "They didn't attack me."

"We know," she says. "Penny, we're having trouble finding evidence of anyone else being out there with you. You'd hit your head."

"You've found nothing?"

"A partial footprint in the ditch, on the passenger side. Which way did you run?"

"That's where he was standing. I ran toward town. Can't you test the footprint, or whatever it is you do?"

"We have samples, but the print isn't good enough to identify the shoe."

"A boot, I think. It was heavy on the road."

She nods. "You said you were leaving the Whitmore farm. Do you know anyone who would want to target you specifically?"

I shake my head gently because it feels like it's being crushed in a vise. "No. Why didn't he kill me? Why run me off the road and chase me? I'd passed out. He could've stabbed me on the ground and ended it all right there."

She takes a seat in the chair by my bed. "That's what we're trying to figure out. Have you had any trouble with anyone? At school, perhaps?"

"No. Only that stupid argument with Ruby."

And we know it can't be her.

"Is Nash allowed to visit in the morning?" I ask.

She hesitates before saying, "There's no reason why he wouldn't be allowed to."

Well, my parents are a reason. I don't think he'll be allowed to visit when I get home, so I need to get him here. My phone was recovered from the crash and is now sitting on the bed beside me.

"Someone called the cops on Saturday, just before midnight, and reported seeing Nash in town. Lurking, apparently. We were supposed to meet up that night, but then the cops showed up at his place, so he couldn't come."

She leans forward, resting her elbows on her knees. "We have a record of the call, but the person didn't leave a name. I didn't know you had plans to meet up."

"We snuck out a lot before . . . his dad, you know."

"I'll be right back, Penny."

She steps outside and gets on her phone.

"Thank you for sharing that information," she says, poking her head back into the room a minute later. "I'll be outside if you need me. You should get some rest."

They might only half believe me about the killer causing the accident but they're not taking any chances.

A chill slides down my spine at the thought of being a target. I don't know what the killer wants from me. I should be dead now, but the feds feel like I'm in danger.

I wouldn't have a personal guard if they didn't.

I check my phone and there's a new message from Nash. The first one since he left. He hadn't replied to me when I tried to contact him.

Nash:

are you okay? We heard a crash and couldn't figure it out at first. Did you see the killer? Did he hurt you? We need to meet.

Nash has exploded all over text. I can only imagine how he's feeling. Grace had just started to come around to the idea of me being back in Nash's life—and hers—and now she's been questioned because she decided to help me.

Penny:

That's a lot of questions. I'm okay, have a concussion and broken wrist but they have me on the good stuff. The killer was there but the feds have only found a partial footprint. I'm not sure they're convinced I'm telling the truth. I wasn't hurt at all by the killer. That's weird, right?

Nash:

You were so still on the ground. I thought you were dead. It's totally weird but maybe he saw or heard my car coming down the drive and split. We didn't see another vehicle.

That's a possibility, I suppose. You can just about see Nash's farm in the distance from where I was. The killer could've seen their headlights.

Penny:

Visiting is at 10 a.m. tomorrow. I think I'll be able to go home at some point.

Nash:

I'll be there at 10.

I fall asleep, waiting on information about who called the cops on Nash the night I snuck out. I have a feeling that if we find out who that was, we'll be closer to catching the killer.

19

FRIDAY, OCTOBER 29

I'm on my feet by eight in the morning, dressed and ready to go home. I've eaten a slice of toast, had a shower—awkwardly because of the cast on my broken wrist—and passed my vitals. Okay, I know it's not something you pass or fail but if they're okay, I get to go home, so it's the same thing to me.

My parents showed up already, rather angry that Nash was going to visit. Mom talked Dad down, though, reminding him that Nash came to help me. Neither of them have said much about me sneaking out, but that doesn't mean they're not going to.

It's only a matter of time.

Adi, Omar, and Zayn are coming to my house in the evening since the doctor told us I can go home this afternoon.

Tomorrow is Devil's Night.

I don't know what last night was because Jackson never used his vehicle to kill anyone. He also never murdered anyone in the movie theater, so we already knew this copycat was going off script. Devil's Night might not mean anything to this killer now. There's no way to tell if he's gearing up for a double murder.

Dad clears his throat, letting that action do the talking.

"I didn't go to hang out at the park, Dad."

His eyes tighten. "No, you just ran to the house of a known serial killer."

"Who's in federal prison. That place belongs to Grace and Nash now."

Mom places a hand on my arm and Dad's. "Let's not argue, okay. We'll give you some space when Nash arrives but there will be an agent outside your room."

Dad scowls but lets it go.

At exactly ten, Nash shows up and my parents go down to the cafeteria. Before they leave, Dad whispers something to the agent outside my room. I can only imagine what he told him.

Nash sits on my bed and his eyes trace every little red line on my face where the shattered glass cut my skin.

"Hi," I say. "It's a new look, huh?"

"You okay?"

"Fine. I told the feds about the call the night we were supposed to meet."

"They didn't already know about that?"

"Well, yeah, they did. But they didn't know about us meeting up. Obviously. I had to tell them, Nash."

He shrugs. "I'm not the one who wanted to keep any of it a secret, Pen. Do you think the caller is the killer because . . ."

Sighing, I finish his sentence. "We suspect Zayn."

It's hard to think about my friend doing this but would it

explain why I'm still alive? Zayn wasn't really friends with Noah, Ruby. Only Mae.

"If Zayn did make the call, it was to deter me from seeing you, right?" He nods and gestures for me to continue. "Well, maybe the crash was the same thing. He would know my parents wouldn't be happy if I snuck out. That I'd be locked down after."

"And the accident was a way to ensure they found out."

"I've spent years with him, Nash."

"And I spent my whole life with my dad. You don't always know, Penny."

Fair point.

Behind Nash, Zayn is the last person I want to be the killer. Along with Omar and Adi, of course.

"He's coming to my house tonight. They all are."

His eyes widen. "You can't let him near you."

"I have to. I'll know when I see him."

"How?"

"I don't know," I say, laughing. "I'll get a feeling."

"You really did hit your head hard."

"Not funny. What did Grace say about last night?"

"She was pissed but calmed down when we got home. The cops wanted to get us off the road, and I didn't want them taking our statement at home. Hopefully they know we're not behind it now."

Nash has been with me three times when the killer has struck or been seen.

There is no way it could be him.

"Good. Nash, if I tell you something, you have to promise me you won't get defensive or think I'm nuts."

"Now, there's a promise I want to make . . ."

"Please."

He sighs. "I promise."

"I saw that truck in your driveway the day you were questioned at the station."

He blinks twice but otherwise doesn't react. "Grace's truck?"

"Grace wasn't in the truck, Nash."

Frowning, he asks, "Then who was?"

"I was hoping you'd tell me."

"I have no clue. The boyfriend, maybe?"

"I feel sick."

He stands and looks around the room. "Do you have a bucket? Should I get someone?"

"I feel sick because you're lying to me."

He stops midstep as he goes to leave the room for help.

"Who is he, Nash?"

His shoulders slump as he turns around and shoves his hands into his pockets. "He's my uncle."

What?

My jaw drops open. "But you don't have an uncle."

"Yeah, well, that's what we thought too. Dad told us he was an only child. Turns out he lied about his past just as much as his present."

"Nash! Are you serious?"

He takes a seat on the bed again. "This needs to stay between us."

"Come on . . ."

"Please, Penny."

"Fine," I relent, feeling uneasy about it. "But I want to know everything."

"They were close growing up until my uncle fell in with a bad crowd in his early twenties. They drifted apart and my dad took it hard, felt abandoned, is what Jensen said. He tracked us down earlier this year after finding out what my dad did. He wasn't even surprised that we didn't know about him."

What the hell . . .

"Does he live with you?"

"No, he's visiting."

"How long has he been in town?"

"He's not the killer, Penny."

"How long?"

"A month."

"Is he still here?"

"Going home next week. I know what you're thinking. I can see it written all over your face. He's not like my dad."

I throw my hands up. "The man is your dad's brother! He turns up a few weeks before the first kill and plans to leave right after Halloween. That doesn't seem suspicious to you?"

"No. This isn't the first time he's stayed."

Is he for real right now?

"Nash, you really haven't considered this?"

Scratching his forehead, he replies, "Of course I have! When it first started. But he was home with me the day Ruby was killed."

Except when Nash was at the pumpkin patch, but Ruby was

already in the toilet by then. "Why haven't we seen him in town at all?"

"We asked him not to go out. There's a . . . resemblance to my dad."

Yeah, I know. Glad I wasn't going crazy after all.

"You can't keep this to yourself. It's a miracle the cops haven't seen him yet."

He shrugs as if he's not concerned. "He doesn't answer the door and before the murders started, no one had come by for a long time."

He might as well have said *you* haven't come by.

"Nash, you can't keep this to yourself."

"You mean *you* can't. Penny, if anyone knows he's here . . ."

"The murders might stop!"

"You don't even know him."

I groan, exasperated that he's not thinking clearly. "Neither do you! It's not even been a year since you met him."

"It's not him."

"Look, if there's more than one person doing this, it could be him. Whoever it is isn't following your dad's path anymore."

"He hates my dad and their fallout happened *before* he killed anyone. Why would he suddenly follow in the footsteps of a younger brother he didn't care to know?"

"That's only what he's told you. Have you asked your dad?"

"Hell no. Grace said he won't talk about Jensen at all."

"So you only have Grace's word for it?"

"Are you saying she's lying?"

"I'm saying you need to hear it. You're more objective when it comes to your dad. Can you set up a call with him?"

Shaking his head, he stands and tugs his arm away from me as I reach for him. "Don't. I can't talk to him."

"Someone is messing with *me.* I'm mixed up in this. Jeez, Nash, I have to have an *FBI agent* outside my door. Maybe next time the killer won't walk away."

"Dammit!" he hisses, shoving his hands into his hair. When he looks back over to me, he's broken. "I never wanted to speak to that man again."

"I know, and I'm so sorry, but you have to. Please."

He takes his phone out and glances at the screen. "If he has enough minutes left, he can call me."

"How do you get him to do that?"

Taking a deep breath, he says, "By getting in touch with the prison and asking for an emergency call."

"Hey," I say softly. "Thank you."

He nods, refusing to meet my eyes, and makes the call. It takes a bit of convincing that this is an actual emergency, but I'm sure the prison is aware of what's happening.

I feel awful. My stomach churns with guilt.

Nash hangs up and stares at his screen in fear.

At some point soon that phone will ring, and he'll speak to his dad.

It looks like the last thing in the world he wants to do.

"When does visiting end? Midday?" he asks.

"Yeah, but we have thirty minutes until my parents come back."

I will Jackson to hurry up. Nash wills him to ignore the request.

"I still think there is something going on with Zayn," he says, breaking a tense eight minutes of silence.

"Yeah, me too."

"You don't want to believe he would run you off the road?"

"Would you?"

Nash's phone starts to ring. He holds it in his hand like a grenade and stares at it.

"Nash," I prompt before it rings off.

I watch him swallow and close his eyes before he answers.

"Hello."

Silence for a moment and then he blows out a breath. "I don't want to talk about me . . . Jensen . . . Why did you never tell us about him?"

Nash balls his free hand into a white-knuckled fist. I reach out and put my hand over his. It was supposed to comfort him, but he tenses further. I think he likes me about as much as his dad right now.

Still, he doesn't shove my hand away.

"When did you last speak to him? It's important! I was five then . . . Not at all since? All right. I'm safe." His eyes narrow and I know there is so much more that Nash needs to say to his dad. So much to get off his chest that he won't allow himself to.

"I don't know . . . I'm with Penny . . . No, she was attacked by the sick bastard playing *you*."

"Nash," I say, my eyes flicking to the agent outside my room. It's a different one now and he's drinking a cup of coffee and talking to a cop. The last thing we need is for them to hear Nash yell at his dad.

"Yes, she's fine," he replies tightly. "So, you have no desire to contact Jensen and he hasn't tried contacting you? Okay. No, I don't think we'll be doing this again . . . Why do you think?" His jaw tightens as he says a blunt goodbye and hangs up.

"Are you okay?" I ask.

Standing abruptly, he tells me, "He's not spoken to him. See you tomorrow."

Then he leaves without another word, and I feel like absolute crap.

And, if possible, even worse when I realize that one of my best friends really might be doing this.

20

I've sent an obscene amount of messages to Nash, and each one has been ignored. He's getting real good at ghosting me. That's something he could probably say about me too.

In about ten minutes, I get to go home and prepare to see my friends.

To see Zayn.

Mom and Dad are fussing, making sure I have all the pain meds I need and follow-up appointments are booked. They've not mentioned the sneaking out thing yet. I'm certain that Mom has forbidden Dad to bring it up until my concussion has healed. I don't trust the silence, and I know they have a *lot* to say.

My impending punishment isn't something I can worry about right now because I'm too worried about Nash's call with Jackson. And the fact that I made him do it.

Mom sends Dad to bring the car around to the front of the hospital and I use that as a chance to get her away, too, so I can speak to Rosenthal. She returned early this afternoon, relieving the other guy.

To give myself a minute with Rosenthal, who's still outside my room, I ask Mom to go grab me some snacks from the vending machine outside the ward. It's close enough that she will do it and far enough to have a private conversation.

Rosenthal steps inside my room as Mom leaves. I'm glad it's her out there today; she's the only one who has stopped looking at me like I've done something wrong.

"Everything okay? I thought you were leaving?" she asks.

"Mom's just grabbing me some snacks. I'm craving sugar. The Jell-O here is not good."

She nods, lips pursed, like she doesn't believe me. Smart woman.

My shoulders slump. "All right. I wanted to talk to you. Did you find out who called the cops on Nash that night?"

"We're looking into it, Penny."

That's a big fat no, then.

"Burner phone?"

"I can't say."

"You just did."

"You should consider applying to the academy."

No, thanks.

I smile but I'm not sure I look very happy.

"Do you need anything else?" she asks.

"Any information you can tell me?" I ask back.

Tilting her head, she smirks and replies, "Nice try."

Well, that was a total waste of time. It wasn't like she was going to divulge confidential information anyway.

Mom comes back with a packet of M&M's and a Snickers. "Everything okay?"

"Everything's fine. I was just checking on Penny. We'll have someone stationed outside your house before you arrive."

"Thank you, Agent. I don't want my daughter alone ever again."

That sounds awful.

"We're here to protect her."

I should tell her about Nash's mysterious uncle, but I don't want to do that before I've spoken to him again. First, I need to see what the hell is going on with Zayn.

Dad is waiting for us outside the hospital, the car idling by the entrance. Mom helps me into the passenger side—a seat that's reserved for when I'm ill or only with one of them.

"I don't think we need to tell you that you won't be going out. Ever again," Dad says. The last part is a joke, but I definitely don't think I'll be going anywhere for a while. Mom clears her throat, but he doesn't notice her not-so-subtle prompt to shut up. Or he doesn't care.

"Dad, I wasn't going to leave Nash to search for his sister alone. What if she was dead and he found her? Can you imagine how awful that would be?"

"Oh, honey. You should have told us," Mom says. "You took such a silly risk. We could have lost you."

"I'm sorry. I didn't mean to scare you. The plan was to drive to

Nash's and then I'd be with him." We'd still be in a group of two instead of three or more, as recommended, but what could we do? "You guys haven't been very open-minded about Nash."

"You know why that is, Penny. Sneaking out and getting into an accident isn't the way to show us you and Nash should be friends."

I don't bother responding because it's a conversation we've had a hundred times before. It's led to countless arguments, and I don't have the energy to fight right now . . . plus they're right. I've not made them want to give Nash a chance.

At home, I wave to the agents in the car outside and curl up on the sofa. My head is sore, and my broken wrist only seems to hurt more and more.

Mom tucks a blanket around me and reminds me that I can't have any pain meds for another hour. I knew that; I've been counting down the minutes since my wrist started throbbing like it has its own heartbeat.

They putter around, never leaving my side for more than a few minutes. If one needs to make a call, the other one stands guard. It makes napping impossible.

"I'm not going to leave the house again, you know that, right?" I say, gently tapping the ache in my wrist.

"I'm well aware, Penny," Mom replies.

"Then you really don't need to watch me every second."

"The doctor told us to keep an eye on you because of the concussion."

That's her excuse for being way over-the-top about this. All right, I snuck out, got into an accident, and was chased by a killer, *but* I'm alive and home. I think it would be okay for us to be in separate rooms.

I message our group chat to pass the time. I've resisted for a while in case they take my phone away, but I'm slowly losing my mind.

Penny:

I'm home and going crazy. parents won't leave me alone for a second. entertain me.

Zayn:

We'll be over later. School's been canceled.

Omar:

yeah, thx for getting attacked, Pen

Adi:

OMG omar u have no tact!

No, he doesn't but he makes me smile. Someone is being real, at least.

Omar:

She knows I'm kidding! Zayn and I have decided to be your personal BODYGUARDS.

Adi:

She has literal FBI agents, moron!

Zayn:

they don't care about her like we do.

I wish I could see Zayn's face. His expression would tell me everything. At least I think it would. I'm starting to doubt my face-reading abilities since he admitted to keeping in touch with Nash. I had no idea and whenever I brought Nash up, Zayn would confidently tell me he'd not seen him.

But maybe I'll be better at it now because I don't blindly trust him anymore.

Penny:

Hurry up and come over. I need a break from people asking if I'm okay.

Adi:

On our way!!

Mom and Dad give me a bit of space when my friends arrive. They close the kitchen door when they retreat in there.

"Your car wrecked?" Omar asks, and I'm so glad he didn't ask how I'm doing.

"Oh, yeah, massively."

"She rolled it, idiot, of course it's wrecked," Adi says, whacking him with a cushion. "What was it like?"

"Really loud and really quiet."

"That doesn't make sense," Zayn replies.

"I know, but that's what it was like."

"The killer was really chasing you?" Adi asks. "It's just . . . Why did he leave you alive?"

I look at Zayn as she asks the question. His gaze doesn't falter, not even a tightening of his jaw. Just curiosity in those dark, guarded eyes. He's waiting for answers—same as me. I don't know if he's the one who can give them to me.

I'd maintain a poker face if I was guilty too.

"I have no clue why he didn't kill me. It would have been so easy. I mean, I passed out."

"Well, maybe that's why. Hear me out," Omar says. "This guy is a sick dude, right? Where's the fun in killing someone who's out of it?"

"That actually makes sense," Zayn replies. "Well done."

Omar flips him off.

"So, you're saying if he comes for us, we should play dead?" Adi asks, her voice high-pitched like she can't believe what crap is coming out of his mouth.

"I mean, don't randomly lie down on the ground, but yeah," Omar replies.

That makes me laugh, and I realize it's been a while since I've done that.

"You're going to end up dead," Adi tells him.

Scowling, Omar asks, "Why would you manifest my death?"

"I'm not, idiot, but your advice could get us all killed."

Omar kicks his feet up on the coffee table, always making

himself at home. "Whatever. Hey, Pen, next time you want to sneak out, you should call one of us. You shouldn't be alone."

"You're a terrible influence," Zayn tells him.

We've known this since we met him in kindergarten and he got us to paint ourselves green. The teachers tried to wash us up, but we still went home looking like the Hulk's love children.

"It was weird. As scared as I was, for, like, a second I wanted to confront him. To be brave and tell him just to come and get me."

"Not a great time to have a Jennifer Love Hewitt moment, Pen," Zayn says.

"Well, she does know what he did last October," Omar replies, chuckling at his own stupid joke.

I shake my head and wince at the pain. "Obviously I wouldn't actually be that stupid. But I'm over being scared."

For a second, I feel a surge of bravery. We can't live in fear forever. We can't give our town over to the darkness, and I won't allow whoever this is to make me hide out. For a whole year we've been scared.

Omar passes me a chocolate from the pumpkin-shaped bowl on my coffee table, trying to cheer me up. "You're safe now."

"The mayor's set up a memorial in the square tonight. Are you going?" Adi asks.

"She has? My parents haven't mentioned it."

"They probably don't want you to go," Omar points out. "Might not be a good idea, Pen. You know, since you nearly died and all."

"Stop being so damn casual about this," Adi says.

"I'm keeping it light. That's what Penny wants."

"I'm not staying here if the whole town is gathering for Noah, Ruby, and Mae," I tell them, pulling the conversation back.

It doesn't make sense for town events to be canceled and a curfew enforced only to then plan a big memorial in town. Plus, it's premature; the killer hasn't been caught yet. Unless they want the killer to show.

After my friends leave, and I'm still totally unsure what Zayn's deal is, I ask my parents about the memorial.

"It's not a good idea. I've already told the agents we won't be going," Mom says.

I lift my jaw, standing tall and holding my ground. They're going to try giving me some bullshit about needing rest. I've been resting for over twenty-four hours and, despite a lingering headache, slight nausea, dizziness, and a painful wrist, I'm okay. "Why, did they ask you if we'd go?"

"That's not important. All that matters is you rest and heal. You were in a serious accident."

"But I'm *fine*."

"The concussion and broken bone say otherwise."

"Mom, please. These were my school friends, Mae especially. She was always so kind to me. I want to be there. Besides, I have an FBI agent and you guys with me at all times now. I'd be safe."

Dad sits very still on the sofa, absorbing both sides of the argument. It's a shock that he's not a flat-out no. His brows knit together as he frowns like this is an impossible ask. But I can tell he wants to go. He knows the parents of Noah, Ruby, and Mae.

"Love, let's think about this for a moment. Penny wouldn't be alone," he says.

Mom gasps. "Are you serious?"

"Closure is important. I've spoken to the parents of every one of those kids. I've played soccer with Noah's dad and given Mae's mom a lift home when her car broke down. I would *never* put Penny in danger, you know that, but I don't believe she will be."

Mom chews her lip. "Right. All right. But you don't attempt to leave our side for even a second, Penny. I mean it. No more running to Nash or anyone else. You need to be smarter."

"Deal. Totally deal. Besides, the FBI wants me there because the killer might show up to see me, right?"

They exchange a look. Dad wrings his hands. "No one is using you as bait."

But that's what this is about. That's why I *want* to go. I'm the perfect bait. The killer spared me, for whatever reason, and I can't imagine he's thrilled about how yesterday went down.

"I'm going to get ready," I tell them, and shuffle upstairs.

I take a shower with a plastic bag over my wrist, awkwardly wash my hair, and get ready to leave.

My phone has been going off all day since word got out about my accident and attack. I only responded to a handful; I don't want to speak with people who only contact me for gossip; I know my messages would be screenshotted and shared in group texts all over school.

I'm not making it that easy.

"Nash is coming today," I tell my parents as we get into the car.

"All right," Mom says. "He can stand with us if you'd like?"

I'm sorry? I heard that, right? My hearing wasn't damaged in the accident. So, what's happening right now? Did it take a near-death experience to get them to ease up on him? Do they know I'll continue to find a way to see him? It's better to let that happen with their supervision.

Whatever it is, I'll take it.

"Er." I blink as her offer sinks in. "Sure."

Dad laughs from the driver's seat. A sound I've not heard in a while. "You'll both stay where we can see you."

That's the one, then. If I'm going to see Nash, it's best they keep an eye on us. Doesn't mean they're happy about it but when they see he's still the same, maybe they'll chill. They used to like him.

We park in the supermarket lot, and they walk on either side of me, two agents trailing close behind. We either look famous or like we're in an action film, walking away from an explosion.

The police presence is heavy. Every direction I look there are cops and feds. If the killer does anything here, they're a total idiot.

Nash and Grace stand at the edge of the square. Since it got out that they had legit alibis at the times of the murders, no one has said another bad word about them.

I can't help the small smile tugging at my lips at the thought of them being accepted in town again. They've been alone for too long. It just sucks that it took all of this to get here.

Then I feel bad because three people are dead.

It takes a second for me to notice town because I was so

focused on the Whitmores. But everything is gone. The square is now bare. No decorations, no hanging bats or dressed-up scarecrows.

A pile of pumpkins made up of each store's decorations sits off to one side. Now they're at the edge of the road, waiting to be disposed of. In their place are teddy bears and flowers and cards. Small tributes to Noah, Ruby, and Mae. The town letting their families know that we care.

Halloween has been canceled but the horror still hangs in the air like a bad smell.

It looks spookier now than it ever did with the decorations. A ghost town.

Adi, Omar, and Zayn are standing by Nash and Grace with their parents. No sign of the new uncle. Which makes sense considering his likeness to the guy who caused this same event to take place a year ago.

It's weird. It's suspicious. I don't trust Nash's intuition when it comes to him.

And I'm desperate to meet him.

"Hi," I say as we approach the merged groups.

If my friends' families don't like Nash or Grace, they don't make it obvious. They wouldn't be popular if they made a big deal out of it tonight, though.

My parents make small talk with the other adults. The agents split their attention between me and the surrounding area. They stay close as if they're waiting to pounce and cover me with their bodies if I'm attacked.

The killer is too smart for that.

Grace is the one to say hi as if only one of the Whitmore children can like me at a time. Nash is looking anywhere else.

"You look better than you did yesterday," she says.

"Yeah, I feel better than yesterday too. Sorry if the lying-in-the-road thing scared you."

She waves her hand. "I'll forgive you. I'm, um, glad you're okay."

"Thanks."

"Do you know what's up with this one?" she asks. "He's been in a mood since this morning."

Well, that would be because I made him call your psycho dad in prison.

Nash side-eyes me, an expression that I can read very clearly: *Don't say anything.*

"Can't blame him for feeling weird, right?"

"I guess. Mayor's here."

The town's pastor steps up to the podium beside the mayor and together they hold a moving service about grief, love, and resilience.

We're encouraged to stick together and look out for one another. It echoes something said last year . . . weeks before the town shunned Nash and Grace.

Once the service is over, people mill around, no one wanting to run off straightaway.

The only reason I'm still here is because my mom is talking to Mae's heartbroken mother. I watch her with a heavy heart as she wipes tears from her face, only to have fresh ones fall a second later. Her eyes are red and raw, and it doesn't look like she's slept for a second.

The atmosphere is somber, the laughter from the Halloween

fair having died days ago. Now people speak of tragedy in hushed whispers all around me.

We're all on edge, waiting for the killer to strike again. The police and FBI presence are supposed to make everyone feel safe but I haven't seen anyone who appears calm.

A lone witch's hat tumbles along the grass on a gust of wind. A forgotten decoration that was once part of a display outside Maxi's Stationery.

Dad and the two agents are still with me. The rest of them are watching. Walking around, trying to blend in as they look for whoever fits the profile of a killer.

I wish I knew what that was.

They've released vague information. They're looking for a male who blends into the community but will be absent for periods of time. They have a vehicle and are physically strong. They would have followed Jackson's murders and been obsessed with them.

If you exclude the Jackson obsession, they've described about 70 percent of the men in town.

A group of people congregate by the tributes to the victims, reading the notes and praying.

Mom stays with Mae's mom as they look at the stuffed animals, quite a few being horses since Mae liked to ride on her farm.

Zayn wraps an arm around my shoulder. "I'm splitting. See you tomorrow."

"What, you're leaving already?"

"Mom wants to. She keeps crying and just wants to be alone. I think she wants to get me out of here. See you later."

Nash and I both watch him leave with his mom. As does an

agent on the edge of the crowd. Could my friends be targets because I am?

"What do you think?" Nash asks, still not quite looking into my eyes. His posture is that of an ice sculpture and his attitude to me is just as cold.

"Hard to tell."

"Because he's not done anything to make you think he's guilty or because you don't want him to be?" The tone is snippy, making it crystal clear that I'm not forgiven.

"You surely understand that."

This time he does look at me and it's with a scowl deep enough to give him wrinkles. I'm certain that he has lots to say but it's too risky to mention Jensen when we're in public. It makes no sense to keep him secret. It's not like he was close to Jackson.

Why hide him?

"Come on, what do you actually think, then?" Nash asks.

It's a challenge. He wants to know if I'm going to tell anyone.

"I wish I knew. My head's all over the place. The concussion doesn't help; it's given me a wicked headache and nausea."

He turns to me, eyes full of worry, and my Nash is back. He does the same letting his concern override his anger thing my parents are so good at. "You're eating, though, right?"

"I'm eating," I assure him.

Chocolate and Jell-O count as a meal, right?

Grace steps in front of us. "Brant is over there. I'll see you at home, Nash."

He catches her wrist, looking from her to this Brant dude. "Wait, are you serious?"

"He'll bring me home later. I won't be alone so don't panic."

"Are you sure you can trust him?"

She huffs. "For the last year he's been the only one I can trust. Besides you, obvs. I promise I'm okay. You get home safe."

Nash nods and we both watch Grace push through the crowd and hug a guy I've seen around a couple of times but never paid attention to.

He has the lightest hair, nothing at all like Jackson's. I'm glad because that would've been way too weird.

"Maybe you should follow them," I say, chewing my lip. "We don't know that guy."

"No one is going anywhere," Mom tells us as she walks up. "Nash, do you need a ride if Grace is going with her friend?"

Nash does a stellar job of not falling over in shock. "Oh, no, thanks. I drove."

"Pastor Young is opening the church. We'll light a candle and say a prayer for your friends before going home. Come on, before word gets out and the place is packed. Rosenthal wants to get you home and I agree."

The agents follow as we walk with the pastor across the square and up the steps to the church. I shudder when the sky darkens in an instant as clouds band together, threatening to soak us.

I hold my head, looking up while the pastor unlocks the door.

"Penny?" Mom says. "Darling, I have your medication. We'll get you some water inside to take them."

"Yeah, thanks," I whisper. Boy, do I know it when the Tylenol is wearing off. "I'm good for now."

It's a total lie. My head feels like it's being drilled from the inside out, I'm exhausted, and the world is a little bit fuzzy. But I really do want to light a candle for Mae.

Nash holds my elbow as if I've broken a leg. But then I did tell him I'm suffering from the effects of the concussion. Dizziness is one of them too. One that I'm now experiencing.

We walk in and I pass the collection of candles. Melted wax stuck to the sides of dozens of white sticks. I blink hard to wipe away my blurry vision.

"Help her sit down, Nash. I'll get the medication and Andrew can get her water."

Omar and Adi hang back with their families, watching over me with concern. I've never been one to be in the spotlight . . . unless a piano is in front of me.

Nash guides me to a row of pews like a small child. "I can walk. It's just a headache."

"Humor me."

I lean on him as the pain in my head intensifies and my stomach flips over. I'm not so sure I'll be able to eat the takeout pizza Dad promised me tonight.

"Sit down ov—" Nash halts, his arms tightening around me.

"What?" I ask, rubbing my eyes.

Blood drains from his face and his eyes widen as he stares at something behind me.

"Move back!" he says, tugging me along.

His sudden outburst alerts the agents, who run the few yards toward us.

I look over my shoulder and just before Nash has gotten me out of the way, I see the outline of a body on the floor.

Surfer-style hair fanned around his head like he was thrown down. One hand covered in blood splatter raised above his head.

"Oh my god!" I fall into Nash's chest as he tugs me backward.

Billy Ross.

Body number four.

21

Ignoring the pulsing headache and sketchy vision, I stare off into the distance, trying to make sense of what we just discovered.

How long has he been there?

He wasn't at the memorial . . . at least I don't think he was. Adi is the one with a Billy radar.

"I've seen three of the four," I say as we sit in the small church hall. When my aunt got married, we used this room to get ready because my uncle wouldn't be able to see her from inside the chapel.

Now the only thing I will remember about this church is Billy's lifeless body.

Adi's going to be *crushed.* He was so shy around her but also so sweet. They never had the chance to go on a real date.

Mom and Dad are close by, talking to a cop, both animated in their distress. There was a fed was in the room with us when we found Billy, but we've still given statements.

Not many people were inside the church at first, so there's only a handful of us—as in my parents, me, Nash, and the pastor. Adi, Omar, and their families were behind us, so none of them saw anything. Thank the Lord that Adi didn't see. They were ushered out so fast, I don't know if she's aware that it's Billy yet.

Nash, leaning closer, whispers, "My dad called again."

Gasping, I look up. He's still a touch blurry around the edges, but I think my vision is getting better. "Did you speak to him?"

"No, I didn't answer but . . ."

"You wanted to."

His shoulders slump like he's admitted something deeply shameful, like he should be able to forget that Jackson's his dad. "It's sick, Pen, I know. I shouldn't want anything to do with him."

"He's your *dad*. Nothing will ever change that, and I think you've earned the right to ask him a few questions."

I don't know how he's managed to keep his distance. If it were me, I would demand answers.

Shaking his head, he replies, "I don't want to go there. I'll never forgive him, and it's not as if I'll like what he has to say."

"Maybe you don't have to like it. Maybe you just have to hear it."

"I don't know, Pen."

I stand and turn to him so I can try to reason with him and lessen his guilt when the lights go out. I blink in complete darkness.

"What's happening?" the pastor asks.

I strain to adjust to the dark, but my sight isn't the best today anyway. All I can make out are silhouettes. We're nowhere near the chapel with the candles now. The room is pitch-black. I'm on one side with Nash while the FBI agents answer questions from my parents and the pastor.

"Nobody panic, just stay still." I recognize the booming voice as the male agent who took my statement earlier. There's a click and then a beam from a flashlight. One by one, he checks that we're okay and then radios his team.

"Looks like a power cut, but we're going to get you outside. I need you to follow closely behind me."

I take Nash's hand and then my mom's to make a chain and all stick together.

"I'll go at the back," Dad says, putting his hand on Nash's shoulder.

Together we shuffle forward. I ignore the ball of anxiety in my stomach and the dizzy spell that almost makes my knees give out.

"What's that?" I ask, hearing a crackle in the distance. For a second I regret talking in case it's in my head. Another symptom of the concussion.

But it's not and somewhere ahead of us, someone yells, "Fire!"

The door in front of us opens and smoke billows through the opening like a flood.

I let go of Mom, stumbling to the side and choking as the smoke fills my lungs and stings my eyes.

I cover my face with my free arm, my cast scraping my forehead.

Panic settles in my stomach like it's part of me now, refusing to go away. I could be attacked by the killer or burned to death.

"Mom!" I cough out as thick smoke clogs my throat.

The flashlight shines around but there's no way of seeing properly. I stumble to the side and try to find my way out.

Muffled shouting and screaming fills the air but I can't make anything out.

Where is my mom?

Nash, still holding on tight to my hand, pulls me to the floor.

I drop heavy on my knees. Down here I can just about see his striking eyes as we lie on the stone. "Stay low and cover your mouth," he shouts through his fingers. "We need to get out."

"Where are my parents?!"

I can hear my mom, distraught as she calls for me, her voice breaking my heart because I can't see her.

"We'll find them. Let me get you out first!"

Nash tugs my arm, and I relent, letting him lead me away. We crawl along the floor, following the beams from the flashlight ahead of us. The church isn't huge, but it's full of smoke, and making it hard to see.

My heart pumps harder as I frantically search for the exit on one hand, an elbow, and my knees, choking on smoke and petrified that this is it.

Nash is beside me, sticking close. We move forward as fast as we can but I'm slower without the use of my wrist. I know where the side fire exit is and that's probably our best shot. If the pews are going up, the fire will take us whole.

Nash seems to have come to the same conclusion and leads us along the short corridor, which feels very long right now, and toward the exit.

"Mom! Dad!" I cough out. Nash grabs my arm and pulls me

along, not giving me a chance to look for them. I want to go back. Dad was behind me and Mom in front. Why wouldn't we have at least found her?

I can hear other people shouting, mostly my name because my parents are in here, too, but I can't see anything with smoke consuming the church.

But there is something my eyes pick out of the thick gray smoke. Behind us, a bright white mask.

"Nash!" I scream, gagging as my lungs burn and feel like they're about to give in and stop working. Every breath is a miracle at this point. There's very little oxygen that the fire hasn't stolen.

If the killer doesn't get us, the smoke might.

Nash grabs hold of me and shoves me toward the door faster. I can't move much, and my elbow slams against the stone floor as we shuffle as fast as we can. I instinctively want to stand and run, but it would be no use—the smoke is a blanket that covers everything.

I whimper, crying as I keep my head down low, knowing that at any second, I could be struck. But if we slow or turn around, we'll have no chance. This is our only choice.

We must be close now; we have to be. I move forward and look back, searching for my parents and trying to figure out where the killer is. My stomach clenches at how close the killer is to us. It would take him seconds, that's it. Two, three seconds and his knife could be plunged into my body.

Why isn't he bothered by the smoke? I can't see if he has anything behind that mask to help him breathe but he must.

His outline disappears as he retreats. Where's he going?

The voices I hear screaming my and Nash's names could be coming from any direction. My parents can't die because of me. I have to find them.

"There!" Nash shouts, nudging me sideways toward a door. I knew it was around here. "Where is he?"

I look over my shoulder, my heart missing a beat as I prepare to see him standing over us. But there is nothing but gray and the crackling of fire in the near distance.

He pushes and the door gives way. It has been used recently—hopefully by my parents. We fall through the door onto the freezing ground outside.

Coughing, I get to my feet in the open air. "Where did he go?" I choke out. "My parents!"

I scan the crowd. Rosenthal and her colleague run toward us.

"The killer's inside. I can't find my parents! You have to save them!"

Nash catches me as I try to run back inside.

"Mom! Dad!"

"Back up!" Rosenthal barks at Nash. "Don't let her move. Agent Jones here will ask you some questions. I'll find your parents."

"Where are they?" I sob, covering my mouth to cough.

We step back and the enormity of the fire hits me straight in the gut. Smoke pours from the church as fire engines battle to keep the flames down. Hoses spray water through smashed windows. Agent Jones asks us to describe everything that happened, then goes to help someone yelling his name.

"Stay here," he shouts over his shoulder.

"Did you smell gas in there?" Nash asks, clearing his throat.

"I . . . I don't know," I reply. "I only remember losing my parents and seeing the mask. How can the killer get out with the feds all over? Oh my god, Billy's still inside. He can't get out, Nash. He's dead."

"Shhh, it's okay," he says, but his eyes widen in horror. If they don't stop the fire, Billy's body will burn.

"Nash, he could've killed us," I say, sobbing into his coat.

"We're okay," he replies, his voice empty, sounding anything but okay. This is taking a toll on him too.

"Penny!"

Gasping, I turn in time to see my parents right before they scoop me up in a tight hug.

"You two are okay," Dad says, placing his hand on Nash's shoulder. "Thank God."

I nod and cough again. "We're fine. Did the pastor get out too?"

"Yes, he's fine. I'm so sorry, Penny. I couldn't find you and an agent pulled us out of the building."

"It's okay, I couldn't find you either."

"Thank you for getting her out," Dad says to Nash, shaking his hand.

Nash nods and it's the first time he's been shy in a long time. They won't be treating him like the enemy anymore. All it took was all of us almost dying in a fire.

"What do we do now?" I ask.

"There are paramedics checking everyone over. Come on," Dad says. "I want you two cleared."

“So much smoke,” I say. My eyes still sting from it . . . and I don’t think my throat and lungs will ever stop hurting.

We wait outside the charred church for what feels like hours. Wrapped in blankets and finally cleared by paramedics.

“This is insane,” Nash says. “They’ve been searching for ages.”

“How can there be no trace of the killer?” I rant. “He was in there! I saw him.”

“Are you sure, Penny?” Mom asks.

“Yes! Nash saw him too.”

“He was right behind us. Penny’s right, he was there.”

“What do you remember about him?” Dad asks.

Nash and I already answered this when the fed asked.

“Not much,” Nash replies. “I was too focused on getting away.”

I shrug. “Masked. That’s it.”

“Tall or short? Slim or built?”

I try to think back but there’s nothing but smoke and a mask. The day I saw him in the corn he was tall and built. “Tall and built. It was too hard to see properly.”

“How did he get out unnoticed?” Dad asks.

Good point. I have no idea.

“Well, there’s a back door that the pastor uses but wouldn’t the police and FBI have been there?” Mom says.

Rosenthal stops beside us and shakes her head. “Not necessarily. Our instant response was to get everyone out of the building and control the fire.”

How much of our conversation has she heard?

"We were out within minutes," Nash says. "Was there anyone on that door when Penny and I got out?"

"Right before," I say. "He disappeared just before we got out."

"I don't know, Penny. I'm sorry," Rosenthal says. "You are all free to go home. It's getting late. Nash, we will have an agent outside your house tonight."

It's almost midnight now and, yeah, I'm dead tired.

"You think I'm in danger?" he asks.

"Given your relationship to Penny and the fact that you escaped the fire with her, we cannot rule anything out. It's not a risk I'm willing to take."

The killer watched Nash get me out.

"It still doesn't make sense that I'm being targeted," I say.

"It's something we're still looking into. Until we have more answers, we need to protect you. That also extends to Nash and his sister. Who is . . . home?"

"No, she's went off with her boyfriend. Brant. They work together. I don't know his surname."

"We'll find them."

Good, and when they follow Nash to his house, maybe they'll find his uncle and start questioning him.

22

SATURDAY, OCTOBER 30

My friends are keeping me company because since yesterday, I feel on the edge of a panic attack. One more thing and I'll fall.

It's early morning on Devil's Night and they're here for breakfast since none of us are allowed to go out. I'm still dealing with the effects of smoke inhalation; the cough isn't helping my concussion headache, but at least I'm alive.

At least I wasn't in the building for long.

My mom leaves the kitchen, having plated up stacks of chocolate chip pancakes.

Adi hasn't done much besides stare at her hands. She's devastated by Billy's death.

"How are you doing, Adi?" I ask.

She shrugs one shoulder. "Don't know. It's weird. Doesn't feel like he's actually gone, but I know I won't see him again."

"I'm so sorry."

"Did he look like . . . Do you think it hurt?"

My stomach twists into a knot so tight I think I might throw up my two bites of pancake. It tastes like ash. "I . . . um . . . I don't think so."

There were stab wounds on his chest but not as much blood as what was on Noah and Ruby. Which would mean his heart stopped beating quite quickly, I assume.

Zayn turns to us and clears his throat. "Have you guys heard there's a party at Sarah's house?" he asks.

Sarah's parents are always absent, so it's not surprising that she's having a party, even now since she's so self-absorbed. I have a couple classes with her, when she bothers to turn up.

"Seriously?" I ask. "The killer murdered Billy yesterday, set fire to the church and almost killed a bunch more, and Sarah's partying?"

The fire was brought under control fast, and it hadn't reached the pews. Thankfully Billy's body wasn't burned. He will still look like him when he's buried.

"Pen, you must've been so scared," Adi says. It's the most understated thing she's ever said. It's the first time she's mentioned anything about me, her thoughts, rightly, on Billy. It means she's starting to join us and get out of her head.

"It was awful," I say, and shudder at the memory. "I couldn't find my parents and I felt like I was suffocating on the smoke. Then we saw the killer."

"You were lucky Nash was there and he knew where to go."

I nod. "We all know our way around that church, but I was lucky. I was panicking about my parents, so I don't know what would've happened to me if he hadn't been there."

"He saved your life," Omar says.

"Yeah, I think he did."

"I just got a notification about the party too," Adi says, holding her screen up and scoffing. "How disrespectful. Billy died yesterday! I hope karma gets her."

That's a pretty iffy thing to wish right now. Noah and Ruby weren't nice people. Karma could be wielding a knife.

"Nope." Omar shakes his head. "No way. I'm not going to any parties on Devil's Night. I will go from my house to Penny's house to my house again. That's it."

"I'm with him," Adi says. "I don't want to go to a party. Billy won't ever . . ."

"Will anyone even turn up?" I ask, giving Adi a side hug.

Zayn shrugs. "Apparently quite a few are. I wasn't suggesting we should go when I mentioned it, by the way. Rule one when there's a killer on the loose—*never* go to a party."

I shudder again at the thought of the killer finding out about the party.

"Should we tell someone?" Adi asks. "I kind of want to ruin it."

"They'll only move locations, you know that," Omar replies. He wiggles his brows, mischief shining in his dark eyes. "If we're calling it in, we should wait until the party has started."

We've been to a couple parties like that. The cops are called about a "disturbance" so you all leave, and then run to another house or to Benji's.

"You really want to snitch?" Zayn asks, smirking.

"They could *die,*" I say. "Who cares about being a snitch when—"

Raising his palms, he cuts me off. "Hey, I'm with you, Pen. If there's ever a time to be a snitch, this is it. Ryan said it starts at eight."

"So, I'll call just after eight," Adi says. The rest of us don't argue. It's right that she's the one to ruin their fun. She's doing it for Billy.

"Or Penny can just shout to the agents from her doorstep," Omar teases. "Where do they go for the bathroom?"

"Is Nash coming?" Adi asks, dropping a pancake on her plate and ignoring Omar.

"I messaged him this morning. I asked Grace, too, but I'm not sure."

I think he's still mad at me for making him call his dad. Or maybe for the fact that he now has an agent outside his house.

Last year being his friend made me a target; this year being mine does.

"I thought you and Nash were back to—" Omar snaps his jaw shut when Adi nudges him. Neither of them discreet. "What? Was that a secret?"

I roll my eyes. "We're friends but it's still . . . complicated."

I cut into my pancake and force myself to eat a third bite. The nausea from the concussion—plus the stress of everything that's happened—is slowly wearing off, but I still don't have much of an appetite.

"I can't believe the feds are no closer to catching this guy," Adi says between big mouthfuls of pancake. "I mean, how is he evading them? They were yards from him yesterday! If they'd done their job, Billy might still be here."

"We don't know that they're not," Zayn replies. "They would

hardly share all the developments. They don't release information about suspects until they have evidence."

That's true. I mean, no one else besides me and Nash know that they're looking into whoever called the cops to make them go to Nash's house the night I snuck out. Or the first night I snuck out, anyway.

"He's right, they must have someone in the frame. Four murders in a week." Omar shakes his head. "This guy must have left evidence by now."

I shrug. "He spent a lot of time with me when he ran me off the road and left nothing but a partial footprint that can't even be analyzed."

I can't believe that was only two days ago.

"This one has learned from Jackson's mistakes," Adi murmurs, her eyes downcast. "What if they never find him?"

"You think he's going to end up the only man standing in town?" Zayn asks, and it's probably the most Omar thing he's ever said.

She stares up at him, open-mouthed. "Really?"

"I'm just saying, eventually he'll be caught. You can't kill off an entire town."

Adi raises her voice. "No, but after being so close to getting caught by the feds, he might've skipped town."

"Okay, eat your pancakes!" Omar says. "Everyone remain calm and eat."

"Have you two pulled a Freaky Friday?" I ask.

Omar laughs and shrugs. Zayn does nothing but scowl at his plate.

As we eat, I watch my three best friends. Omar looks down at his phone as it dings with a notification. Adi stares off into space as she starts on her second pancake. At least she's eating. Zayn watches me like he's worried I'm going to drop dead.

"What?" I ask.

"You're pale."

"Seems to be the thing with me right now."

Omar slowly turns his head to look at Zayn. "She's been in an accident and then almost burned to death, dude, what do you expect?"

Plus, I was chased through a cornfield.

Can I get a little bit of grace?

"That wasn't an insult. You must've noticed how pale she is?"

"I have," Adi replies.

"Do I even need to be here for this conversation? It's been a rough week."

Omar laughs. "A rough week. Do you want us to leave so you can sleep?"

"I'll nap after breakfast."

I do want to be alone—as alone as my parents will allow—but when they're here, I know they're safe. But thirty minutes later, they're making excuses and walking to the door, wanting me to rest.

As if I'll be able to sleep. I spent last night tossing and turning.

"Straight home. All of you," I tell them.

"We all came together," Zayn says, his eyes sliding to our friends. "I'll drop Omar and then Adi."

My heart skips a beat. Zayn and Adi will be alone for the five minutes it takes to get from Omar's house to hers. He wouldn't do anything to her, even if he was somehow mixed up in all of this.

Come on, Penny, he wouldn't hurt anyone!

He's tall and muscular. Then so is Omar and Nash. And almost everyone else in sports at school. We're big on sports.

Me not so much anymore.

I'm not big on anything but surviving.

With uncertainty curling in my stomach, I grab Adi's hand. "Hey, I'll message you in a second."

"Okay . . . why?" she asks.

"I'm worried about you."

"I'll be okay, Pen. You don't need to keep tabs on me."

"Right. It's just . . . boy stuff."

"Ah," Omar says, and slaps Zayn's shoulder. "She doesn't want us in on this one, dude. 'Oh my god, Adi, does Nash love me or not?' " His voice is ten octaves higher, pretending—and failing—to be me.

"Come on, dumbasses!" Adi pushes them out of the house and toward Zayn's car.

The two agents watch the entire time. One gets out and stands beside the car.

"Everything okay, Penny?"

"Yeah, they're just leaving."

I close the door as they drive off and run to the kitchen for my phone. My parents are still in their office.

Penny:

hey you guys good?

Adi:

Tell me about Nash. i need the distraction.

I don't actually have any Nash news; I just need to keep her messaging me and I wanted Zayn to know I was going to be in constant contact with her.

Penny:

He's avoiding me. didn't reply to my invitation to breakfast

That'll do. Anything to keep her talking.

Adi:

U called him?

Penny:

Not picking up.

We go back and forth, discussing my faux issues with Nash. I feel massively insensitive talking about him when she's just lost Billy, but I know it will keep her talking.

After a few minutes, she tells me that they've just dropped

Omar off and are now heading for her house while also encouraging me to call Nash.

I tell her that I'm too scared in case he asks me to give him space. She's probably ready to tell me to grow the hell up—I would—but if her being irritated with me means I can make sure she's home safe, it's a small price to pay.

Suspecting one of my best friends is the worst, but Zayn has been odd recently.

I want it to be someone else. He can't be the one killing people. He was with me when I found Ruby and he was as shocked as I was.

How can you fake that?

He's never been a brilliant liar.

But then, I had no clue that he was speaking to and visiting Nash for months.

We all have secrets.

Adi finally tells me that she's home and Zayn is on his way to his place. And I can relax; the ball of anxiety uncurls a fraction.

In my room, I close the door and sit on my bed.

I call Nash, eager to find out if he's still mad at me and if there's anything I can do to fix it.

"Penny," he breathes, picking up on the first ring. "Now isn't a good time."

"Please, just a couple of minutes."

"What do you need?"

"We missed you at breakfast."

"I never said I was going to come."

Someone's cranky.

"We still missed you. Are you and Grace okay? And your . . . uncle?"

"We're fine. Grace came home from Brant's last night after Rosenthal got hold of her. Jensen is going to stay as long as the killer is around. Doesn't want us on our own."

Convenient.

"That's good of him."

Nash laughs down the line. "That almost sounded sincere."

"I do want someone to look out for you guys."

Like federal agents with guns who have taken an oath to protect citizens from their crazy uncles.

"But?"

I'm not the best liar and he can see straight through me. "But I'm not sure if he's the right person. The murders started after he arrived, Nash. Doesn't that worry you?"

"He's no more guilty of my dad's crimes than me or Grace are."

"I agree, totally. But you know *nothing* about him. Not really."

"I know he doesn't like my dad, more so after what he did, so that's good enough for me. The man is a teacher, Pen. He volunteers at homeless shelters."

"Do you know how many killers have been described as 'such a nice person' before they were caught?"

"It's *not* him," he says, exasperated.

"Where was he when Billy was killed?"

"I don't know. When his body was discovered, Jensen was home."

"How can you know that because you and Grace were at the memorial?"

"Penny, jeez, will you stop?"

"No. Nash, I understand that you want to believe he's innocent but be smart about this!"

If I lost everyone but my sibling and an uncle turned up, I would want to believe that he was good too. I don't get how he can ignore all the red flags, though. They're blowing at full mast.

"Stop. Please, stop."

"All right. I'm sorry. Are you okay?"

"Yeah. Are you . . . after yesterday?"

There is absolutely no time to stop and worry about how I'm doing. "Fine. That was scary. I don't think my heart will ever be normal again. I'm glad I was with you, though. That would've sucked so bad if I was there alone. I'm not sure I would be here now."

It was a few minutes tops, but it felt like a lifetime.

The killer cut the power, doused the service room in gas, and lit the place on fire. Then he vanished without a trace like the morning he drove into me.

"Yeah," he replies. "I'm glad we were together too. I think I'll smell smoke for the rest of my life. It lives in my nose now."

I laugh. "Yeah, same. Nash?"

"Listen, I've got to go."

"Wait. Have you heard there's a party tonight?"

"*Don't* go," he says, and hangs up.

Wasn't planning to.

I spend the day in my room out of the way. My parents pop in almost constantly to check on me.

All I do is snack on M&M's when my nausea allows and trawl social media for everything to do with the case.

I get more details for the party tonight. It's at Sarah's unless the cops shut it down. The alternate location hasn't been revealed. There are a few places they could go but Benji's is the most likely since a lot of parents are staying home. I'm hoping at least one of them is smart and they send everyone to another location when they arrive.

That way the killer won't know where they are.

Assuming the killer is an adult like Jackson.

Hello, Jensen.

Nash and Grace could be sleeping in the same house as a killer. Would he kill his own family? It'd be super risky. Like Nash once said, killing someone close to you is the fastest way to get arrested.

Jackson never hurt them, and he had plenty of opportunity.

I can't believe no one knows about him. Jackson didn't have much of a background because his parents both died before he was eighteen. Nash said that Jensen had left before that.

The sun sets slowly. I watch it descend and disappear behind the neighbor's house. My heart goes with it because it's now Devil's *Night.* One year ago to the day that Jackson killed two people. As morning broke on Halloween, he was arrested.

I hope that this will be over by sunrise, but I don't think it will be. Why would he stop when Jackson did? What's to say that Jackson would've stopped if he weren't caught?

• • •

By eleven that night, I'm going out of my mind. My parents are asleep. The agents have swapped; this time one agent is joined by a cop.

I told Mom it's probably because they want as many agents as possible out there tonight. She told me to go to bed and not think about it.

Like that's possible.

I lie in bed on my side, my back to the door so I can pretend I'm asleep if they come in. Unlikely, though, as they sleep heavily.

I've sent a message to Nash and Adi but neither of them has replied. Omar's online, posting TikToks and comments. Zayn has been quiet, but I don't really know what to say to him. Either my gut is off and I'm an awful friend or he's mixed up in this and I've lost him too.

Zayn and Nash both spend a lot of time alone.

Don't think about that.

Both have been with me during . . . discoveries, and Nash was in the church when we saw the killer. Zayn had left.

Stop. Thinking. Like. That.

Zayn has never made me doubt him before. To be fair, he's probably not made me doubt him; it's the whole situation. The call, secret meetings with Nash, and tracking my phone.

A message flashes from a number I don't recognize.

I hesitate for a second before opening it.

It's a picture.

My breath catches in my throat.

Slowly, I sit up and stare at the screen, willing it to be a joke.

I rub my eyes, hoping the concussion is making me see things. But it's not. I can see clearly. The picture is Adi. Hands bound, blood trickling down her forehead, eyes closed, tears staining her cheeks, lying on the back seat of a car.

Unknown:

See you at the party

Adi no!

There is no threat of what will happen to Adi if I alert the police.

It's not needed. I've seen what this person can do.

My hand trembles so hard that I drop the phone onto my mattress and scramble to pick it back up.

The killer has Adi.

Oh my god. *Think.*

I have to help her.

How the hell am I going to get out of here with the feds parked in my drive?

It's cold, so their car door will likely be shut, the window wound up. If I'm silent, I have a shot. I'll hop the back fence into the neighbor's yard and hope that I'm not seen.

I fly out of bed and pace my room on tiptoes. My mind has gone blank; there's nothing there but tumbleweed and blind panic.

Adi, Adi, Adi. I don't know how hurt she is. She looked like she was sleeping, so he must've knocked her out.

I have to go to the party but what happens when I get there?

This person didn't say which room in Sarah's house to go in, and I only saw Adi in the back of a car. I don't even know who it is or where they'll be.

I change quickly, putting on sweats and Nash's hoodie that I stole last year. Dark colors. I put my phone on silent and creep downstairs, leaving the lights off so I don't alert the agent and cop outside.

Walking through the kitchen, I grab a knife from the block. I hold it for a second and watch the soft light from the moon outside glow against the blade. I look out the window to the darkness of my garden.

The moonlight isn't going to help me escape but I think I'd be more scared if it was total darkness out there. I'll just have to be extra careful not to get caught. My neighbor has a bushy yard; they're always out there gardening.

It's all I've got, so it'll have to work.

Adi's life depends on it, and I won't let her down.

I walk to the back door and stop by the counter. There's a small notepad and a pen. I could leave my parents a note in case I don't come back.

No. Don't think like that.

I pop a couple of prescription pills. The last thing I need is my head or my wrist slowing me down. They scratch my already tender throat, but I ignore the pain and without a single thought of self-preservation, I unlock the door and step into the cold night.

There's no light coming from inside, so I haven't woken them up. Yet.

Keep going. He has Adi.

I walk along the back wall of the house to the fence and then head down to the end of our property. The fence is high, but I'll be able to use a chair to hop it. I pocket the knife and drag the chair with me, hearing the gentle scrape of the metal leg on the grass.

Before I swing my leg over the fence, I take one look back at my house and wonder if this will be the last time I see it. I press my hand to my chest, pushing down the heartache and a sob that might give me away.

I jump down the other side into the neighbor's garden and shuffle along their fence through many bushes. I don't hear a car door, so I've not made enough noise to alert the feds in my driveway.

The killer took Adi before eight, as she was going to call the cops on the party right around then. Now it's almost midnight.

That's four hours he had her before sending me that picture.

Has she been passed out all that time?

I can't dwell on that, or I'll lose focus.

This guy hasn't been torturing his victims, as far as I know. It looks like he just stabs them. My heart pounds harder at the thought of Adi being with him for hours already.

She must've been so scared.

When I get past the house, I run. Sarah's house is only a couple blocks from mine, hidden like Nash's, only on the opposite side of town. I'm getting farther away from someone I know would help me. He might be mad at me right now but if I was in danger, he wouldn't hesitate. I *know* that.

Vapor pours from my mouth as I pant with the effort it takes to sprint, flat out, for the two blocks. I pass the last row of houses and see the start of Sarah's property. Her family lives on a lot of land but her parents work in the city and spend most of their time there.

She has a big house and acres to herself most of the time.

Before the murders, I used to think she was so lucky. Now, if I were her, I would be scared all the time.

I stop dead halfway along her drive.

Something's not right.

Turning slowly, I look around and see nothing but grass and trees. The air is still and quiet. The only sound is from the rustling of some final leaves that refuse to yield to fall.

Where is the music? Where is the light inside her house? Why are there no drunk people throwing up in her yard?

The party isn't here anymore. I don't know what to do. I can't go home. Adi is somewhere with this guy, and I can't leave without her.

With my pulse thudding wildly, I move closer to the house and ignore my gut telling me to run. I listen hard but I can't hear a sound.

I check my phone again, looking for any notice of the venue changing. Adi must've called it in and then . . . what? The killer took her from her house?

It doesn't make sense.

She was under house arrest too. The killer shouldn't have been able to get near her.

Unless . . . Zayn.

She would leave with him.

My skin prickles with goose bumps as the temperature plummets.

I look over my shoulder as I walk around the house, my feet gently padding on the damp grass.

At this point, I don't know what I'm walking into. But there's no time to stop and think it through when Adi is in danger. I'd never forgive myself if I was too late.

She might already be dead. It's not something I really want to consider as I walk around alone in the middle of the night to meet a killer.

Adi and I are going to need each other to get away. That is, unless she's still unconscious and I have to drag her.

With one busted arm.

After I disarm the killer alone.

What the hell am I doing?

I can't do this alone.

As I unlock my phone to call Nash, it dings with another message.

The same number.

Two words.

Unknown:

Come in

I gasp, my hand flying to my mouth, and I can say with total certainty that I do *not* want to go in there. Like, I would rather take math tests every day for the rest of my life than go in there.

Sarah's house has always been somewhere you just walked in; the parties are endless, and she has everything you could want or need, including a cinema room and a gym.

Now it's more like a haunted house.

I approach the front door, looking up at the security cameras that face the porch, and slide my phone into my jeans pocket. In my hoodie is the knife. It hasn't poked a hole through the material yet, so I don't think I made the best decision grabbing that one.

It's too late now. Hopefully I won't have to use it. I don't want to.

Opening the door, I take one quick look behind me in case he's waiting to pounce while I'm going inside.

He must be inside, though, because there's no one out here. The trees are too far away. I didn't look around the house to see if the car is there, but why message and tell me to come in if he didn't want me to?

This is his endgame.

God, I don't want to be part of it. Somehow I've gotten myself mixed up in whatever is happening. Maybe because I found the first two bodies. He could've then focused on making me a lead in his movie.

It's not a role I want.

I make my way into the kitchen and flick the light, taking shallow, even breaths. The room is super bright with the white walls, cupboards, and countertops.

But there's no killer.

No blood.

No sign that they've been in here.

I look back to where I've been, keeping an eye on what's happening behind me, too, and then move forward. Her house is too big, and there are too many rooms for my eyes to be everywhere but I'm trying.

Poking my head around the door to the living room, I flick

the light next to me, and my hand shoots to my mouth to cover a scream.

Jesus.

In the corner of her living room is a life-size cutout of Jason Voorhees. There are Halloween decorations on every wall. It must've been for the party. Where did it move to?

My stomach churns.

Not a real person. It's just cardboard. I let out a breath and wring my hands. My wrist aches and I know it won't be long before the pain is back if I keep using it, despite the meds.

Whatever, my wrist can wait. Adi is relying on me to help her.

I want to shout her name but if she's not still out of it, she might be gagged. The killer will know where I am based on the fact that I'm leaving a trail of lights behind me.

It's a dead giveaway.

When there's nothing in the bathroom, cinema, or gym, I know I have to go upstairs.

I stand at the bottom of the steps and listen to my heart thudding away.

For Adi, I tell myself over and over.

She would walk up there and confront a killer for me, no questions asked.

The house seems smaller now as I make my way to the second floor. It's darker and less inviting. Has it always been like this or has the killer ruined it? What will Sarah's parents do if Adi and I die in here tonight?

I reach the top and as I'm about to open the first door, which I think might be a guest bedroom, my phone dings again.

Startling, I slam myself back into the wall and reach for the knife in my pocket.

It's just the phone. It's fine. It's fine.

I only have one good hand and it's not my dominant one. My fingers brush the wooden handle of the knife as I let it go and take a breath to settle my nerves.

There's another message on my phone.

Unknown:

waiting for you

I kind of want to reply and ask which room to save me the mini heart attack at opening every door and anticipating a knife-wielding freak show on the other side.

But I'm already here and don't want to play into it anymore. Besides, I wouldn't believe what he told me anyway.

This might be how I die but if I'm going down, so is this asshole. I open the recording app, set it up, and put the phone back in my pocket. If I die, the cops will find this and hear everything. I'll say their name to ensure the cops get the right person.

Then I place my hand on the door handle and push it open.

Shouting, I take a step back in shock.

"Nash," I breathe.

23

Dashing forward, I drop to the floor where he's lying by the bed, a trickle of dried blood on his head just like Adi. There's a red patch on the cream carpet underneath him.

He groans and tries to push himself up.

"Nash, are you okay? Who did this to you?" I ask, helping him get up. He leans heavily on me as we slowly stand. He doesn't seem in a hurry to get away.

What the hell is going on?

"Nash!"

"My head," he mutters, rubbing his temple and looking around. "Asshole whacked me as I was taking the trash out and I woke up . . . Where are we?"

"We're at Sarah's. The killer lured me here after sending a picture of Adi unconscious in his back seat. Where were the cops? You were supposed to have someone outside your house."

"What? God, the cops left. Got a call but said they'd be back."

"The killer lured them away. Why didn't they do that with me? The feds are still sitting outside my house."

He shrugs, blinking heavily. "They believe you're a target, so the feds won't leave you."

"No one else is here. The party must've moved."

"What?" He rubs his head again and groans. "Damn, this hurts. Wait, you said Adi's unconscious? Where is she? Why are we here? Is Sarah doing this? I'm so behind. All this must've happened while I was out, so in the last..." After looking at his watch, he adds, "Like, thirty minutes ago. Unless you just didn't call me."

"Take a breath. Everything happened so fast, Nash. I don't know where she is or why we're here. I don't think Sarah has anything to do with it."

"So why here?"

"This is where the party was supposed to be." I glance back at the door. "Have you heard anything?"

"Nothing until you called my name. What does this guy want?" He stands steadier, letting go of me and supporting himself.

"Your head is really going to hurt tomorrow."

"Thanks, Pen. I needed to hear that right now.... What're we going to do first? Look for Adi or go get help?"

"Calling anyone is too risky when he still has Adi. I guess we keep searching the house. Do you feel up to fighting if he jumps us? I'm not sure I can take him alone."

Arching his eyebrow, he smiles and takes a step forward, testing how stable he is on his feet. "I'll take him. You stay the hell back."

"I'm not leaving you al—"

"You need to get Adi. You said she was out of it in the killer's back seat. She might be badly hurt. This is the plan. I'll go for him. You find her and get as far away from this house as you can. Okay?"

"I don't have a car. And, I mean, not even my parents' car since I totaled mine."

"And I got a ride in his vehicle, I guess." Nash winces. "There must be something you can use here. Sarah has quads in her barn. There were a couple wagons when we were here last summer. Remember, Omar and Zayn were racing down the hill in them."

"You want me to chuck Adi in a wagon and run away?"

"Do you have a better idea?"

I do not.

Shaking my head, I reply, "Fine. That's the plan. I have a knife on me."

He does a double take as he's about to walk out of the room and clutches his head.

"No sudden movements. I learned that the hard way with my concussion."

"A knife?"

"When you're summoned to meet a serial killer, you come prepared." I take the knife out of my pocket and hold it up. I'm not sure if I'm trying to prove to him that I'm serious but I feel kinda silly right now. "This is your hoodie. I'll try not to poke a hole in it," I say lightly.

"Do not hesitate to use it if he comes for you. Which rooms have you checked?"

"Downstairs is clear. This is the first room I've come in up here."

"All right." He inhales for a long time. "Stay behind me."

We walk out of the room and cross the large landing. There's a door opposite this one that I have absolutely no desire to go inside. I don't want to keep doing this; the anxiety creeping up my throat is strangling me.

The house is too silent.

Nash looks over his shoulder as he places his hand around the handle. I nod once and he pushes it open. We both step inside, seamlessly stepping in opposite directions, instinctively knowing that this guy can't split himself in half and take us at the same time.

The room floods with light when Nash snaps the switch. Another bedroom, Sarah's judging by the numerous *Stranger Things* and Harry Styles posters.

That's all there is in here, though.

No creepy Halloween decorations and, thankfully, no killer. I don't know if my heart can take many more scares.

"Penny, call him so we can hear where he is," Nash says, stepping behind me so that he's blocking the door. He'll be the first one the killer reaches if he comes at us from wherever he is in the house.

"Are you kidding me?"

"He messaged you, right?"

"Yes, but I don't want to call him!"

"Give me your phone and I'll do it."

"Do you really think it won't be on silent? Or that he'll answer?"

Holding his palm out, he says, "There's one way to find out."

I hand him my phone because I'm not going to be the crazy

one here. Except for the fact that I'm here and that's hardly the action of a sane person.

Nash scowls at my phone, probably seeing the picture of Adi. Maybe the record app too. "Didn't you say she was tied up?"

"Yeah, she is." I tap the screen but it's facing him, so I have no idea if I'm anywhere near Adi.

"Look," he says, flipping the phone around.

I squint as I look closer. Her hands are together and bound. "What?" I breathe as I finally see. The rope around her hands isn't tight. It's loose, like it's barely touching her. "Maybe he just didn't tie it tight enough."

"Yeah, maybe . . ."

My heart beats harder at his tone. That "yeah maybe" was unconvincing. Nash suspects Zayn and *Adi*.

I shake my head. "No, don't even go there. She is not part of this. She wouldn't hurt Billy, especially. Neither of them would kill anyone. They're my best friends."

"We need to move, Penny."

"She's not behind this. We have to find her." I snatch my phone back. "You weren't tied up. How do you explain that?"

"I was out of it. You're right, maybe he knew she wouldn't be able to fight back so didn't bother securing the rope."

"I am right," I tell him, and turn so we can check out the rest of the rooms. His accusation of my best friend has irritated me so much I'm filled with renewed courage.

"I'm still not leaving you alone with her," he mutters under his breath as we open the door to another room.

"Ah!" I shout, leaping back and slamming against Nash's chest.

Written in what looks very much like blood on the mirror is one word: BENJI'S.

"Nash . . ."

"Yeah, I'm seeing it. This asshole wants to take us on some sick treasure hunt." He turns to look at me. "There's no electricity in the old theater, Penny. It's a bad idea. Let's just call the feds."

"What do you think he's going to do to Adi the second he hears sirens or sees flashing blue lights? Besides, if the party has moved there, there will be a generator."

He shakes his head. "We can't go in there alone with just your tiny knife."

"I don't see you with a weapon."

"I didn't have time on account of being out cold on the floor!"

I chuck my hands up. "Let's go."

There's no time to stop and argue with him. I race down the stairs and out the front door. Nash is right behind me.

"It'll take about fifteen minutes to get to Benji's. What if we don't make it?"

"He wouldn't be doing all this if we wouldn't be able to make it. Why get you to find me first, though? You didn't get a message about me, right?"

"Nothing about you. We need to keep out of sight, stick to trees at the side of the road so we're not seen," I tell him.

We step into the ditch along the main road and walk in the squelchy mud.

At least I'm nowhere near my accident site. I don't think I'm ready to see that again. Unless I close my eyes at night, then I'm right back there. The fear I felt that morning isn't something I will ever forget.

As scared as I am tonight, it's not on the same level.

Not yet anyway.

"You're mad at me," Nash says.

"No, I get it. Besides, you're still mad at me."

"I don't want Adi to be involved in this either, you know? She's my friend too. I'm not mad about the calling my dad thing anymore. He didn't try to reach me yesterday."

I don't turn around because it's dark enough out here and I'm trying to walk in an uneven ditch.

"How do you feel about that?"

"I don't want anything to do with him."

"He won't ever stop being your dad."

"I don't need a dad. Grace and I are doing fine."

"With Jensen."

"He's not living with us."

"Wait, Grace! Where was she when you were attacked?"

"Passed out on the sofa after talking to Brant for two hours solid on the phone."

"And the uncle?"

He chuckles under his breath. "The uncle is back home, three hours away, covering a couple classes this week for some dude whose wife is giving birth early."

That's a good story. Backed up with the woman in labor. Who would question that? Well, me, that's who. It's a bit convenient that he's gone on Devil's Night.

"When's he back?"

"November fourth is when his coworker is back, so unless the killer is caught, he'll stay home until the holidays. He asked us if we want to move in with him."

"What?" This time I do turn around, and Nash almost walks into me. "You can't leave."

"Why not? Grace and I are hardly welcome here."

"But . . . we've just started hanging out again. All of us. No one said anything when you were at the memorial."

If I sound desperate, it's because I am. They can't go.

"Can we deal with this later?"

Right. Adi needs us more right now. I place my hand over the knife in my pocket and trudge along the ditch again. The air is much colder now. I can feel the crisp grass under my feet when we pass the muddy ground.

"Penny, are you going to be able to use that knife?"

"If it's life or death, yeah, I'll use it. I can still grip; it just hurts to right now."

I'm not giving up my knife for anyone or anything.

"Okay."

We take the back way, avoiding the renovated part of town. The remaining buildings all sit around an identical grassy square. The movie theater is the closest one to the new town.

"What's the plan?" I ask.

He clears his throat and looks me dead in the eye. "We go to a party, I guess."

I don't have a good feeling about this.

24

We walk up to the first step and take in the looming, derelict building in front of us. It's never appeared so sinister until tonight. Covered windows and chipped brick and cobwebs so thick it looks like ice has settled on the awnings. I check my watch. Eleven-forty-five. Not long until Halloween morning.

A cold shiver rattles down my spine. "The party will be in theater room three. Same as always. We stick together and find Adi," I say.

"Do you think the killer is partying?"

I shrug. "Adi was out of it, so she's probably somewhere else, still in his car maybe. The message said come to the party."

"So we start there. See if someone is looking out for us when we get inside. We have to get him to take us to Adi."

"Should we split up? You find Adi and I'll go to the party?" I ask.

"Okay, I'm going to pretend you didn't suggest that."

"Nash, we don't know how long she has."

"And he told you to come to the party. We need to play by his rules for now because we don't know what it means for Adi if we don't."

"He didn't tell you to come with me."

Nash tilts his head to the side and looks at me like I'm simple. "He sent you to me first."

I sigh in frustration, second-guessing myself and not knowing what to do.

"Penny, he knows we're together, so let's not deviate. Should we call Zayn and Omar to help?" He frowns and adds, "Or at least Omar. Hold on, we call Zayn and see where he is. Before we go inside and it's obvious we're at the party."

"What if the killer sees we're making a call? He could be watching us from a gap in the boarded windows right now."

"He never told you not to call anyone."

"You don't think it's implied?"

"Oh, it's heavily implied," he replies, and holds his hand out for my phone.

"Where's yours?"

"Back home, I guess." He taps a few buttons, knowing my passcode, and calls Zayn.

I glance back at the building, knowing we have to go in there very soon. Adi might be upstairs. I can't think about what might keep her where she is.

"Hey," Nash says, bringing me back from my thoughts. "Yeah, it's Nash . . . She's with me. Where are you?"

"What's he saying?" I whisper.

Nash holds his finger up, telling me to wait. I don't do waiting very well. I'm crawling out of my skin on the sidewalk, needing to get going.

"We're being careful. No one knows she's with me." He laughs but it's a bit hollow. It'll probably convince Zayn, though. "I'll take her home and make sure she gets in safe."

He hasn't told Zayn where we are, so he probably assumes we're at Nash's house. I don't think he'll be able to hear the music down the phone. Nash no longer has Find My enabled on his phone either. I don't know how else he would know where we are.

While Nash chats as if he's having a regular conversation, I look around, scanning the few windows in the theater that look out our way. Streetlights from the town drift this way and give enough light for me to see if there's anyone lurking around.

"Yeah, dude, see you later."

Nash hangs up and gives me the phone back.

"Well?"

"He said he's at home."

"You don't sound convinced."

"Maybe. I could hear music, but I don't know if it's the same as what'll be in there. He could be playing some at home . . . He also could've gone in another theater room to take the call. There's no way to tell."

"Excellent. So we can't rule him out. I *really* want to rule him out, Nash."

He sighs. "I know. I do too. Ready for a party?"

"No. You?"

"No. Let's go."

"You've got to be kidding me," I breathe as Nash pulls the door open. Music drifts through the building, bleeding onto the street.

Nash and I step into the theater, quickly closing the door to contain the noise, and pass a couple people hanging around in the foyer, laughing. The smell of cheap beer hangs in the air.

"Hey," a couple of them say to Nash, his old teammates not caring that he's been absent for months or that his dad's a murderer.

Nash nods, not giving them a chance to strike up a conversation because now is not the time, and we walk through the door to theater three.

My breath catches as we scan the room from the doorway. Most people inside are dressed up.

Monsters dance to "Anti-Hero," holding cups in the air, sloshing beer everywhere. A few have masks, most face paint. In the low, colorful lighting and dark costumes, it's nearly impossible to tell who anyone is. The generator Sarah must've taken from her farm will be whirling away. If we're lucky it won't cut out early like last time.

But we're not lucky.

"Nash . . ."

"Yeah," he replies.

We have no idea who the killer is and there's no way of telling even if we find someone watching.

"Do you think he'll be in *that* mask?"

Someone bumps into me and walks past. Nash tenses and looks over his shoulder to see who it was. Someone in a black cloak with the hood up over their head and face painted like a vampire.

"I don't think that's him," I say.

"Why?"

"Not tall or built enough . . . and might actually be a girl. Hard to tell with the hood," I tell him as we both watch whoever that was disappear around the wall.

"What's past there?" Nash asks the football guys who're laughing and teasing each other about failed throws.

One shrugs. "Dunno."

"Toilets," the other says. I don't recognize him at all, so I think he must go to another school.

"Should we follow?" I ask Nash.

"You don't think it's the right guy."

"It's definitely not the person who chased me through the cornfield or ran me off the road."

"Then let's keep moving inside. Watch out for anyone with the mask. Stay close."

Swallowing a rock-hard lump in my throat, I move ahead, and Nash walks right behind me like a bouncer.

I scan the crowd of people, my eyes moving quickly past people with painted faces and any costume that isn't black with a plain white mask.

I'm totally on edge, my heart wild against my rib cage as I try to find the killer. He could be tucked away in a dark corner, watching us search for him. What's the plan when we find him?

Should I cause a scene or silently follow to wherever he wants us to go? He can't want us to stay in here.

Something doesn't feel right . . . and I don't just mean the obvious.

"Nash, I don't like this," I say over the music.

"I'm with you."

What's the point of making us come to a second location if Adi is somewhere else? She has to be here. My fear grows, doubling with every step until I'm sure my lungs are going to pop.

"Nash," I say, taking a ragged breath and grabbing his wrist.

We press on, squeezing past a group of people dressed as serial killers from different movies. I look from faces to hands, watching out for any weapons. All anyone seems to have in their hands is either beer or their phones.

Nash moves deeper into the room, half pushing me along because I've completely changed my mind. I want to go back home and get into bed. Not that I would, of course, because I have to get Adi out of here.

"Anything?" Nash asks.

"No, I don't recognize anyone."

Literally. Not a single person, nor a single killer. I remember broad shoulders and height. A couple of the guys on the football team and some of the sportier types fit but I haven't seen those guys here yet.

Unless it's the one who told us he doesn't know where the vampire went.

"Nash, could it be . . . what's his name? Outside in the lobby. Chad or Chace? I can never tell them apart."

Nash shrugs. "It's Chad, but you've seen this guy. Could it be him?"

"Same build. Maybe he does know what's in that room and he's working with the vampire . . . Don't look at me like that. My mind has been doing this all week."

Nash looks over his shoulder at the same time the dance floor erupts. People all around me throw their hands up, spilling beer all over the place, and sing along to "Thriller" at the top of their lungs.

I'm shoved to the side and my grip on Nash's wrist is broken. He turns back to find me but a group next to him decides this song needs a mosh pit, and he disappears into the crowd.

"Nash!" I shout as I'm knocked backward. My voice is drowned out by the music and singing. If the cops didn't know about the party, they soon will. Or at least, that's what I'm hoping.

I push on my toes and try to look over witches' hats and devil horns. A sea of Halloween characters move as one like a wave, creating a barrier between me and Nash.

I stumble forward, trying to push between a solid wall of skeletons and victims with realistic gashes on their faces and fake blood-soaked clothes.

"Move!" I shout, but no one pays any attention to me. "Nash!"

God, will this song just finish already?

Craning my neck to find Nash through the crowd, I spot the mask and blood drains from my face.

Standing near the door, tall broad shoulders, dark clothing, plain white mask. Staring me dead in the eye.

He's come for me.

I know what I have to do but every cell in my body wants me to get the hell out of here.

Stepping forward, I weave my way through the crowd slowly as people are still moving as one. The room is so hot the air clogs in my throat.

I press on, using my arms to push through the stupid mosh pit.

Where did Nash go?

As I move closer, the masked man retreats from the theater room. I shove my way forward quicker so I don't lose him. Running toward the killer goes against every instinct I have.

I burst into the lobby and find no one. No Nash, no Chad, no other team members . . . no killer.

Turning around, I look for any signs of the other theater rooms being used. The dim glow from the portable light doesn't do a lot in the large area but it's better than nothing.

I look up in time to see a door closing on the second floor.

Am I supposed to go up there without Nash?

Nope.

I turn around, looking into the theater room.

"Penny!" Nash shouts, shoving someone who just bashed into him.

Moving forward, I run to him. "Where were you?" I ask. "The killer was in here. He's gone upstairs. We need to follow!"

"Whoa." He looks toward the door as if he can see where he went. "I lost you in the crowd. I was looking for you."

"Come on, we need to go up."

Before we can take a step, we hear frantic screams over the music. I look over my shoulder and a cloud of purple smoke fills the room, heading right for us like it has a grudge.

"Run, Pen!"

We're knocked and shoved as everyone pours through the doors of the theater room and into the lobby.

"It's the cops!"

"It's the killer!"

"No one say shit to anyone!"

"Get out and go home!"

"He's coming for us!"

I cough as the colorful smoke fills my lungs. I cling to Nash harder, my mind tugging me back to the church.

Nash pulls me out of the crowd that's sprinting for the side door. A couple guys are by the main entrance redirecting everyone to the side exit down the alley. Even with the threat of a killer among us, we still can't have parents or cops knowing we snuck out.

Smoke flows out of the theater, following behind the crowd like it's determined to swallow us. Thin purple vapors float toward the ceiling.

With a deep breath, I head straight up the stairs.

"Where to first?" Nash asks, running to catch up.

"The room with the broken cabinet. That's the door I saw move when I came out here."

Downstairs quickly falls into silence as the music stops and the last few people scurry home. I can't even hear anything outside, no low murmur of voices. Everyone is being extremely quiet as they sneak back out of the theater.

"Erm, where's that room?"

Right, he wasn't with us when we came in here last time.

"Here." I shove the door open and my stomach clenches at the sight of an adult male body sprawled out on the floor.

"Penny!" Nash shouts, yanking me back and coughing out a sob.

"No! No!"

Nash falls to his knees, staring at the lifeless body of his uncle, who should be at work. I step into the room, fisting the knife in my pocket . . . but the killer isn't here anymore.

Jensen is worryingly still and slumped on the floor but . . . he doesn't look like the other ones did.

He's not as pale. The blood around him is fresh, bright red and slowly trickling from a stab wound in his abdomen.

"Penny," Nash breathes. His voice rattles, and I desperately want to wrap my arms around him and tell him that it's going to be okay. But there is no time for grief. We have to get Adi and get out of here.

But we can't just leave him.

"Something's not right," I tell him, stepping forward again. My breath hitches and I tighten my grip on the knife.

Would one stab wound, resulting in a small amount of blood, be enough to send you to the ground?

Behind me, I hear Nash jump to his feet. "Whoa, what do you mean?"

I step closer again and curl my fingers around the handle of the blade. "Keep a lookout, Nash."

"What are you doing?"

I crouch down and stretch out my bad arm to check for a

pulse. If he is the killer and jumps me now, I'll stab him with the other hand.

As I get inches away, Jensen gurgles and his eyes open, rolling back into his head.

Nash and I shout. I fall back on my butt and shuffle my legs to get away, my heart almost giving out at the shock.

"Jensen!" Nash calls, dropping beside his uncle. "Hey, look at me. It's okay. You're going to be okay."

Jensen's chest rattles and he lets out one final chilling breath.

"Nash," I say, pushing myself to my feet and placing my quaking hand on his shoulder. "I'm so sorry. He's gone."

"No. No, he just took a breath! He can't be gone. We can help him. We have to do something. CPR!"

Nash presses on his chest, and I watch the doorway.

"Come on," he pleads. "Breathe."

My breath catches as I hear a noise outside the room, a thud. The killer is up here and we're sitting ducks.

"Nash, he's out there."

He doesn't hear me.

I shake my head, my heart aching for him as he tries to save his uncle, but Jensen is already gone. Still, Nash tries and tries but minutes pass and nothing happens.

"Jensen, come on!" Nash pleads. "Don't leave us. Penny . . ."

"I'm sorry," I say, refraining from telling him to stop because we're too late. Calling 911 wouldn't help because the killer still has Adi.

"It's not fair, and I'm so sorry. We need to move because we're not alone up here."

He falls back on his heels and drops his head, broken. "We couldn't save him."

"No, we couldn't, but why was he here?"

He blows out a ragged breath. "I don't know."

The killer couldn't get to Jackson so maybe Jensen was the next best thing.

25

"He should've stayed away from us," Nash murmurs. "Grace and I are cursed. God, I'm going to have to tell her about this."

"I'll do it with you. She has Brant too. She'll be all right. You both will. Nash, are you ready to go? He's here and Adi could be . . ."

Clearing his throat, he looks up at me with a shattered expression that makes me wonder if he will ever be okay again.

"Do you want to stay with him?"

"I'm not leaving you." He pats his uncle's arm and stands. With renewed energy and a whole lot of anger that I'm sure could take on the killer single-handedly, he adds, "Let's get this asshole."

This new pissed off Nash is exactly who I need by my side right now. We're on a rescue and revenge mission.

"Where do you think he got Jensen?" he asks.

"Did you hear from him today?"

"No. Grace went to Brant's because his extended family were

over and wanted to meet her. It was a good excuse to get her out of town tonight."

"Where is that?"

"His house is about twenty minutes away. She's safe."

"So *you* were left alone?"

"With a federal agent outside my house. No one thought this guy could get through him."

"I don't understand this. Why start off copying your dad if this killer was just going to do his own thing?"

"I don't know, but my dad is involved somehow. I was attacked and Jensen . . ."

"Right, you both look like him, no offense, so you're both good substitutes. Why didn't he kill you too?"

"God, I don't know, Pen. Do you think my dad is this guy's hero or does he hate him?"

"Good question." His eyes follow me, waiting. "Oh, I don't have the answer."

He stops at a door. "Doesn't matter, I guess. We just need to stop him."

"Shall we?" I ask, nodding my chin toward the door.

Last time I went first, and I think I'd rather give Nash a turn this time.

"Keep hold of that knife, Pen, but keep it concealed. He has to think he has the advantage."

My stomach clenches and adrenaline streams through my veins, preparing for the fight of my life. I'm so ready for this to be over. I want to get Adi and stop this guy, whatever the cost.

Nash pushes the door open, and we step over the threshold.

It's dark without a window in here but I use the flashlight on my phone to see. The air is thick and musty inside; dust particles float around, tickling my nose. The smell is awful, like rotten food and dirt and despair.

Gross. I cover my mouth and gag.

The room slants down toward a huge screen at the end. Rows and rows of chairs still sit proudly in the space. I remember Adi and I being here a few years ago, stuffing popcorn and M&M's in our mouth without a care in the world.

Nash takes my hand, holding it a little awkwardly because my cast is in the way, and we walk toward the screen.

"There was a body between pews in the church," Nash reminds me. It's a hint to look between the rows of chairs for Adi. I shine the light along each one, and my stomach clenches every time, preparing to see another body.

To see my best friend's body.

If I find her dead, I don't know what I'll do.

"Nash, I'm scared," I whisper, sticking close to him.

"It's okay," he says, his voice holding no conviction. He's telling me what I want to hear so I don't fall apart.

We both know it's not okay and maybe nothing ever will be again. This is it. Whatever this guy has planned, it's going down tonight. Right now. Nash and I are part of it whether we like it or not.

We reach the last row of seats.

"Well, what now?"

"Now we check out the last screen up here, I guess."

That's it, only one room left. He has to be in there . . . with Adi.

We both jump as a thud from behind the screen echoes through the theater. My breath catches in my throat, and I swing around to face the direction of the sound.

"Behind there," Nash whispers.

"Yep," I reply, hyperaware of what's going on.

"Penny!"

Nash and I swing back. I shine my light to the door of the theater, my jaw hanging open and hand tightening around the knife.

Zayn.

Nash looks back over his shoulder, checking our surroundings. I'm now completely focused on Zayn walking toward us. There he is, tall, broad shoulders, watching us like he's also confused.

"What are you doing here?" I ask him.

"Remember there's someone behind the screen," Nash mutters.

I hadn't forgotten, actually. But what if Zayn is working with them?

Zayn throws his hands up. "Looking for you two. What the hell are you doing here? Didn't we decide this party was the worst idea ever? You don't go to parties when there's a killer around."

"Shhh," I hush. "Were you at home?"

"When Nash called me? Yeah, I was. Thought I could hear music in the background and figured you'd be here. I saw someone up here and then the smoke downstairs. The killer is here, isn't he?"

"Did you go to Sarah's?" I ask.

I tense as he gets closer, ready to strike if he does. He's wearing jeans and a red Nike hoodie. Not exactly what the killer has been running around in, but I would keep it casual if I wanted to convey my innocence too.

"Why would I when the party was moved here?"

"Who moved the party?"

"Sarah when the cops were called. Penny, what's wrong?" He frowns as he reaches us. My flashlight is shining just below his face, lighting him up as if he's about to tell a ghost story around the campfire.

Dust dances between us like tiny flecks of glitter.

"Who called the cops?"

He shrugs. "Adi, right? She said she was going to."

"When did you last speak to her?"

"Er, I don't know. Not since we were at your house. I've been playing *Halo* most of the evening, bored out of my mind."

That could be true. There's no way to find out.

But he looks innocent. He looks just like the friend I've always relied on.

"Did you call the cops the night Nash and I were supposed to sneak out?"

"What? No, of course I didn't."

"Someone did," Nash says. "And whoever that someone is, is probably the killer."

Zayn's dark eyes bulge. "And you think I did that? Wow, it's nice to know what you think of me."

"You told me you were worried about me sneaking out and

came to find me," I say. "Then Adi said you were on your phone most of the evening at her house. What are we supposed to think?"

He scratches his forehead. "Adi is the one who called the cops, Penny. I came to pick you up because I knew he wasn't going to show."

"What?" Nash breathes.

"No, she wouldn't do that."

His eyes narrow. "But I would?"

"No . . . I . . ."

I have absolutely no idea what to think right now. Why would Adi do that? Why would Zayn?

I'm about to argue again when I hear another thud behind the screen. My heart skips a beat.

"That noise again. He's behind there," Nash says.

"Again? Why were we arguing here if you knew where he was?" Zayn snaps.

I should explain. We thought he was working with the killer, but he's not exactly thrilled with us for suspecting him.

Zayn steps forward, putting some distance between himself and the end of the screen but moving so he'll be able to see behind it.

"Stay here, Penny," Nash says as he follows Zayn, not wanting him to face this guy alone.

I walk along a row of chairs to the very end and bump against the wall. I can't see behind the screen but Nash and Zayn gasp at the same time.

"Adi!" Zayn shouts, and sprints behind the screen.

Oh my god. Adi!

I place my hands on the chair in front of me and leap over the back, crying out in pain as I stupidly use my bad hand. My wrist instantly throbs but I don't have time to feel sorry for myself.

"Penny?" Nash calls, turning back.

I run past him, saying, "I'm fine," and leap onto the platform. Zayn is shining his light on Adi. Her hands are bound, rather crudely like in the picture, and she has a gag over her mouth.

Wild eyes stare at us as she begins to cry.

I drop to the floor and tug on the rope around her hands. The binds are tighter now. "Are you okay?" I ask as Zayn removes the gag.

"Penny," she sobs, shoving the rope away and chucking herself at me.

"It's okay," I whisper. "You're safe now. Are you hurt?"

Shaking her head against my shoulder, she mutters, "I . . . I don't know what happened."

"How did he get you?"

"I can't remember. Was I in bed? I don't know. I don't know!"

"It's okay, Adi," Zayn says softly, stroking her hair to calm her down. No, there's no way he's behind any of this. "We need to get out of here, though."

"Did you see who it is?" Nash asks.

Adi sits back and shakes her head. "No."

"Is that a definite no or you don't remember?"

"I . . . I could've seen him, I guess. I can't remember anything, Nash, okay?"

He holds his palms in the air. "I wasn't suggesting anything.

I was whacked and woke up in Sarah's house. Didn't see anyone either."

"Wait, what?" she asks.

"There's no time to explain. We've wasted enough already," Zayn says, pulling Adi to her feet. "Can you walk?"

"I'm not dead, Zayn."

He looks across at me. "She's going to be fine."

Zayn helps Adi to walk the first few steps and then she brushes him off. She could be limping with her arm hanging off and she would still try to go it alone.

I turn back toward the steps so we can get the hell out of here when the door opens again.

Adi gasps. Zayn jumps. Nash steps forward. I grab my knife.

Nash takes another step.

"Jeez, Grace, you scared us! What're you doing? Where's Brant?"

"Nash," I say, grabbing his arm as he goes to take another step.

He hasn't seen yet.

The manic expression on her face or how her eyes are completely void of emotion.

"It's Grace," I whisper.

26

"What do you mean?" Nash asks, looking from me to his sister. He's slowly piecing it together, but he doesn't want to. "Grace, what are you doing here?"

She's still by the door at the top of the theater. I don't know where the emergency exit is in this room because there's no electricity to illuminate the sign and show the way.

Grace begins to make her way toward us and my stomach clenches.

What's she doing? It's four against one. She has no chance, so why would she walk toward us like she's in charge and we should be scared?

"Took you all long enough to get here."

"Grace, what the hell is this? What are you doing?" Nash demands, shaking his head. "Tell me this is some sick joke. Grace!"

"Calm down, Nash. You're getting hysterical!" she snaps. "Let me start by saying that if I see anyone dialing 911 or if I hear sirens, my body count will go through the roof. I'm *not* playing, so don't test me."

I push away the urge to call for help because I believe her . . . because I've *seen* what she's capable of.

Nash runs his hands through his hair, finally letting himself accept that Grace is behind all of this.

Grace is quite tall but not broad. She could have easily worn something to alter her appearance, though.

With his dad in prison, his uncle dead next door, and his sister a killer, Nash has now lost everyone. He's the only remaining sane and breathing Whitmore.

"Why?" he breathes.

"Sick bitch," Adi mutters. "I knew there was something wrong with her."

"Shut up, Adi. God, I wish I'd killed you. Always thinking you know best. Miss Perfect. You make me sick."

Grace has stopped walking. She splays her arms, beckoning us to watch her show. I can't look away. I need to know why.

"Is this about Dad?" Nash asks. "Did he get into your head?"

She rolls her eyes like she was expecting that, and Nash is way off. I keep my phone light shining on her, but my hands shake and make it look like her shadow behind her is getting ready to box, to knock us all out. KO. Grace wins.

"Why?" I ask. "You called us all here, so you don't want us dead just yet, do you? First you want to explain. You want us to understand exactly what you're doing before you murder us."

There must be more she wants than blood. She had the opportunity to kill us all already.

A sick smile spreads across her lips, and I no longer recognize her at all. “Isn’t that what we all want? To be understood?”

That’s crap. You don’t murder to be understood.

“Not like this,” I reply. “You can stop all this craziness, Grace. It isn’t too late.”

She laughs. “It’s entirely too late and you know it.”

“No,” Nash says, stepping forward and putting himself in front of us. Does he think that she won’t kill him because he’s her brother? She’s already proven that sharing blood doesn’t mean much to her.

But she grew up with Nash. Surely she wouldn’t hurt him.

“Gracie, talk to me. I had no idea . . . What the hell has been going on with you? You’d left for Brant’s, and now *this*.”

“God, he’s so dull. It’s a relief to ditch him.” She shakes her head, smiling as if we’d understand how irritating she finds her *boyfriend*. But the smile fades and her expression turns hard. “The whole town, Nash. You know this. I hate them all. If I could burn the entire place to the ground and kill every single person, I would do it. I would do it without hesitation.”

“What?” he breathes.

“It started years ago. This isn’t about Dad. We’ve always been the ones on the outside. The scrapyard. We were less than all of them, and you can’t tell me you didn’t notice how they turned their noses up to us.”

“That’s not true,” Zayn says. “You were always part of our group.”

"I'm going to have to ask you not to interrupt me again," Grace tells Zayn. She keeps eye contact with him as she pulls a knife out of a holder around her waist.

I bite my lip, my heart dropping to my toes. Her knife makes mine look like it belongs in a dollhouse.

"Grace," Nash says again, trying to get her attention on him.

We can't call the cops, so we need to try to gain control of the situation, keep her calm. I'm not so confident that he can talk her down. No one had any idea that she was behind this. I didn't even suspect.

Grace has killed five people. Where can she go from here? If she's caught, she's going to spend the rest of her life in prison. A maximum-security one, same as her dad.

"How you've felt this last year is how I have felt my whole life, Nash. Do you know what that does to a person?"

"Nothing good," I mutter under my breath.

Zayn snorts but Grace doesn't appear to have heard me.

"That doesn't make this right, Grace. We're going to let them go and we'll go talk."

"I don't think so, bro."

"We have to. Come on, you can't do this."

"I'm not finished."

"I'm not letting you hurt them."

She tilts her head to the side. "You're not going to have a choice."

Nash visibly shudders in front of me. "Grace, come on . . ."

His voice is rough and broken. He sounds like he wants to run away and pretend that none of this is happening.

"Would you choose *her,* Nash, really?" Grace sneers. "I'm *blood.* I'm the only one who's had your back. The only one." Her teeth snap together, and she glares at him, holding in her barely contained rage. The beam from my flashlight sticks to her like glue, and I don't take my eyes off the knife she's holding.

My recording app is still running. I can't risk calling the cops after Grace's threat, but at least they'll be able to listen to this and know what Grace has done.

We're still too far away for her to reach us with it but she's irritable and irrational, so I don't know what she's going to do. She could pounce at any second and it looks like she wants to come straight for me.

What does she think will happen? She could maybe get one of us with that knife but the rest of us would be on her in seconds.

"Why here? Why now with us all together?" I mutter under my breath. *Think, think, think!* It doesn't make sense to come alone. Brant? She said she'd ditched him but what *exactly* does that mean?

"Grace, where's Brant?"

She shrugs, staring at me like I'm simple and have asked a boring question. "How the hell should I know? I walked out of his boring family party hours ago."

Maybe not Brant, then. At least he's okay. Is it possible that she's doing this alone? She was at the memorial, but the body could've been placed in the church earlier, same with the movie theater. But dead weight is a bitch and she's not exactly strong.

Grace takes another step. Zayn, Adi, and I move backward. Nash doesn't move an inch.

He truly believes she will not hurt him.

I think she's capable of anything.

"Grace, why them?"

Smirking, she addresses me directly. "No reason, Penny. They were in the wrong place at the wrong time."

I don't believe her.

"Did your dad tell you what to do?"

Nash does a double take, looking from her to me and back.

"Now, why would you assume I need his help?" With a growl, she adds, "Why does no one believe that I'm capable of this all on my own? You think that because I didn't go to some fancy college that I'm not intelligent enough to orchestrate this whole thing?"

"No one thinks that," I say. "We all know how smart you are. The teachers said you could get into any college you wanted."

"Yeah, we know you're the smartest person in the room," Zayn adds. "Remember when we used to meet around the back of the library? You told me you were getting into NYU no matter what you had to do. What happened to that dream, Grace?"

Nash glances over his shoulder at Zayn's confession. Yeah, I didn't know they were meeting up either.

"Do you really think flattery and reminiscing about old times is going to work? You ignored me for months, Zayn. All of you did."

"Grace, what do you think's going to happen?" Nash asks. "What's the point to all of this? You're going to end up in prison just like Dad and I'll be alone. You . . . you killed Jensen."

She relaxes her shoulders and smiles at her brother. "I'm

getting bored of this now. Let's give them the answers they want so we can get the hell out of this dead-end town."

Her words ring through my ears on a loop.

I play them over and over until they make sense.

Let's give them the answers they want.

Let's.

My heart clenches hard and I shuffle back with Adi and Zayn, staring at Nash like he's just cut out my heart and chucked it in the trash. He was working with her all this time.

Nash turns to us, wide-eyed and hands up in surrender. "No, don't listen to her. Penny, you know me. Grace, what the hell! I'm not behind this, I swear."

He goes to take a step forward but stops when I draw the knife out of my pocket.

"Stay back." I shake my head, my eyes welling with tears. The betrayal hitting me harder than my window in the accident.

Nash shakes his head, his eyes wide and panicked. "No, Penny. She's lying. Come on, you know me."

Grace laughs. "Come on, bro. She's not going to believe you now. We might as well finish this."

"Shut up!" he bellows. "What the hell is wrong with you? Grace, you need help!"

"Oh, hush, little brother."

"Penny, I promise I'm innocent. I had no idea she was . . . God, she killed my uncle." Nash shoves his hands into his hair. "Zayn, you know I wouldn't do this. You know me, come on."

Zayn holds up his hands, putting a barrier between us and

Nash. "Stay back, dude. We don't know shit right now, except that your sister is holding a knife and confessing to murder."

"Actually, I never confessed . . . ," Grace sings. "I didn't kill anyone."

That's when another voice pipes up. One I recognize very well. "I did."

27

Startled, I shout and spin around to face another one of my best friends.

Omar.

"No," I say, shaking my head. "Omar, no."

He runs his finger over the tip of the blade he's holding. Blood has dried all over it, turning it rust-colored. Jensen's blood?

"I'm afraid so."

The way Nash stares, with his jaw slack and eyes wide, gives me hope that he really is innocent. But I don't know who to believe. Thirty seconds ago, I would've trusted Omar with my life.

And three minutes ago, I thought Zayn might be guilty.

"No. Hell no," Zayn says. "Dude . . ."

Omar takes a deep breath. "I'm sorry it's come to this. I really am. We tried to keep you out of it but, Penny—God, Penny—you just couldn't stay away from Nash, could you?"

"What? Omar, what does that have to do with any of this?

Please think about what you're doing. We're friends. You're not going to forgive yourself if you hurt us," I ramble, my head still not quite catching up.

"Grace didn't want you near him anymore," he replies. The answer is so simple yet so underwhelming. As if not wanting your brother to spend time with his ex is reason to *murder* five people.

"Omar . . . did *you* kill them all?"

"It's not challenging, Penny. You just"—he shrugs one arm lazily—"stab."

Nausea bursts in my stomach. "You tried to hurt me. I could've died in that crash."

"I chased you through that cornfield and you still didn't stay away," he tells me, scowling like I'm a naughty child. "What choice did you leave me? Even after the crash, you still ran to him."

Grace scoffs but Nash cuts her off. "You don't get to decide who my friends are! What the hell happened to you? I know you've been speaking to Dad, but this is insanity, and you know it."

"Don't talk to her like that," Omar spits, his demeanor changing from cocky to furious . . . murderous. Grace has a hold on him that I never could have guessed. She's turned him into her personal weapon.

I stare at him, trying to figure out how I missed this side of him. My sweet, sarcastic friend who never takes anything too seriously.

"What are you going to do now, Omar? Kill all your friends?"

"He only needs me," Grace says, answering for him.

"She wasn't talking to you," Zayn snaps.

"I tried to warn you!" He throws his hands up, the knife pointing in the air. The blood glistens in the beam of my flashlight.

"So what's the plan?" I ask, taking a step forward. "Omar, we've known each other since we were five. You've been my friend for twelve years. I trusted you, and I don't want to lose you now."

"That's not going to work," Grace says.

"Stop talking for him," I tell her. "He has his own mind."

The problem is, right now, Omar isn't using it. He's doing everything she wants him to, *killing* when she wants him to. When we saw them talking outside the theater, they must've just dumped Mae's body. He was only gone for a few minutes, so Grace had to have helped him.

Parked close by with Mae in the trunk, taken her through the staff entrance down the alley. It'd be much quieter but still so risky . . . but then so is killing. Mae liked Omar. What must she have felt when he attacked her?

"Omar, please think about this. What this means for you. She hasn't killed anyone. She got you to do it all. *You're* the one who will end up in prison, not her. Please don't do this. I know you don't want to hurt us."

"You brought a knife too," he says, and I'm sure his little smile is full of pride.

"I don't want to use it. Please don't make me have to defend myself."

"I tried to warn you, but you wouldn't listen."

"How was I supposed to know any of this was a warning to stay away from Nash?"

Tilting his head, he smirks. "Would you have stayed away if I'd made it more obvious?"

I purse my lips and consider lying, but he will see through it. Omar has known me far too long for that to work. "No, I wouldn't."

"All right," Adi says, raising her hands and moving closer to Omar. "I don't know what is going down between you and her, but I can tell you she's using you. Open your eyes."

"Hey!" he snaps. "Watch your mouth."

"No, we're honest with each other, and I'm not about to stop that now. We say it how it is regardless of how awkward it can be. That's always been the deal."

That was the deal before last year. We've all kept secrets since then.

"Shut up!" he shouts, taking long strides toward her.

Adi screams and runs backward, hitting the chairs and falling onto the dust-covered seat. She covers her face with her hands. Nash, Zayn, and I fly forward.

"Hey, hey," I say, blocking Omar from coming closer. We face each other, both of us holding a knife—his much bigger than mine. His breath is as ragged as my own. We could be alone now. Neither of us can focus on anything but each other as we plan our next move. Me trying to find a way to talk some sense into him. Him . . . I couldn't even guess at this point.

There is so much I never knew about Omar. Like his relationship with Grace for one. What's the deal there? He had a crush on her, but she never gave him the time of day.

"Penny, move back," Nash whispers.

I shake my head as a surge of adrenaline makes me braver than I have ever been. "No. Omar and I will sort this out."

"Good girl," Omar replies. "We might be on opposite sides here, but I am proud of you."

His words send a bolt of anger through me. He's completely unable to see how Grace is playing him. "Don't do that. You're holding a knife at me; you're prepared to kill me. Don't pretend that you care about me anymore. Why are you doing this for her?"

"I love her."

Well, that much is obvious.

"Someone who loves you doesn't ask you to kill for them."

"Shut up!" Grace snaps.

Why aren't they trying to attack us? They have no choice now; we all know the truth.

"What did she say to you?"

He takes a deep breath through his nose and moves his weight from foot to foot. "I haven't been manipulated, Penny. I told her I want to help."

I can't even imagine how that conversation went.

"I don't understand."

Grace laughs manically. "It's fine, you can tell them, babe."

My voice recorder app is still counting off the seconds.

Adi stands and huddles against Zayn. They both watch Omar, waiting to hear about our friend's secret life.

He is the last person I would ever think could hurt someone. He has, on occasion, been quite cold and joked about things you probably shouldn't, but not this. He's not who I thought he was.

"Omar, please. Can you explain what's going on?"

"I like it, Pen. *I like it.*"

"See, this is always who he was going to be. Dad knew it," Grace says as Zayn shines his light on her. I keep mine on Omar.

"Dad knew it?" Nash asks. "You spoke to him about what you were doing? He knew. Oh my god. He told me . . ."

Grace rolls her eyes. "He said he'd spoken to you."

"Grace, tell me what Dad knew!" Nash's patience is melting away.

"He told me that Omar was bad news." She winks at Omar. "Wanted to protect me. I mean, until he figured it all out."

"Figured what out? Stop talking in riddles."

"You really don't know, do you?"

"No," I breathe. "Your dad warned you away from him. You don't mean recently. Oh my . . . You're the one behind it *all.* Grace, your dad's innocent, isn't he?"

"What?" Nash whips around, mouth open, eyes wide, and face white as a ghost. "What are you saying, Penny? Grace, what the hell is she saying? That's not true."

Behind us, Omar cheers. "I *knew* she'd get it eventually."

"Tell me that's not true right now," Nash demands.

We need a plan. Keeping them talking is only delaying whatever they're going to do.

"Omar and I have been seeing each other for about two and a half years," she tells us. "None of you had a clue."

"You don't know how much I wanted to stab you, Zayn, when you asked her out," Omar adds.

Zayn tenses and shuffles a bit closer to Adi so that the four of us are together, ready to face whatever is about to come.

Four against two. We still have the upper hand in terms of numbers. But they have two knives to my tiny pitiful one. I want, more than anything, for my parents to realize I'm not home and raise the alarm with the feds outside my house. But they will come with sirens, and then who knows how quickly Grace will lose it.

Still, it feels like we're running out of time, because she's not coming around.

It hasn't been thirty minutes yet since everyone left the party. I would think the cops would turn up any second if someone ignored orders and raised the alarm.

"Grace!" Nash snaps, sounding like he's seconds away from a breakdown. He's had a lot to process in the last thirty minutes.

"I've wanted to hurt a lot of people for a long time. I found out very quickly, thanks to beer and being left with Omar at a party, that he feels the same. It took another three months for me to mention it again. So many people thought they were better than me. Than us, Nash. Every time someone stuck their nose in the air when I passed, I imagined jabbing a knife into their gut. It was in my head so often that I knew I couldn't ignore it anymore."

Omar chuckles. "I thought I was the only one who does that. And we don't just mean the odd dark thought when someone has wronged us. I'm talking vividly imagining killing them, watching the life drain from their face. The blood. Everywhere."

My stomach churns at the thought of him liking that, wanting that.

Difference is, Grace has acted her fantasies out through Omar.

"We hung out in secret and planned. We planned for months

and months what we'd like to do until it turned into a compulsion. It could no longer stay a fantasy. We *had* to." Grace taps the tip of the knife against her cheek but doesn't press hard enough to cut.

"Omar and I agreed at the same time. It was fate. That first kill was . . . Words cannot describe it. You will never understand."

"Good," Zayn sneers.

"Watch your mouth," Omar warns him. He places his hand over his pocket and tilts his head.

"Did you kill Mac?" I ask Grace. She was the first one to die last year. Up until this point, we've only had a confession from Omar.

"No. We're a team. Omar is the one who does the killing. I like to watch and cover it up."

Zayn growls. "Open your eyes, Omar. She's using you!"

"Hey! I need to know everything, so everyone who isn't my sister, shut the hell up. How is Dad mixed up in this?" Nash asks. "Why is he in prison and not you?"

Grace scoffs. "God, he was so overprotective, it was suffocating."

He actually wasn't. Nash and Grace always had a lot of freedom. Unless she's telling us Jackson forbid her from slaughtering people and that's what she means by suffocating.

Seems reasonable to me.

"He began to suspect that I was hiding something."

"How?" Nash asks.

"He overheard a few things I'd said to Omar on the phone. Wanted me to go to anger management classes," she says, and laughs. "He was really worried, apparently. But he didn't speak to anyone, didn't ask for help, didn't go to the cops. Not even when I came home with blood on my T-shirt. He watched me burn it in the yard and said nothing."

Nash shakes his head.

"Things got worse for him after that. Omar and I killed again, this time in masks. Dad found one of them in my room. I bullshitted something about it being my costume, but he didn't believe me. Not after the bodies were racking up. He begged me to stop. That was it. Just begged and pleaded and offered me all the help in the world. He was so weak," she says, laughing to herself.

He should've called the cops on her.

"How did he end up taking the fall?" I ask, stealing a quick glance at Nash. One light is still on Omar and the other on Grace, but I can make out the absolute horror on Nash's face.

He's hated his dad for a long time.

"He followed me the night we took Kelsie and Brodie. Omar was getting his truck so we could load them up when Dad found me." She takes a breath and then a wide smile spreads across her evil lips. "I put on the performance of a lifetime. Cried and begged him for help. Told him that I know I'm not well, blah, blah, blah, and want to get better so I can give NYU a shot."

"You're sick," Nash breathes.

Grace ignores him as she continues with her story. "The crime scene was a bit messy. We hadn't had time to clean it up and we could hear sirens in the background." She rolls her eyes. "Kelsie was so freaking loud when Omar was stabbing her. Hurt my ears, so it wasn't a surprise that someone heard."

Bile hits the back of my throat at the thought of Kelsie fighting so hard to live.

"Dad pulled a strand of his hair out and laid it on Kelsie's body. Told me he would make this better and in return, I would never see Omar again and focus on getting my life back on track. In hindsight it was a horrible plan. But the feds were coming, and he panicked. He sacrificed himself for me."

"And what does he think now?" Nash growls through gritted teeth.

"I stopped answering his calls when we killed Noah. I knew it would get back to him, knew the cops would question him again, so I could hardly pretend nothing was going on, could I?"

"So you ignored him."

"And still he covered for me." She shakes her head. "So, you see, Nash, we are going to finish this and then you're coming with us. Somewhere we can start over without this poison."

Grace is the poison.

Nash shakes his head. "I'm not going anywhere with you."

"What are you finishing?" I ask.

She waves her hand. "You three. Omar, get it over with, will you?"

Adi, Zayn, and I gasp. We spin to face our friend, who's just been ordered to kill us.

"Omar, no!" I shout as he leaps forward and, without hesitation, sticks his knife into Adi's abdomen.

28

A scream echoes around the theater, cutting through my heart.

Adi falls to the ground like a rag doll and Zayn goes with her, shoving his hand against the wound to stem the bleeding.

Omar moves back a few steps and looks to Grace, instantly getting a smile of approval.

He's so far beyond reason, I don't know how I'm going to get through to him. Grace has him brainwashed. He touches his pocket again. What does he have in there? A second knife maybe.

"Apply pressure!" I shout to Zayn as blood pours through his fingers.

"I am, I am, I am!"

Nash and I stay on our feet, as much as I want to help Adi. We're sitting ducks if we crouch down too. Somehow we need to stop them and get help before Adi bleeds out.

"If you even think about alerting the cops, Pen . . . ," Omar warns.

My phone is in my hand, locked, with only the flashlight app on. Still recording everything that's going down. "But aren't you going to kill us anyway?" I ask. "They'd never get here in time even if I did."

"No cops. And Grace wants to keep Nash . . . unless you try to play hero and call for help," Omar replies, and smiles as if he's just offered me a milkshake.

Grace wants to keep him, as if he's a pet or a possession.

"What's your plan, Omar, huh? You're going to run away with her and do what? The feds are going to figure this out and they'll come looking for you."

"We'll be in another state before they realize."

"I doubt that. Jackson's brother is dead in the next room and you three are missing."

Omar really isn't the brains of this operation. For a guy who's quite intelligent, he sure turns pretty stupid when it comes to Grace.

"Do you honestly believe everything she tells you? She let her dad take the fall for what she was doing and had her uncle killed. Why wouldn't she turn on you?"

"Or we could stop talking about me like I'm not here. How about that?" Grace says.

"She's losing too much blood," Zayn interrupts, panicked. "Penny, we need to get her out of here."

What the hell can I do right now?

There's no other choice. . . . I hit the emergency button and a call goes through to 911. I don't know if the call will stop the recording app, but that doesn't matter anymore.

The call operator begins talking; the volume is down so Grace won't be able to hear, but I also can't say anything to alert her. The operators will send help when they hear.

"More pressure! Omar, you need to let us take her or she's going to die. This is *Adi,* one of your best friends. You can't be responsible for her death. Come on, you will never forgive yourself," I plead, frantically trying to get him to listen because I'm petrified that my best friend is dying by my feet.

"Not happening," Grace says, answering for him.

"Omar, *please.*"

"Shut up, Penny!" Omar shouts, clenching his fist.

I swear I can see a flicker of doubt in his eyes. It's a glimmer of hope, and I cling to it in a death grip. Talking about killing his friends with Grace and actually doing it are very different things.

He glances down at Adi and back up.

Come on, Omar . . .

This is affecting him; I don't care what he says to Grace. He doesn't *want* to do this.

"Why did you get Zayn to come here?" I ask, pulling the focus to Omar's friends and trying to get him to see how toxic Grace is and how much she's controlling him.

She doesn't want him to have anyone but her.

A true narcissist.

He looks at Grace before answering me. "He was getting in the way, talking to Nash and encouraging you to do the same."

Those sound like Grace's words.

"And Adi? Why would you take her, Omar? You two have been tight almost your whole life. *How could you?*" I blink rapidly, clearing tears that I have no time for.

Come on, where are the cops!

He shakes his head once, as if he's trying to rid himself of any blame.

Grace might be manipulative as hell, but he didn't have to do it.

"You can still put this right, Omar."

Dark eyes flit to Adi for half a second, and then he rolls his shoulders. "No," he says, shaking his head again and moving to the side.

I tense, shuffling in the opposite direction with Nash. I've lost him. He doesn't care. I hold the knife out, pointing it straight at him as he walks around us and makes his way up the steps to Grace.

He stands by her, making his choice official.

"Omar, no." I brush tears from my eyes. "Please don't do this."

"You don't understand, Penny. You will *never* understand. This is the only way."

Grace touches his arm, smiling up at him like a total psycho.

"We need to move, Omar. Finish Zayn and Penny. Looks like Adi's already gone."

Pain cuts through my body like Grace has used that knife. I glance at Adi for a second, limp on the floor, eyes closed. Zayn stares at her, his face twisted in the same agony I feel.

Our Adi has gone.

"There is no way I'm standing by while you hurt them," Nash tells her, staring at his sister like she's a stranger. His words tear my attention from my best friend.

She sneers at him. "I wasn't asking your permission."

"After everything you've done to me, my friends, to Dad and our uncle, I will kill you myself if you come near them. I suggest you turn around and leave. Take Omar and run off into the sunset. Never return."

I can't believe what he's suggesting. I want them to pay. The hate I feel for them is so completely overwhelming I want to charge them with my knife. But I know better than that. There's nothing I can do to help Nash and Zayn get out of here if I'm dead.

She turns her nose up. "And wait for you to call the feds. I don't think so."

"We won't. This is the deal. Their safety for our silence."

"Nash—"

He raises his hand to stop me, asking me to trust him. I do because he knows that I will never follow through with a vow of silence.

I'd chase them myself.

Grace looks up at Omar. "What do you think?"

What?

Wait . . . why is she asking him that? She seemed committed to her crazy-ass plan five seconds ago.

"Do it," he replies without hesitation, and I see a flicker of the friend I know and love. "We can leave and never look back, Grace. No one will ever find us."

Grace's eyes cloud like the sky before a hurricane. A shiver rolls down my spine at the change in her demeanor.

What's that about? This should be the perfect solution for them. We keep quiet and the case goes cold. The police only got an arrest last year because Jackson planted false evidence.

It could work. To save my friends, I would make it work.

"Omar, no!" I shout as I realize what that change was about.

I gasp as Grace plunges her knife into Omar's side. The blade disappears into his flesh. I watch, mouth open in horror, as she stabs once, twice, three times.

I scream his name as his eyes bulge, looking at Grace with betrayal etched onto his face. He trusted her, believed in her, did everything to make her happy, and she hurt him.

As if in slow motion, he stumbles toward us down the walkway and gently sinks to his knees.

No!

Nash catches me as I attempt to run to him. He's so close, just five strides and I'd reach him.

"Omar! Omar! Let go, Nash!"

"Jesus!" Zayn shouts. "What the hell, Grace!"

Nash says nothing. His arms are frozen around me as he stares at his sister in disbelief.

"Call the cops," he whispers in my ear, and lets go.

I already have.

"Whoa, no!" I say, tugging on his hand as he tries to pass me and moves toward Grace. She's snapped, and I can't count on her not hurting him.

"I have to do this. Get Zayn and get out, Pen."

"No, no, no. We can end this together," I say, clawing at him like he's about to disappear. Fear and panic push down heavy on my shoulders.

Grace lowers the knife, and it drips with Omar's blood. Her head tilts to the side and she smiles. Her first kill . . . and she liked it.

Omar's lying on the floor, eyes wide as if he's staring up at her, forever shocked.

No!

All Grace has done is tip the scales in our favor because Nash will never let her hurt me or Zayn.

"Grace, please, you have to stop this. It's you against the three of us now. You don't have to do this," I plead.

"Shut it, Penny! God, you're next and I'm going to *really* enjoy this."

The call is still live, but I can't hear anyone talking anymore. This will be recorded.

"Okay. Okay, Grace, just calm down a minute. It's going to be all right. You need help, and I can help you," Nash says, moving in front of me again.

"The cops are coming," I whisper to Nash since he's blocked Grace's view of me.

I think he heard, but he doesn't acknowledge it. He needs to know so we can keep her talking.

I don't think anyone could ever help her. She's orchestrated *twelve* murders, killing one person herself. She's set fire to a church and run me off the road. She let her dad go to prison for her crimes.

How do you save someone like that?

But I know what he's doing. If anyone can get through to her—if that's even possible at this point—it will be her brother. The one person she wanted with her. That has to mean something. It's all we have until the cops and feds arrive.

She looks up and screams, the sound shrill, and it rings through my ears. Holding the knife out, she runs toward us. It doesn't matter. All I need to focus on now is stopping Grace before anyone else gets hurt.

Zayn grabs my hand and tugs me back. "You need to go!" he shouts, dragging me along.

I need to go. Not *we*.

"No, I'm not leaving either of you!"

"Come on, Pen!"

"Nash!" I yell as Grace advances on him, desperately trying to tug my arm out of Zayn's grip. They walk toward each other along the walkway. She steps over Omar's body without even a glance, like he's nothing.

Nash raises his hands. "Grace, stop. Talk to—"

I hear the scream rip from my throat, but I feel like I'm in a nightmare.

No, no, no.

Choking, Nash grips his abdomen where Grace has just plunged her knife.

"She's going to kill you, Penny. Just let me get you out. I'll come back for her. I'll make her pay for Adi," Zayn snaps, yanking me harder.

"Nash! Nash!" My voice doesn't sound like my own. Pain radiates through my wrist as my phone drops to the floor. The room is cloaked in darkness again. The only light is from my dim screen, faceup, with the emergency call still live.

We need to get him help.

Nash takes two uneven steps forward and sinks to his knees the way Omar did.

Grace stands over him, about halfway to the door, but she's not watching her brother; she's watching me and Zayn. The two bodies at her feet are ignored.

Omar and Nash are so close they could reach out and touch each other if they were able.

I sob, teary-eyed, and follow Zayn over a row of chairs. My entire body aches and the world tips sideways as I leap over the next row at the same time Grace walks down closer to us. We hop the next chair and come level with Grace.

She has a knife and so do I. My vision has just about adjusted to the dim light but my head pounds with a headache that makes me want to vomit. Concussion, terror, and heartache pulling me apart at the seams.

"Penny, hurry up!"

"Get out, Zayn."

"Listen. I hear sirens!" he says. "Don't be a hero and let me get you to safety."

I don't hear them, not yet. I don't know if Nash is dead, but I would also die protecting Zayn. I'm not going anywhere. It's me she wants anyway. I don't think she'd care if Zayn left, as long as I stay.

Zayn reaches for me again, but I move too fast, dodging him. He was about to jump the next row, but I run along the seats, toward the center of the room, toward the steps to the door . . . toward Nash and Omar and Grace.

She's higher up now, farther away from Nash but still blocking my way to the exit, penning me in.

"Go, Zayn!"

I don't expect him to go anywhere because he wants her dead. He wants to avenge the death of his friends. I feel that so deep in my soul, there is nothing that can make me leave.

Just like him, I'm staying until the end. I won't hide in safety while Zayn takes her on.

"Run, Penny," Nash grits through his teeth, clutching his abdomen. "Go."

This bitch has killed too many people I care about. I'm not giving her a chance to escape. There is no way I'm leaving Nash alone. Not again.

Grace smiles. "I like this side of you, Penny. Maybe I should've picked you to join me."

"Thanks, but I would rather die."

"Unfortunately for you, that's exactly what's going to happen."

I hear the faint sound of sirens outside, approaching the building. There they are. The cops and the feds are coming. She won't get away with this.

"Don't be too sure about that," I reply.

I move out of the aisle and drop to my knees beside Nash. I want to start screaming that we're up here, but Grace isn't advancing, instead reverting to gloating about what she's done and going to do, so I have the opportunity to buy more time.

The sirens are getting louder, lots of them, but I don't know if anyone is in the building yet.

Zayn steps between me and Grace as I check on Nash. His breathing is labored, the rattling sound in his chest sending chills down my spine. I don't know if it's the stab wound or the shock.

I cover his hand with my own and the bleeding instantly slows.

He looks up at Grace, whose focus is now on Zayn, and back to me. "Penny."

"See, it's slowing. You're going to be fine."

Zayn and Grace don't seem to have noticed the sirens as Zayn moves a step toward her, hands raised as he tries to protect all of us. The cops must be right outside now.

I gasp as Zayn picks up Omar's knife.

"Zayn, don't," I say. We don't need to be goading her right now.

"It ends here," Nash murmurs as the sirens are on top of us now. He leans over, groaning in pain, stealing my attention as he reaches for something . . . in Omar's pocket.

My stomach ties in knots as he pulls out a gun. Omar had a gun! The one his dad bought recently maybe.

Why hadn't he used it? Could be the same reason he wanted Grace to run away with him. None of this was Omar's idea and he'd had enough. He wanted Grace to stop; he wanted his friends to live. Or he liked the blood, as he said.

"Nash, what are you doing?" I mutter.

Zayn advances on Grace. He has a knife pointed at her; she has one at him. Both of them are prepared to end this right now.

"Zayn!" I shout as he lunges forward. Grace snarls and pushes her knife out, her arm stretching impossibly far, so close to Zayn.

"No!" Nash shouts, aiming.

Bang.

ACKNOWLEDGMENTS

I want to say a massive thank you to my amazing team at Delacorte Press and Random House. You're all rock stars and I so appreciate everything you do.

Jordy, you never fail to create beautiful covers. This one is perfect.

Ariella and Amber, thank you for being by my side. I couldn't do any of this without you.

Sam, Vic, and Elle. Where do I even start? Thanks for the laughs, the GIFs, the mimosas, and the dodgy bike rides.

To my husband, sons, and new puppy, I love you all like crazy!

And as always to my readers, bloggers, vloggers, and everyone else who reads and promotes my books, THANK YOU SO MUCH.

Published by Delacorte Press, an imprint of Random House Children's Books,
a division of Penguin Random House LLC, New York.

Prologue

I upload my latest trailer to TikTok advertising my new YouTube video, *Killer in the Family,* and I sit back. Within seconds the numbers under the little heart start climbing as if Jeff Bezos were watching a livestream of his bank balance.

He's building rockets. Malcolm Wyatt, a rich dude who invited *me* to his amusement park, is building islands.

Tearing open a packet of Hershey's Kisses with my teeth, I wait. Chocolate passes the time. I get a bunch of comments telling me how awesome it is that I've posted, but it'll take about thirty minutes for people to head over to my YouTube channel to watch the full video, then come back to TikTok to let me know what they think.

My hard-core followers comment on both. Then on Insta too.

I can wait. If I go downstairs right now, I'll just hear my parents arguing over Malcolm's invitation.

That invitation might just be the single coolest thing that has *ever* happened to me, without exception, and they're not certain they're going to let me go.

Not. Going. To. Let. Me. Go.

When Dad initially said no, I thought I was going to pass out. I was light-headed and everything.

There is no option: I *have* to go.

Things got so desperate I even had to send an SOS to my brother in college to call Dad and fight from my corner. Blaine is much better at wrapping our parents around his little finger. It helps that he's a literal genius and gives them excellent bragging rights.

If anyone can convince them, it's him.

How will I be able to look at myself in the mirror if I have to stay home that weekend while someone else takes my spot?

Nope, it's not happening.

I'm getting on that island, even if it kills me.

Only six of us have been invited. Six influencers. An exclusive weekend on a new island resort. An amusement park so remote that you can only reach it by boat.

It's a freaking dream come true.

The owner, Malcolm, wants us to endorse it. Influencers are taking over the world. If I hadn't accidentally made it big, I might be in a little despair over that fact.

People listen to someone online they've never met more than they do to their parents, teachers, doctors. It's tragic, really, but I'm not complaining. I'll be able to go to a top college and leave without any debt. I can buy a house when I'm done.

I've already got a brand-new BMW that my brother was *so* jealous about. It was glorious. His was two years old when our parents bought it.

I lean back in my office chair and peel the wrapper off a chocolate.

The count climbs. When it reaches more than one hundred thousand in minutes, I lock my phone and go to eavesdrop on my parents.

I'll come back in a bit to see what people are saying.

When I leave my room, Mom and Dad are still debating, as I expected. It's been two days and my trip is all that's been discussed. I tiptoe along the hallway and listen to Mom tell Dad that spending a weekend with other successful influencers who aren't focused on murder might "do me good."

Mom's not a fan of my content.

"She might start blogging about makeup like that girl Ellie's obsessed with, Gregory."

Ellie is my thirteen-year-old cousin. She's constantly glued to her phone watching some TikTok-er named Ava dance and vlog about beauty tips, hacks, and tricks.

"I don't think that's going to happen, Cheryl. She's obsessed with this death stuff. We don't know anything about this place or this billionaire who's invited her. It's perverse. Who does he think he is, asking my seventeen-year-old daughter to his island for the weekend?"

"Oh, Gregory, be real. Malcolm Wyatt is completely legitimate. And this trip? This is what being an influencer is. There's a group of them, all around her age. And a woman . . . Camilla something, will be their chaperone while they're there."

Camilla Jenkins. She's Malcolm's personal assistant and is apparently the one who's coordinating everything. She'll be watching out for us until the boat picks us up on Monday at lunchtime.

"Don't you see an issue with the fact that you're only pushing for this in the hope she'll come home and start doing dances online . . . or whatever it is these kids are posting?"

I close my eyes and cringe. Lord, shine a light.

"Even Blaine agrees with me," Mom says. She's smug; I can hear the triumph in her voice. Dad will be rolling his eyes.

See, Blaine is their golden child. He's the one not reporting on crime in his spare time.

He's at Princeton studying biochemistry.

"Oh, you know he can never say no to her. He'll agree with whatever she wants to do. Besides, this isn't up to Blaine."

Oh yeah. My brother might be their golden child, but he's always had my back and let me get my way.

"Forget Blaine. This is about Paisley. It's a great opportunity for her, Greg. It's no secret that I don't love what she does, but we can't argue that it's taking her places. She'll make some good connections."

She's probably referring to the billionaire.

There are a couple of millionaires on our street, but anything beyond that is blocks away, deep in the posh suburbs. This kind of money isn't part of my world. At least not yet.

Dad's sigh travels up the stairs. That's his sigh of resignation.

I know it well. It's the same one I heard after Blaine and I spent a week pestering him for a puppy. Bailey, our sweet Lab, is asleep on my bed.

Yes! I leap into the air in silent celebration, punching the air above my head.

I take out the invitation from my hoodie pocket and leap again.

At the end of the month, I'll be spending a whole weekend on Jagged Island.

1

THREE WEEKS LATER

From the mainland, Jagged Island looked tiny, but as the boat speeds toward the rocky cliffs, I see that it's much larger than I thought.

It must be, to fit a whole amusement park, hotel, and restaurants on it.

Large hills and hoops of wooden roller coasters jut out of the ground and stretch high into the sky.

Sharp black rock that looks as if someone has carved vertical shards from the surface frames the island. The amusement park sits high off the water. Waves crash against the cliff face and white foam races back into the sea.

Trees are sparse on the island but the few there are full of bushy green leaves. From here, the park is dark, wooden, and void of color.

Even with the blue ocean and clear, sunny skies, the island appears more gloomy than glamorous. I kind of like it. The Magic Kingdom isn't my thing.

Our boat jumps over choppy water as we hurtle toward the jetty. I grip the side of the boat as my butt leaves the padded seat I'm trying to sit on.

"This looks creepy as hell," Ava says. Ava as in BeautyFulAva. The TikTok girl who my cousin is obsessed with and who my parents want me to be more like. Absolutely not going to happen. Before I left, Ellie made me promise to ask for her autograph, but so far, Ava's been a total brat.

Her contoured face twists in distaste as she stares at the island. Her glossy blond ponytail whips behind her in the wind. She's as sharp as in her videos, savagely rating brands that don't live up to her expectations. Her reputation for brutal honesty gets her a lot of attention.

Here, it might just get her hated.

We're not her followers.

When we arrived at the harbor, she dragged three large bright pink suitcases on board the boat and acted offended when Gibson, our rather hot driver, questioned if she needed it all. I'm trying to not judge her too harshly, but she's referred to Gibson as "the help" twice and we've only been on the boat for fifteen minutes.

He looks ready to throw her overboard.

"Nah, this looks awesome," Liam replies. Liam is a gamer, though from his appearance and muscular physique he seems like more of a jock. He has a dominant personality and perfectly styled brown hair. I focused on him straightaway. It's hard not to.

His YouTube channel is massive and he's TikTok-famous—his TikTok has exploded. He's a big fan of any game with violence and hits back at negative comments in the way a jock would—with complete and utter annihilation of his opponents.

He's gorgeous and probably wouldn't give me the time of day if we went to the same high school.

"No," Ava says more forcefully. "It's *creepy.* Who's going to look at an ad for this place and want to come here . . . besides goths, freaks, and serial killers?"

I wonder how much trouble I'd get in if I shoved her into the water. I doubt Gibson would care.

James wraps his arm around her shoulder. "I'll look after you."

It won't be the rough sea that makes me hurl.

Ava smiles up at him with her flawless bat-winged eyes. James is a movie buff. He reviews them, makes them, dissects the continuity, and rarely rates anything higher than three stars—his only five-star review last year was for *Squid Game.* He's tall and on the skinnier side, but you can tell he works out between all that movie-watching. He has striking features. His jaw is squared, his eyes are a very dark blue, and his hair is blond and curly. He's the only guy wearing aftershave. It's strong, woody.

And he makes Ava giggle a lot.

I don't know what she was expecting. The invitation was black with intricate red and gold gargoyles etched into it. All gothic and perfect and authentic.

The aesthetic is so on brand for me.

A couple days ago, I covered the tragic, historic story of

five-year-old Maggie, who was murdered at the Rocky Point Amusement Park in Rhode Island. It created a buzz among my followers. Half of them are saying a private island is the perfect place for murder and the other half thinks I'm crazy to stay somewhere I can't leave immediately if I want to.

It's only perfect if no one but you and your victims know you're there.

I'm sure I'll find an edge to the resort; the gothic vibe will help.

We're almost there now. I have to tip my head up to see the island. A few birds circle above like they're searching for prey.

This weekend we get to check out the park, spend time on the rides, and hang out at the hotel spa and pool. Then Malcolm is hoping we shout great things and send all our followers to the island.

The invitation described the resort as unconventional and extraordinary. One of a kind.

The boat leaps over another wave.

My stomach flips.

Gibson is the only one who doesn't look slightly green as we rock over choppy water. He steers the boat and smiles into the sun as we cut through the sea. His eyes are hidden behind dark aviators.

I think he's around our age, maybe a year or two older. His earlier use of "sup" when he helped us onto the boat threw me a bit, but he's fresh-faced and dressed in jeans and a white T-shirt. His light hair is cut quite short with a shaved line down the side.

He looks happy. Like he could race around on the ocean all day and never get bored.

Beside me, a girl named Harper grips the edge of the boat. She's a book blogger. She reads at least one book a day and posts so much on TikTok I can't keep up with her. But her reviews are awesome, and we had a short conversation a few months ago when she raved about a true-crime novel that I later devoured.

Her skin is dark, and her Afro is tied on top of her head. She smiles at me with her bloodred lips and pulls a well-read thriller paperback out of her bag with her free hand. The pages are so curled at the edges that it's not a surprise she doesn't mind the odd splash of water on the cover.

I'm not convinced reading's going to help her nausea.

"It's funny," Harper says. "I've swam almost every day of my life. We spent two years living in the UK, where I swam the English Channel. England to France—not all at once, like some more hard-core swimmers. But you spend all that time in the water and a boat still makes you feel sick."

"Impressive," I say. "How old were you?"

"Fifteen. We moved back to the States soon after. My dad did the swim too."

"Wow. I love swimming, but I wasn't good enough to make my school's team," I tell her.

"My parents don't accept anything less than impressive. Or, rather, perfection." She rolls her eyes and clings harder to her book.

"Why does it look depressing?" Ava says, her voice grating.

She's gripping her long ponytail and twisting it around her hand. "I'm supposed to be living it up in luxury, not slumming it on a grim, run-down island."

"It's not grim," Gibson says.

Will, who's mostly remained silent, finally speaks up. It's not surprising that it's a reply to the very hot Gibson. "Nothing weirds me out."

Ava mutters something inaudible, but from the look on her face it probably wasn't kind.

Will's a rival beauty blogger with a slightly larger audience than Ava's. That must be killing her. He has shiny brown hair, a fake tan, dark eyes, and smooth skin I would *literally* kill for.

I snap a picture of the ominous setting for a TikTok I'll post after Malcolm takes us on the island tour. Which the itinerary boasted would happen right before we check into our rooms.

The top of the hotel comes into view. Constructed from stone with sharp points, two turrets, and carved gargoyle, the hotel is stunning. The six of us get it all to ourselves for a long weekend. We hit the jackpot.

Each of us has more than 500,000 followers. Liam is at 499,900, so he'll be joining us soon—probably by the end of the weekend.

The second I found out who else was coming, I did my research. I'm probably most like Harper and Liam. Though we're from wealthy families, our follower counts are higher than our bank balances.

"So, is this rich dude a psycho or something?" Will asks casually.

Ignoring the strong urge to push him off the boat too, I reply, "Just because he appreciates Gothic architecture doesn't mean there's something wrong with him."

He flashes his fluorescent white teeth. "Course not, crime girl."

He's done his homework too.

If I wanted to be petty, I would tell him his foundation doesn't match his skin color, but one, I'm not petty, and two, it's as perfect a match as Blake Lively and Ryan Reynolds.

Instead, I look away. It's not the first time someone has insinuated that I'm strange. My mom regularly tells me to blog about something else. "You're too cute and friendly to cover such a dark topic, Paisley." As if you needed to be hideous with boils all over your face and a missing front tooth to report on crime.

News flash: plenty of serial killers are good-looking and act friendly.

There is no "type."

Gibson slows the boat and throws the rope to a man on the jetty who's so gorgeous he doesn't look real.

This is a resort for wealthy *and* beautiful people.

"Welcome to Jagged Island!" says the man, easily catching the rope. "I'm Reeve, head of maintenance. You'll see me more this weekend since the island is running a skeleton crew until we open to the public."

Reeve is tall with dark skin, and his muscles have muscles. He has the darkest eyes I've ever seen in my life and cheekbones so sharp they could cut through steel. He's sort of a slightly older version of my ex-boyfriend, but I won't hold that against him.

"Thanks," I say as he helps me off the boat. He gives me a Hollywood-worthy smile, and I trip over my own feet.

Smooth.

Ducking my head, I focus on tugging my suitcase out of the way of the others getting off the boat and not on my burning cheeks.

Why do I blush when every cute guy looks at me? I am such a loser.

At least Reeve has made more than just *my* head turn. Will, Ava, and Harper also do double takes and smile at him hopefully. We're all sixteen and seventeen, so I don't think he's going to give any of us a second glance. He'll probably forget we even exist when we leave on Monday.

He claps his hands. "If you all want to follow me, I'll take you to Malcolm."

I guess Malcolm doesn't come to greet his guests.

We walk up the ramp next to the steps. Both are long, winding, and carved into the island. Sweat beads at the nape of my neck as I wheel my suitcase behind me.

Ava has Reeve pulling two of hers. She just handed them off to him. I could never be so bold.

Even Reeve's irritated expression is cute.

Ava had asked Gibson to take her stuff, but he has to take some staff back to the mainland. Something about orientation this week but them not being needed over the weekend. She brightened when he said he'd be back in around an hour; James just sulked. I got the feeling he was used to girls falling all over him.

"At least I don't need to go for a run today," I say as we climb the slope that seems to stretch on forever. My bag gets heavier with each step I take.

Harper grunts. "I brought books with me. This *hurts.*"

"What do you set your Goodreads challenge to?"

"Three hundred and fifty a year."

"Wow. I can only manage about fifty."

"Are they all crime?"

"Mostly. Lots of nonfiction."

"Hey, I run too if you want to go out together tomorrow?" she asks.

"That sounds good. I lost my running partner when my brother moved to college." I grin over at her. "How incredible is this place?"

"Right? I didn't want to say anything in front of the princess. Can't be bothered with the drama."

I like Harper already.

I switch hands and tug the case to the top. That's when I get my first real look at the park. It's exactly what you'd expect of a theme park, except it went heavy on stone and dark wood.

Reeve unlocks a large gate with sinister-looking gargoyle heads carved into the pillars. On the other side of the gate is a white cart professing the best ice cream in the world and largest choice of toppings.

A little bit of fun to lighten the darkness.

The roller coasters are all on thick wooden tracks that conceal the metal ones so the aesthetic of the park isn't compromised.

A group of staff members passes us, heading to the boat. They're all wearing dark navy shorts and red polo tops. They look us over as if we're a circus act.

My parents weren't happy that the island wasn't fully staffed, but it doesn't need to be. You don't need hundreds of people working for six guests.

Blaine convinced them to be happy that the owner and his assistant would be with us. And that this was an opportunity that came once in a lifetime—and that I'd managed to get all on my own.

I wish I had his powers of persuasion.

"It's cool, but this place is kinda weird," Harper says, looking around.

I open my mouth to reply but Reeve beats me to it, explaining that Malcolm wanted an exclusive park with a unique angle. A theme park for the rich, but he didn't want it dripping in gold and diamonds.

No glass and mirrors and caviar.

That was overdone, apparently.

"Malcolm grew up traveling the world, but it was his visit to the Burgos Cathedral in Spain when he discovered his love for the Gothic era," Reeve explains as they walk up the cliff.

I get the feeling that his speech is rehearsed. Part of the orientation. Watch a video about the new boss's life.

I can imagine how enthusiastic the staff was to learn about a billionaire's private-island dream while they're probably getting paid twenty dollars an hour to serve guests and control rides.

Reeve leads us around a corner, past the entrance to a rather adult-looking poltergeist train. "I'm *definitely* going on that later," I mumble to myself.

And then I look up and, *holy hell,* that must be Malcolm. Standing at the thick double-pointed-arch wooden doors of the hotel is a tall, lanky man with curly black hair and a pipe. He's wearing a long burgundy coat—despite the summer heat—and a black turtleneck.

He spreads his arms wide. "Welcome to my island."

STAY UP ALL NIGHT WITH THESE FOUR UNPUTDOWNABLE READS!

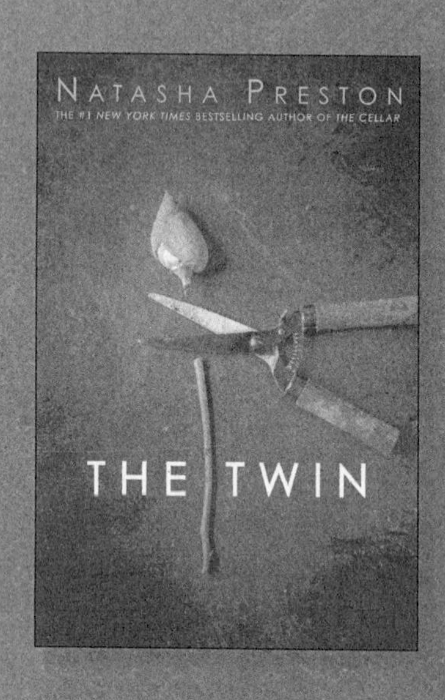

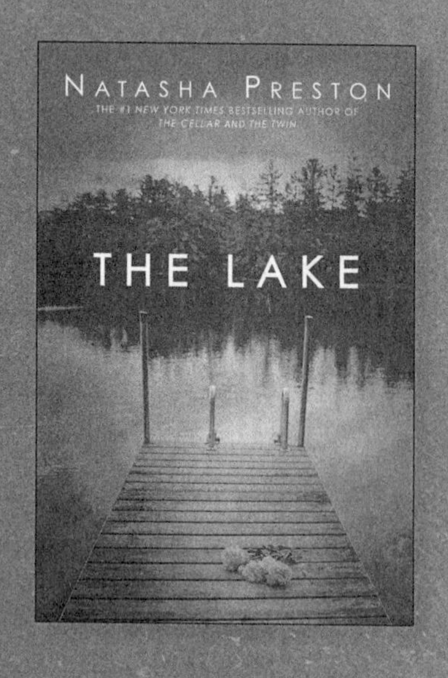

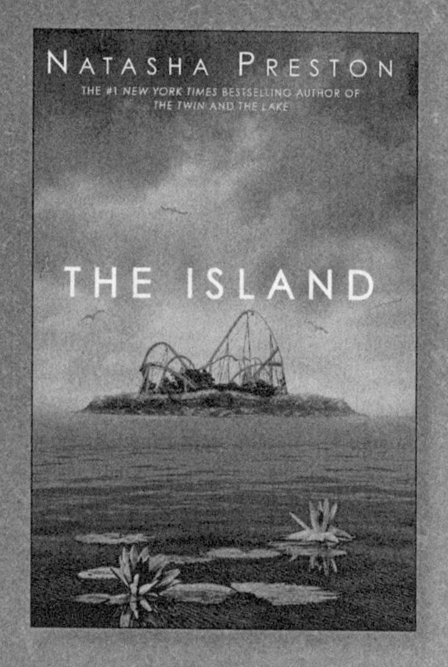